Charmed, Texas, is as warm and welcoming as it sounds. But even in a small town, when it comes to love, sometimes you've got to take the bitter with the sweet . . .

Carmen Frost hates honey. And bees. And in her hometown of Charmed, Texas, which practically invented the stuff, that's a problem. The good news is that the summer Honey Festival is finally over. Even better, so is the annual Lucky Hart carnival, a road show that made off with her dreams years ago—including the boy she loved. Now she's got a divorce behind her, and a successful law career in front of her, but in a tiny town, big memories die hard. Or they don't die at all—as Carmen discovers when she runs into an all too familiar pair of eyes—older, wiser, and just as heart-melting as ever . . .

Sully Hart has had enough of the nomad lifestyle. Travelling with his father's carnival gave him adventures, but it cost him much more. Now he's home to stay, contracted to create an entertainment complex in Charmed. He wants roots, a house with a yard and all the mundane pleasures that go with it. But the girl he loved has become a woman who still wants freedom. Can she still want him? It seems he and Carmen are at each other's throats one minute—and on each other's lips the next. Someone's gotta give . . .

Sharla Lovelace's works include

"Enchanted by You", a novella included in
The Cottage on Pumpkin and Vine

The Charmed in Texas Romances
A Charmed Little Lie
Lucky Charmed

Published by Kensington Publishing Corporation

Lucky Charmed

Charmed in Texas

Sharla Lovelace

LYRICAL PRESS
Kensington Publishing Corp.
www.kensingtonbooks.com

LYRICAL PRESS BOOKS are published by

Kensington Publishing Corp.
119 West 40th Street
New York, NY 10018

All Kensington titles, imprints, and distributed lines are available at special quantity discounts for bulk purchases for sales promotion, premiums, fund-raising, educational, or institutional use.

Special book excerpts or customized printings can also be created to fit specific needs. For details, write or phone the office of the Kensington Sales Manager: Kensington Publishing Corp., 119 West 40th Street, New York, NY 10018. Attn. Sales Department. Phone: 1-800-221-2647.

Lyrical Press and Lyrical Press logo Reg. U.S. Pat. & TM Off.

First Electronic Edition: July 2017
eISBN-13: 978-1-5161-0125-2
eISBN-10: 1-5161-0125-1

First Print Edition: July 2017
ISBN-13: 978-1-5161-0126-9
ISBN-10: 1-5161-0126-X

Printed in the United States of America

For my husband, who keeps me sane—or at least joins the crazy train when I go off the rails. Love you baby.

Chapter One

"C'mon people," I muttered, crossing the grocery parking lot for the third time. "The sales aren't that good this week. It's time to wrap it up."

I could go to the bigger supermarket in Charmed, but I preferred Brewsters, a smaller one in Goldworth, near my office. Fewer people. Less judgment.

Fewer parking spaces.

Spotting a mom shouldering two reusable canvas shopping bags with two kids in tow, I cranked the wheel in her direction. She smiled quickly and pushed her kids in front of her as she approached an SUV, as if she was used to being stalked. As anyone who shopped here should be.

I groaned under my breath at the big cartoonish honey bee sticker on her back window saying, "It's sweeter in Charmed!"

I was so tired of honey. I despised it, honestly. That might sound like a random and insignificant fact, but living in Charmed, Texas—which lives and breathes the stuff—it can become a thing. Not that I was averse to sweets. Chocolate, for instance, could easily run from my tap and I'd celebrate, but I had issues with a substance that was made by one insect throwing up on another, who then spent the next couple of days playing in it.

There should be a disclaimer on the *World Famous Honey* welcome sign for a town that breeds bees: You'll get to know a little too much about the process.

Summer was the hardest to stomach—no pun intended—with the annual Honey Festival kicking off right after school ended. It was even more everywhere than usual. Every retailer sported a stash of jars from whatever apiary hit them up first. Every restaurant sold them at the checkout. Hell, even the Quik-Serve convenience store had a supply on the counter last time I was in. I couldn't pop in for a coffee and a package of chocolate donuts without being accosted by honey jars.

This summer was a little better. My best friend, Lanie, was back in town with her new hubby (wink, wink) and so the consummate honey frenzy was overshadowed by a tinge of gossipy drama. The festival's annual dance had all eyes on her, and no one noticed that I showed up to help her out. I don't usually go. Most of the good townspeople of Charmed don't care much for me, and that's okay. I gave up on that fight a long time ago. Small towns are good at holding onto the past, whether it's ancient grudges or high school drama. I get it.

Once upon a time, my eighteen-year-old self was scandalous. Heaven forbid. My sins then evidently tainted the next decade, the sainted (cough) man I married, and my mother, who apparently could never again hold down a job. (Side note: she wasn't holding down a job the previous decade, either.)

So anyway, there was the festival, including the ridiculous Honey Wars, with crazy people hawking their self-labeled jars on every sidewalk, and then the Lucky Hart carnival a month later. It wasn't honey-driven, but it's crazy too. Or it was, anyway. I hadn't stepped foot inside that carnival in six years, since my divorce from said saint, now-the-mayor, Dean Crestwell.

As honey-bee-reusable-bag-mom drove away, I pulled into the spot and got out, ready to load up on chocolate anything in those evil plastic grocery bags that I'm gonna go to hell for. My cell buzzed. I laughed as I answered, entering the store.

"Just couldn't stand it, could you?"

"I know. I'm worse than a mom."

It was Lanie. Calling from Vegas, where she and Nick were vacationing after renewing their vows. With real rings. That's a story for another time.

I was envious of the trip, but not completely, because of the other reason I was feeling all jiggy over this summer. I was going on vacation. A long one.

Vacation!

"Are you kidding me?" I said. "You *are* a mom. You fawn more over that dog than anyone I've ever seen."

I was house-slash-dog sitting while they were gone. Lanie kind of inherited a Rottweiler when her old neighbor skipped out, and while it was a little iffy at the beginning, Ralph had won her over. The jury was still out for me in that regard, but I had to admit, Ralph was kind of sweet. When he wasn't licking himself.

I would have nothing for Lanie to sit for when I left on my vacation, except maybe an unfortunate plant on my porch. That wasn't as sad as it sounded. I liked it that way. No strings. No obligations. No arrangements to make if I wanted to suddenly pick up and go to Tahiti. Not that I'd ever done that, but I might. Stranger things could happen. Stranger things just might.

"He's family," Lanie said.

"Well, he's fine," I said. "I shared my blueberry muffin with him this morning, and gave him a bacon treat before I left."

"See, Carmen, you're a softie, too," she said.

"Don't ever say that out loud." I stopped in front of an end cap of chocolate syrup. I'd seen some vanilla bean ice cream in Lanie's freezer and that would be a great complement. I kept walking, though. It was a maybe. I could always come back. "How's Vegas?"

"I'm down a hundred already today," she said. "So I'm playing the penny slots and waiting on my handsome hubby to finish his game and come whisk me off upstairs for naked room service."

I was hit as always with that mix of being so damn happy for her, after she fought through her baggage to find her soul mate, and feeling so damn envious.

"So you're calling me why?" I asked.

"I saw a slot machine themed with pancakes and I thought of Ralph," she said.

"Of course you did."

"Did we miss anything interesting at the carnival?" she asked. "Or did you skip it?"

I snorted. "What do you think?" I picked up a bag of peanuts and then put it back down. Salty wasn't the thing tonight. It had been a long day at the office, and besides, celebrations were all about the chocolate.

It was over. As of yesterday, that damned infernal beast that descended upon the little town of Charmed every year was over. Forever. Not everyone shared my view or saw the summer carnival as beastly. Kids loved it, of course. A lot of adults still rolled out for it in spades, probably grabbing the one last chance to mingle and see who was doing what—or who—since the Honey Festival the month before.

I always looked at it as one more year in the bag. One more summer of successful absenteeism. That festival would probably go on till the end of time, but now, with Charmed taking on a new entity—a planned outdoor entertainment area that everyone was buzzing about—the carnival itself would stop here no more.

The Charmed city council had voted in a bid to build a permanent mini-theme park, boardwalk, and restaurant-and-retail row on Bailey's Pond near my mother's trailer park. Lots of sales-tax dollars from surrounding towns, more local jobs, something for people to get excited about beside flying insects and honey (thank God). And an end to the yearly nomadic reach of Lucky Hart Carnivals.

It was a win-win, and I was so friggin' excited, I couldn't stand it.

I'd forced myself to go out there with Dean for years, just to prove a silly point. I would smile, flirt, and go overboard doting over my husband every time a certain hooded gaze landed my way. A gaze that was once the most intense and mind-altering drug I could ever know.

Prove a point to whom? To Dean? To myself? To the man behind the eyes?

Yep. Absolutely. And now I never had to think about it, demean myself, or avoid an event again. Not that I ever should have in the first place. I should have been above it all. But hey, small towns have big memories and every time I tried to forget about the very public *Carmen Frost Public Humiliation of Summer 2001*, someone was always around to remind me.

I breathed in deeply, savoring the satisfaction as I rounded the cookie aisle. Chocolate-covered graham crackers were just the ticket to celebrate.

"I know," Lanie said. "I just thought maybe you'd surprise me. Where are you?"

"Brewsters," I said. "Getting some party food."

"You having a party without me?"

"Can't help you had to go honeymooning," I said. "I filed two briefs today, settled a divorce case in mediation, and spent most of the afternoon avoiding Judge Constantine and his unibrow." *And Lucky Hart Carnivals was trucking along their merry way.* "And in case I haven't mentioned it enough, I'm going on vacation in a few weeks."

"Seems to ring a bell," she said.

"So I'm having a comfort food extravaganza to celebrate."

Lanie chuckled. "Comfort food meaning three batches of brownies?"

I laughed too loudly, and held up a hand to a woman who took a break from studying various Oreo flavors to give me a double-take.

"Sorry, I'm having a moment," I said. "Don't mind me."

I grabbed my package of bad-for-me and turned back. Smack into a wall of broad chest, with a set of arms that felt just as solid. A hand gripped my upper arm as the chocolate grahams crushed between us.

"Oh! I'm so—"

I looked up. Into the eyes of the drug I thought I'd never see again. Eyes that had gotten older and wary and were supposed to be gone. They flashed with as much surprise as I'm sure mine did, in the two-second span we both stood frozen with cell phones to our ears.

"Shit," I exclaimed.

"Carmen?" Lanie voice called from somewhere far, far away.

Backing up a full step so that he had to let go of me, my mind went on a roller coaster ride. *Roller coaster.* That was ironic. Or perhaps I was having a stroke and my life was flashing by as the man I'd spent fifteen years trying to forget stared down at me. Regardless, I got a five-second speed reel in my head of all of it. All of us. Me and Sullivan Hart.

"Sully," I finally croaked.

"Sully?" Lanie said. "As in *Sully?*" She sounded like a bird chirping in my ear.

I tried to be subtle as I gave him the once-over. The thick dark hair wasn't as long as it used to be, but there was enough to be held back by what looked like a leather strap, with a pair of Ray-Bans shoved up on top. His smell was the same heady mix of wood and adrenaline that I'd still know if I were struck deaf, dumb, and blind. And he still had the same habit of running his hand over his face, taking a deep breath and lowering his eyes when he was nervous.

He was nervous?

He mumbled something into his phone and put it in his pocket.

Suddenly, I was eighteen again. Standing in the second empty parking lot of the day and sweating through my clothes. Clutching a duffel bag as the wretched sickly sweet smell of melted cotton candy baking on the asphalt stung my nose. I'd seen him since then, of course. From a distance. Years ago. I was so over it.

So why did this one-on-one give me chest pains? Why were his eyes so friggin' intense? *Ignore it! So what that your fingers are going numb!* Maybe it *was* a stroke. He was supposed to be gone, damn it. Gone with that cursed carnival.

"Let me call you back, Lanie." The phone was halfway down my body before the words were out of my mouth.

Sully cleared his throat. "Hey."

I willed my face to go neutral, but I couldn't really feel it anymore. I would have given anything for superpower speed, so that I could flash out of there the next time he blinked. Assuming he blinked. He hadn't yet.

"Hey."

"How've you been?" he asked.

No. We weren't doing that. We weren't catching up like old buddies.

"I thought—you—" I gestured something with my hands that I hoped demonstrated *go away.*

His eyes narrowed. Crap. He didn't understand the universal sign language for *Why the living hell are you still here?*

"You thought what?" he asked.

"The carnival left," I said. "I assumed you were with it."

He nodded. "You don't know."

"Know?" I echoed, crossing my arms and backing up another step.

No, I clearly didn't know. Was I supposed to? Were there people that knew and left me out of all the things to know? My heart thundered so loudly in my ears, it was all I could do not to clamp my hands over them.

Why was he here?

"About the Bailey's Pond project?" he prompted, crossing his own arms.

A tattoo peeked out from under a shirt sleeve. *The* tattoo. Shit. It was all I could do not to run my thumb across my left breast where its clone resided.

My mouth went dry as all kinds of confusion exploded in my head. *Keep it together. Don't show weakness. He left you.*

He left you.

A calm washed over me and all my strength as a professional business woman, as an adult woman who'd been through and seen a few things, came back and held me up. What did it matter that the love of my life, the man who shattered me into a million pieces in a stadium parking lot, was standing in front of me fifteen years later, looking good enough to lick from head to toe?

I was better than that.

"What about it?" I asked. "Your carnival won't be coming through here anymore."

He raised his right eyebrow. The light overhead flickered, flashing in his hazel eyes. "That's right. Aidan will bypass all of Cedar County from now on."

Something familiar poked at me. Something I should know. Seemed there were quite a few things I should know.

"Aidan?"

"My brother," he said, gesturing to his phone like that would clear it up. *Bingo.* Aidan Hart. I had a vague recollection of a sulky pre-teen boy hanging on the outskirts. Sully's stepbrother. "He's running the road show now."

I blinked, and the warning bells started to ding. Aidan was on the road? *Sully wasn't on the road?* Hell no, he wasn't on the road; he was standing in my grocery store. *My* grocery store.

"And so you are—?" I prompted, a sick acidic burn starting low in my belly.

Somewhere deep in my psyche I knew the answer before he could tell me.

"The major investor in the development," he said smoothly. His tone was deep and the words slightly lazy as they rolled off his tongue, just as I remembered. *Why did I remember?* "The park will be named The Lucky Charm, but that's not public knowledge yet."

I nodded. "Good for you," I said, as my legal brain started ticking away.

Being an investor—especially one getting the name of his company included in the project—meant bringing major capital to the table. Investing that kind of money would mean sticking around long enough to watch the progress. Or it would for me. An accountant would probably set up a per diem for his stay. And seeing as nothing had even started yet—dear God he could be there in Charmed for months.

"So you're here for a while, then?" I dug my nails into my upper arms.

Sully blinked a couple of times, studying me like he was contemplating his words. That was bad.

"I got a house, Carmen," he said. "In Charmed. I'm not leaving."

There was one of those moments where things spin around and lights look funny. I blinked it clear and breathed in lieu of words. There were none. He bought—

"You—" I shook my head and forced a smile. "You what?"

Sully gave me a long look, followed by a glance toward the Oreo lady. *She's not gonna save you, buddy.*

"I assumed you'd probably heard."

I snickered. "Why?" I asked. "Why would I hear about random people moving here?"

I mentally patted myself on the back for making him a nobody. But why *didn't* I fucking hear about him buying a house? I went to those monthly breakfasts at the Chamber of Commerce. Occasionally. Someone there should have known. I couldn't pump gas without someone telling me about my ex-husband's latest hilarious Facebook post. Or my mother's most current medical issues. But let the hot carnie that made me an overnight scandal come back and buy a house in Charmed, and nobody has anything to say?

Sully held up a hand. "I don't know. Never mind." He laid the hand against his chest, and my eyes fell to it.

Damn it, I'd loved his hands. The long, roughened fingers of a working guy, even back then. My mind flashed to what they looked like—what they'd felt like on my skin a hundred years ago, and heat rushed to my face.

"I mean, what do you think? I hang out with Realtors?" That sounded stupid even to me.

"Well, it's actually a rental for now." He backed up, looking like he'd rather be anywhere else. "With an option to buy if everything works out."

Oh dear God, thank you for that. He could still go. Things just need to not work out. Man, that was catty.

"But I guess I figured—small town. You're a lawyer—"

"How'd you know that?" I asked.

His tired expression focused as he tilted his jaw. I saw the spark. The challenge. The grin that pulled at his lips. He grabbed a new package of chocolate grahams from the shelf without breaking eye contact, and switched them out with the one in my hand.

"Well, people do talk to *me*."

Oh. Hell. No.

No, he didn't.

I lifted my chin, and refused to look away. No matter what was liquefying in my chest as his gaze burned through me. No matter what images flashed like a movie reel in my head. I wouldn't give him that satisfaction.

"Good for you," I said, placing the package back on the shelf. I needed them more than ever, but not in front of him. "Welcome back to Charmed."

I started to walk around him, but he grabbed my arm.

"Carmen, wait."

His voice was like hot honey over my body.

I hate honey.

I was proud of myself. My acting ability was stellar. The fact that I didn't suck my tongue down my throat, choke on my own spit, or jerk my arm free like I'd been bitten by a rabid squirrel—was Oscar-worthy. Instead, I patted his hand and smiled up at him, slowly stepping to the side until his fingers slid free.

"We're adults now, Sully," I said, wondering where the hell the words were coming from. "It's all good. Have a great day."

And I walked away. And out. And to my car. The pains stabbing through my middle stole my breath. Thank God I was empty-handed, because being chased down for shoplifting cookies while in a blind haze of what-the-fuckery would have been the final icing on a messed-up cake.

Fumbling for my keys, I hit the button and got in as quickly as possible. I had to leave. Now. Before he came out. Before I could see what he was driving and then obsess every time I saw the same vehicle in another parking lot. Before I could succumb to the temptation of watching to see where he went. Where he lived, what his home looked like.

"Leave," I whispered, my voice sounding vaguely desperate. My eyes burned. I shook my head and tilted my head back. "No. You will not cry, damn it."

I blinked at the roof. I was thirty-three. Eighteen was a long time ago. *Suck it up, Carmen.*

I took a deep breath and looked up, just in time to see him walk out of the store. He'd slid the sunglasses over his eyes, causing a stray lock of dark hair to fall next to his face. He was probably twenty-five feet away, and I could feel that strand of hair on my fingertips.

Without another look, I pulled out and drove away.

Chapter Two

Everything I knew about love I learned from Sully Hart. Everything. Sullivan Xavier Hart made his appearance on the carnival circuit the summer of my junior year. He was nineteen, wanting to follow in his father's footsteps running Lucky Hart, and so he was along for every stop. He was hard to miss. He had taken over the Ferris wheel controls from a coworker and stood there like a Norse god or a vibrant shining star on a runaway freight train. He made eye contact with every single person that gave him a ticket and by the time you passed him you were connected. Sully Hart virtually sizzled with electricity; it was impossible not to be mesmerized by him. And while the sensible part of me knew he probably mesmerized girls everywhere he went, I couldn't help myself. The second we met, and those intense unblinking hazel eyes landed on me, I was his.

It didn't matter that I was sort-of-kind-of already Dean's. We hadn't really said it. We weren't serious, and besides that—Dean was a boy. This guy, in my seventeen-year-old wisdom, was all *man*. And not just any man. A man on the move. A man with a life. Someone who saw different people and places every week. That was like crack to my nomad-needy heart. I couldn't resist it.

It was relatively innocent. Nothing happened that summer except a lot of talking and some very heated, teasing kisses that left me breathless. We kept in touch for a while, until life got in the way. Senior year got crazy; my mother was hell-bent on my getting into a good college and going to law school, and I was hell-bent on getting out of Charmed. Law? Good God, nothing sounded more hideously boring than that, but it *could* write me a decent ticket to anywhere. And then Dean, who I *had* managed to get kind of serious with, dumped me before prom because I still hadn't had sex with him. I was waiting. Lanie waited, so I was, too. And Dean pushing me just made me hold out longer.

My mom and I were constantly butting heads over schools, so I signed up for a local community college to piss her off. So, with a month to go before the semester started, and a fuck-it-all attitude, I went looking for Sully Hart the first night of the carnival. And dear God, I found him. He was sitting on a fence with a few of other carnies, one of whom I recognized from the year before. Her name was Kia, and last year she hadn't been so beautiful and exotic-looking. Jealousy coursed through me as I watched them laugh together, obviously a thing. I started to turn back. But then he saw me.

The way he slid slowly off that fence and looked at me like the rest of the world disappeared, I knew it was on.

There was nothing innocent about it.

Sully taught me everything. And I don't just mean sex. Falling in love with him was easy. It was natural, like we were made to order. Our bodies fit; we finished each other's sentences; our thoughts were always in sync. The feel of him close by was tangible, whether we were touching or not. We fell hard and fast. He called me his *love*, and for twenty-two days, we were nonstop. Incomparable lovers. Best friends. Inseparable. After the carnival left Charmed, I drove to its new city or he skipped out and came to me, but we were never apart. Until the miles became too far, and a decision had to be made.

I made mine.

He made his.

They weren't the same.

* * *

I pulled into the parking lot in front of the trailer-park office, squeezing between my mom's car and Larry's giant ugly SUV in a spot that wasn't really a spot. It's all there was, and I grabbed it. I palmed my keys and sat behind the wheel in a state of sweaty turmoil, knowing I didn't have long. One of the slats in the mini-blinds was bent in the middle at right about her eye level. Either the heat or Mom's curiosity would get me soon, but I had to pull myself together.

I was flushed, my hands trembled, and I wanted to puke. Geraldine Frost would take one look at me and zero in on that like the second coming. My mother had a laser-like ability to detect a problem in my life, and while I could tell her the truth, I wasn't in the mood for another lecture about my teenage sins.

Instead, I squinted like I was having a migraine and rubbed my temple as I got out, waving at Mr. Greene and waiting for the fussing. He was a sweet old guy who had the beginnings of dementia, and yet walked the entire trailer park every day, pointing his cane at people he felt weren't following the rules. I jiggled open the trailer office door before he could fuss, and squinted deeper and more pathetically. You're never too old to play sick.

Mom sat directly to my right, clicking away at something on her computer screen as if she were the busiest, most important person on Earth and wasn't playing Spider Solitaire. She peered up at me over her Dollar General cheater glasses, her dark red hair glowing a little too red in the florescent light.

"What's wrong with you?"

See?

"I have a headache," I said.

"You don't get headaches," she said, frowning at me like she was reading my skin.

"I do, too," I said, feeling one coming on for real. I pulled the brown hair band from its perpetual place on my wrist and twisted up my hair in a messy bun. I needed it off of me.

She grabbed one of my hands.

"What are you doing?" I asked.

"You're clammy," she said, like it was an accusation.

"Okay, I told you I don't feel great, so—"

"It's probably stress. Did I tell you about the migraines I've been getting?" she asked. "All this worry and tension."

And there we were, back on her. "*What* tension?" I asked.

The door opened behind me.

"Hey Car," Larry said. He pushed his way in behind me.

"Hey, Larry," I said, my cheek twitching at the *Car* nickname.

I couldn't stand that, but Larry Landell had managed the Bailey's Pond Trailer Park since before I was born and had seen me grow up there. He called me what he called me. And he had given my mother a job as office secretary, so he could back off some of the admin stuff, so who was I to gripe about something as petty as a name.

"You here to pick up the books?"

Because I'm a lawyer, somehow that relates to all things legal, financial, accounting, and otherwise with certain people. Like reporting their sales tax and checking the books each quarter for anything auditable. Because I was Gerry Frost's daughter and technically trailer-park family, I got to do it for free.

"What's wrong with you?" he asked, giving me a double-take.

Jesus.

"See?" My mother pointed a pen at me. "I told you, you look like shit. All pasty and squirmy."

"Well, good," I said, pulling up a rolling chair. "My ego needed a kick in the crotch today, so now I'm much better."

"Did you hear, yet?" Larry asked, to which my mother reacted by picking up a folder and swatting him with it.

"Imbecile! I told you!"

"Oh, sorry, Gerry," Larry said, looking at her with hurt puppy-dog eyes. Oh lord, he still had it bad for her. *That's* why he suddenly needed a secretary. Certainly not for her hunt-and-peck typing skills. My mom was still a good-looking woman, just a little flighty.

"Tell me what?" I asked, rubbing my forehead. I was pretty sure I knew where this was going.

"Nothing," my mom said.

"Gerry," Larry said, tilting his balding head.

"I swear," she said under her breath, violently shoving the cheaters on top of her head.

"Mom?" I asked wearily. "Is it about the new entertainment complex?"

She blew out a breath. "You do know."

"No secret. You and I talked about it two weeks ago," I said, dropping my hands to my sides and trying to look innocent. "You signed Lanie and me up for that... gazebo thing. The 'let's-hold-hands-and-sing-Kumbaya' debacle."

"The 'Build a Charming Charmed' project," she said defensively. "It's a good thing, Carmen. Don't make fun. And it starts tomorrow, so I expect you there."

It was the city council getting out of paying for some of the new structures for the complex. They got the town all fired up to volunteer, to come together and donate time to build a big pavilion and a gazebo. And—I don't know what else. But anyone who could swing a hammer or tote wood was scorned if they didn't sign up to help. I did not have either skill, nor did Lanie, but ours were the first names she wrote down on her pink clipboard when *she* signed up to be in charge of manpower.

"Lanie's out of town."

"You aren't attached at the hip," she said. "You can show up. This is a *good thing*."

"It's giving weapons to unskilled labor," I said. "Someone's gonna get a cracked skull."

"Whatever." She flicked her fingers. "It's teamwork. Six o'clock."

"I'm going on vacation," I said. "I won't be around for—"

"That's three weeks away. You'll be around for enough," she said. "You being a part of this might help your reputation." She glanced at me. "You're too defensive. And then there's Dean."

"No, there's no Dean." I turned to Larry. "Did you ever find out how the land sale was affecting the trailer park? You never told me."

"Larry says it's not part of it," Mom said. "He says Bailey kept it."

I nodded. "Okay." I glanced at Larry. "Thanks, *Larry*."

Mom narrowed her gaze in on me. "You know who it sold to."

I sighed. There was no winning.

"Yes, I know," I said, closing my eyes. "Lucky Hart."

Larry cleared his throat. "The Lucky Charm, I heard they're going to call it. Silly name."

"It's kind of genius, actually," I said. "Just—"

"The old man's not running it anymore," my mom said.

"He died," we said in unison. I realized I hadn't said a word to Sully about his dad dying. It would have been the right thing to do. The adult thing to do. I wasn't thinking like an adult up at that moment, though. I'd been thinking about eyes and man-chest and how to make it out of the store without collapsing in spasms.

I stared at her coffee cup, which was preferable to her scrutiny. "I know. I… just ran into…hang on…"

"What?" she said, frowning as I put my hands on my hips and narrowed my eyes. "You ran into who?"

"You know who I ran into," I said. Literally. Smack into his chest. "The big question is, why *did* you know? Why was he surprised that I didn't?"

My mother sighed like I made her tired. Yeah. I made *her* tired.

"Carmen."

I cocked my head. "Mom."

"I found out from Susan Harmocker," Mom said. "She works for one of the councilmen, and she gave me the scoop." She winked. "Secretary-to-secretary."

Good Lord. Now she had a tribe.

"And when was this?" I asked.

"Oh, I don't know," she said. "A few weeks back?"

"A few weeks," I echoed. People knew for a few weeks. "Seriously? I don't live in a bubble, Mom. No one could pick up a phone?"

"Do you know he lied?" she said, narrowing her eyes with disdain.

"No," I said, crossing my arms. "No, I don't know. I don't know anything. There's been a town-wide conspiracy to keep me out of the loop."

"He didn't apply for the permit under his own name," she said. "He used a pseudonym to hide it."

Ten dollars said that Susan Harmocker threw that word out there and Mom came home and looked it up.

"LH Industries?"

She frowned. "How'd you know?"

Bigger question was, how did I remember that? The last time I'd heard the name was fifteen years earlier, in a random conversation about his family's company.

"LH is Lucky Hart," I said. "It's the legal incorporated name of the business."

Mom chewed on the side of her cheek and shrugged. "Well, still," she said, straightening a stack of papers. "It could have been a little more above-board."

I widened my eyes. "Look who's talking. How above-board were *you*, not telling me about this?"

She gave me her *I'm your mother and that's that* look.

"You have enough on your plate with your job and Dean and—"

"I have no Dean on my plate, Mom," I said. "I divorced him, so our plates don't play together anymore. That problem went away. Six years ago."

She hated that I'd gotten divorced. Not that she was ever particularly in love with Dean—she found him a bit whiny and controlling—but in her mind, as long as I was married, I was taken care of. And grandchildren could pop out at any minute. Little did she know I'd been on birth control our entire marriage. It never felt right to bring kids into our life. I never knew why, but I hadn't been wrong.

"You know what I'm saying," she said, pushing back in her chair. "You have enough," she repeated.

I really didn't know, but her tone didn't leave room for questions.

"So you felt that being blindsided with Sully Hart was better?" I asked. "Did it not cross your mind—anyone's mind—that a little prep might be nice?"

She cringed. "Don't say his name."

"Oh, seriously, Mom, he's not Voldemort."

"Once upon a time, he was worse." She stood up, grunting from the effort.

So much for avoiding the melodrama.

I couldn't go down this path right now. Not ten minutes after seeing him, smelling him, feeling his hands on my skin. I couldn't talk about him. Maybe he *was* Voldemort.

"He ruined our family. He had you all wound up on leaving here and joining the circus," she said, her hands flailing.

"Carnival," I corrected. "And I never said I was doing that."

Our plans never made it that far, but if Sully had asked, I would have walked on my hands and barked if that would have kept us together.

"You were leaving," she said defensively.

"I was leaving anyway," I said, probably a little too harshly. "All I ever wanted to do was leave. Hell, you wanted me to!"

"For college!"

"Well, between you and Dean, you both got what you wanted, didn't you?" I snapped. "I went away to school, then came back forever, attached to this place with a fucking bungee cord."

"Watch your mouth," she said under her breath.

"You even had that wanderlust as a little girl," Larry piped in, as if we'd been chatting about vacation plans. "I remember you always drawing me maps of the imaginary places you wanted to go. You'd pin scarves to your clothes and tell people you were a gypsy."

I stared at him for a moment, blinking a couple of times to catch up to the spin. He winked at me, and I realized he wasn't being crazy or senile; he was trying to change the subject and cool the collective jets.

I chuckled. "I remember that too, Larry. My friends wanted to be models and actresses. I was much more realistic." I smiled. "Except that I'm still here." I walked to a cabinet I knew too well, opened it, and pulled out this year's ledger. "For now."

"For now?" Mom piped up. "Are you going somewhere?"

"I'm going on vacation."

She rolled her eyes. Literally. Like a preteen. "Oh, this vacation of yours. Really, Carmen? I mean, you've been to Mexico, France, and Jamaica. Actual vacations a lot of people would kill for."

I gave her a matter-of-fact look. "Yes."

"And now you are renting a car for some ridiculous reason," she said. "And driving for weeks to *no place in particular*, coming back *at some point*, and calling that a vacation?"

I nodded and shrugged.

"Yes. Absolutely," I said. "The best kind ever."

"How?" she asked, shaking her head.

I leaned in. "Because it'll be an adventure. And I may love it so much, I'll put a sign on the car that says 'Attorney On Wheels' and travel the states." Okay, I couldn't really do that, but God, it sounded good.

She didn't agree, she just looked at me in horror. My mother never got it. She never got me. She certainly should, given her penchant for needing new jobs and getting so easily bored with the everyday, but it never panned out that way. She could not wrap her head around my need to get out. To experience life. *Real* life. And not from a tour bus. This road trip vacay had been itching in my blood for some time, and it was finally going to happen. No plans. No reservations. Just get in my car and go. Or—not *my* car. The convertible I was renting. Because—awesome.

"That's dumb, that's what that is," she countered. "How would you do work?"

"Just like I do now," I lied. "Everything's online. Everything is done using an iPad and a stylus. Totally doable."

Mom shook her head. "It's reckless. God only knows where you'll end up, and no one will even know where to look to find your body."

"I have GPS on my phone," I said.

She gave me a look. "And if your phone dies, too?"

I shrugged. "I guess the police will have to work a little harder."

My mother opened a drawer and pulled out a bottle of Tylenol. "You give me a headache, you know that?"

"Sorry," I said, holding up the ledger and turning to go. "This will be the year, y'all. The year we put this shit online. I'll get these back to you by the end of the week."

"The end of the week?" she said. "Larry said it normally takes you two days."

"No rush," Larry said, holding up his hands.

"All that *stress* on my plate," I said to her, turning. "See you tomorrow."

"Six o'clock!" she called out as I closed the door.

Chapter Three

It was like some sort of secret society newsletter went out.

The Gig is Up! Carmen Knows About Sully!

In one day, suddenly I was getting Facebook messages, e-mails; people were stopping me at the courthouse to ask my thoughts. Where were all these concerned citizens yesterday? Where was all this unrest and distrust for someone who "snuck in under the radar and fooled everyone" a week or so ago?

"How is Mayor Crestwell with this new turn of events?" one particularly nosy paralegal whispered to me in the elevator.

I stared at her until she blinked away, scurrying off at the second floor.

So much for everything going away with the carnival. And how was the mayor doing, indeed. Had he kept it from me, too? Or was he on the no-tell list as well? I had to assume I would find out in due time, and I needed to try not to stress about being in the spotlight again. God, I hated spotlights.

I had a lunch appointment with an old client at the Blue Banana Grille, and I decided to head there early and score some extra food before he got there. I was friggin' starving and didn't want to look like a ravenous pig. I wanted to choose the diced chicken chef salad and not drool on anything else. Look like someone who cared about health and good eating habits instead of revealing my love for junk and devouring a hamburger and fries.

My mouth watered when I opened the door to the Blue Banana, and I instantly knew I didn't care one fried pickle about what ravenous looked like and that I had a plate of chili cheese fries in my very, very near future. Then maybe the salad. Or not.

Not that chili cheese fries were junk. Especially not at the Blue Banana. Not since Lanie's husband Nick took over as head chef. He made everything taste gourmet. Nick was off having lots of sex in Vegas at the moment, but he'd trained Dave-the-fry-cook in all his dishes before leaving, so hopefully it would still be awesome.

I spotted Allie and waved at her. Allie Greene grew up in the trailer park, too, working in her dad's eclectic little diner till she took it over. Allie was one of those girls in high school that never quite caught a break. Her mom died, then she ended up pregnant at seventeen from a guy who bailed. Allie was always a little bit of a bad-ass, but being a single mom at seventeen enhanced that gene. And now she ran the best establishment in town.

"Hey Carmen," Allie said, waving off the waitress to seat me herself. "Just you?"

"For two," I said. "Meeting a client—" My words were cut off as my gaze landed on Sully. Sitting at the counter, he forked chicken fried steak into his mouth and licked gravy from his lips. Next to him, plucking at French fries, sat Kia, a girl I'd once seen put her foot behind her head. While standing. "—for lunch," I finished.

Damn it. *My town. My grocery store. My diner.* How the hell was I ever going to function like this, seeing him every damn place I went? Them? Did she come with him for this? Were they—?

Oh man, I needed medication.

Allie turned to follow my gaze and gave a small knowing smile. "I assume you'd like a table as far away as possible?"

God bless her.

"Yes please," I said, swallowing hard. She remembered, and not in the mocking way that many others did.

The door opened, and I heard a familiar voice that instantly put me on edge. Allie flushed as she smiled past me, and I knew it was about more than my ex-husband walking in. Bash was with him. Sebastian Anderson.

I gave her a little grin before Dean could take that ability away.

Bash owned Anderson Apiary, the only major profitable bee vomit factory in town. I know that sounded a bit negative. But Bash was good at what he did. I might not understand the fascination or like the product, but I understood good business. Even if he weren't an old friend from a million years ago, I'd respect him for his hardcore approach to his work.

Allie, though... I always suspected she secretly had it bad for Bash Anderson since way back when. And they were lifelong friends, so I just didn't get it. I glanced over to Mr. Chicken-Fried-Steak-and-Sex at the counter. My stomach tightened as he wiped his mouth and sat back, one arm thrown over the back of Kia's chair, his eyes on me.

"Mr. Mayor. Bash. I'll be right back, guys," Allie said, averting her eyes when Bash's gaze settled on her.

Bash watched her walk away with a rare serious look on his face. I turned to follow Allie to my table, sneaking another glance at Sully. I swallowed hard. Fuck him. Allie had the better plan even if she had no reason for it. Just keep walking away.

"Carmen."

Dean's voice came from behind me, his tone sharp with the edge I used to despise when we were married. The one that told me where to shit and how to do it. It was only fractionally better than the whiny kiss-ass one he adopted to reel me back in when I started to rebel.

My jaw twitched.

Rolling my shoulders to prepare for battle, I turned slowly, pasting a polite smile on my face. Sully was still back there. I felt him.

"Dean."

"Did you know about this?" he asked, his light eyes flashing.

I was already tired. "About what?"

"You know what," he said, a little too loudly. "Your old boyfriend." He pointed at the counter as if I'd brought Sully here and deposited him like a toy. "Sitting up at the bar."

It took everything in my power not to look past Dean. My heart slammed against my ribs at the scene he was making, but I would not look Sully's way and somehow indirectly involve him.

I chuckled to hide the bristling. "Did I know he was here? No."

"The pond project," Dean said through his teeth. "Did you know about that?"

"The gazebo project? Are you working on that?" I responded.

He blinked as I threw off his ranting rhythm.

"Of course."

I nodded. *Of course.*

"Did I know about the whole Bailey's Pond thing?" I asked, crossing my arms. "Of course I did. Who hasn't? But I had no idea it was Lucky Hart until yesterday." I leaned forward. "My own mother didn't tell me for weeks, so if you're going to rant about a day, you're preaching to the—"

"He falsified—"

"No, he didn't." I was irritated as shit at being forced to defend the man.

Dean narrowed his eyes to little slits, making him look like an alien. "How do you know what I was going to say?"

"Because I've already heard it," I said. "It's their company's legal name."

His jaw was working so fast, it looked like he was chewing gum.

"Do you know what that's going to do to our industry here?" Dean asked.

"What?" I was genuinely confused.

He took a breath and let it out slowly, as if he needed to dumb it down for me. I felt all those little muscle fibers in my neck grabbing hold of each other, getting ready to tie some knots.

"Leveling all that untouched flora around the pond will directly affect our bee population," he said. "I know you don't care about honey, but this town does, and—"

"Hang on," Bash said, walking up behind him. "No one cares more about the bees than I do, and I'm actually for the project."

Dean stared at Bash as if he'd just run over his dog.

"How can you be for it?"

"Because I've researched it, talked to people, talked to *Sully*," Bash said. "His plans include apiary kiosks, sales in all the stores, and I'm actually opening a sales presence of my own out there." He grinned proudly. "My first extension."

"Congrats!" I said.

"Thanks," he said with a wink. "And the bees'll be fine, Dean."

"You aren't worried about bees," I said, watching Dean grope for something else. "This has been in the planning for months. *Your* city council voted it in. *Your* buddy Alan was spouting about it before the festival last month. You didn't have a problem with any of it until the name was attached it."

"Please," Dean snarled. "I could give a shit about Sully Hart."

"Is there something I can help you with?"

Oh, fuck me.

Sully. Now standing next to Dean with a satisfied smile, eye-to-eye with him once Dean turned around. Only three feet from me, and something in my body knew that. I felt every inch. Dean saw it when he looked back at me, and by his expression, he looked like he could have thrown Sully through the nearest window and not even broken a sweat.

"Guys," I said, glancing around, wary of the crowd watching the show unfold. Where was Kia? My neck went hot when an old client of mine smiled empathetically and then looked away.

"This doesn't involve you, Hart," Dean said. "Mind your own business. From what I've heard, you have enough crap in your own house. Leave Charmed to Charmed."

Sully's expression was carefree, but his body was spring-loaded and tight, probably expecting Dean to sucker punch him.

"I heard my name, so that kind of throws things into the *my business* hat," Sully said quietly. "But you digging around in mine must mean you like me." It was full of snark, but his eyes weren't laughing as he crossed his arms.

It was somewhat of a concession: taking his hands out of the running, disarming himself, giving a little without backing down. I didn't know if Dean would see it that way, though. He only saw red at the moment.

"Boy, you don't want to play with me right now." Dean took a step forward.

Bash jumped between them and put his hand on Dean's chest, but Sully didn't even twitch. It was like watching two bulls preen and then fight to the death. I was stressed, I was embarrassed, and I'd had enough.

"Dean, go find a seat and *sit down*," I said through gritted teeth.

"Have you heard what kind of crapshoot his family runs?" Dean said. "He can't control his own brother's operations, that's why he's here. He bailed. And we want *that* in charge of a major tourist attraction?"

Sully's jaw tightened, but that was the only reaction.

"Sully, if you're done, please leave," I said.

He looked shocked, even more so than Dean. His eyebrows furrowed.

"I came over here to help you," he said.

"I don't need your help." My eyes started to burn. I saw something flash in his. Pain? Anger? "I didn't ask for it. I've been handling my ex's idiocy just fine for years, and I don't need you strutting over here so the two of you can swing things around. I have a life and a job and a client coming to meet me in about thirty seconds."

I sucked in air and contemplated duct tape. I was hot and so mortified that once again my life was on everyone's radar. And probably cell phones. "On second thought, y'all stay here and act like fools. I'll meet him somewhere else. I don't care about your bee drama or honey or parks or any of it. As far as I'm concerned, the little shits can all be kidnapped at gun point and sold for bee porn."

Bash bit back a laugh as he turned around, and I pushed past all of them to intercept my lunch date at the door.

"They're full," I said. "How does Rojo's sound?"

***

Rojo's was a Mexican restaurant a few blocks over, famous for excellent margaritas and homemade salsa. As much as the day so far was screaming for tequila, I had too many things to do to hit that up this early.

Including possibly swinging a hammer. Then again, maybe a drink was the better plan.

Monte Bradford and I both had sweet tea.

Monte had played football for the Charmed Memorial High School's varsity team, the Mighty Charmers. (The name strikes terror, doesn't it? I guess it was either that or the Honey Bees, and that worked better for the drill team.) He was *that guy*. The high school/college star who thought he could do no wrong. Pro scouts were stalking him right and left. Problem was, he was great as long as he was the shiniest star, but put him in a pack of gold stars and he disappeared. He rode the bench for two seasons with the Dolphins, quitting after loud-mouthing it about being shafted.

Yeah. He was that guy. Fast forward about eight or nine years, and now he was a big, muscled man with an equally big ego, a soft middle, thinning hair, and way too many glory-day stories to count.

Monte had gotten enough of a signing bonus to afford a good financial planner, and then hit it big in the stock market, letting him live the fancy life he thought he deserved. Two ex-wives and a big house on the other side of the Bailey's Pond (that he kept—both times) were evidently deserved. The last time I'd represented him, he was convinced that wife number two was cheating on him. (She was. With wife number one.) When I explained that I was a lawyer and not a private investigator (or a stalker), he threw money at me until I agreed to hire a PI and then serve her divorce papers.

The time before that, he sued a laundry delivery service for ruining a nine-hundred-dollar pair of slacks.

My thoughts at the time? *What man is so damn high maintenance that he buys nine-hundred-dollar pants?*

This is why law will never be my passion. Because there is always a Monte.

While Monte headed to the bathroom, I devoured half the basket of chips. I'd already worried enough about food consumption before the dick-swinging began, now I was pissed off and past caring. Let Monte think I was a pig. It wasn't any worse than what the rest of the town would be talking about.

Like I needed to give this never-forget-a-damn-thing town more fuel.

"Hey," Monte said, sliding into the booth across from me. It wasn't sunny out, but he had sunglasses perched on top of his head anyway. Probably to disguise the balding.

Sunglasses…Sully…

He wasn't balding.

Dear God, don't let every road start leading there. *He* had a woman now. One with perfect eyes and hair and skin, and could probably literally fuck while standing on her hands.

"Hey." I shoved another salsa-laden chip in my mouth.

"Want to order some *queso*?" he asked.

"Absolutely," I mumbled around the chip.

Monte laughed. "Hungry?"

"You have no idea," I said. "So what's up?"

"I think someone's getting ready to rob me."

I stopped chewing and looked at him. "What?"

He raised his eyebrows, shook his head, and dipped a chip into the salsa bowl.

"I'm not kidding," he said. "There were guys in boats the other night, just outside my fence. With flashlights and weird bulky stuff. Around midnight."

"Like real boats, or the little rowboats?"

The city of Charmed had bought rowboats for the pond back when I was in middle school. Randomly placed, anyone could use them for free to go anywhere on the pond without checking them in or out, so unfortunately it was a fifty-fifty shot if there would actually be one at the park—the most populated area. Most of the time, they congregated off the high-dollar docks across the way.

"Bigger," he said. "Like flatbeds."

"Did they break in?"

"No, they kept to the rocks and went up the bank to the caves," he said. "They didn't know I was watching from upstairs. Do you know the caves I'm talking about? Off that cove that goes into the woods?"

Caves… cove… sex… Sully… way too many times…

Damn it.

I cleared my throat. "Vaguely."

"So they went that way for a while and then came back," Monte said. "Then headed back across."

I widened my eyes, waiting for the ball to drop. "And?"

"And that's it," he said. "They're obviously casing me out." He shoved another chip into his mouth.

"Jesus, Monte, there are four other homes on that bank," I said, rubbing my forehead. "Not to mention—call the police, maybe?"

"I did!" he said, pointing a chip at me. "They came and looked around, but since there was no actual attempt at a break-in, they won't take it seriously."

I held out my hands. "And so what am I supposed to do?"

"Be waiting," he said matter-of-factly. "Because when it happens, I'm suing their asses."

I shook my head. "You can't be for real."

A pretty waitress stopped at our table. "Are y'all ready to order?"

"Please, God, yes," I said. "And put it on one bill; he's buying."

He smiled at her with his *I'm awesome like that* eye-gleam. "Sure, go right ahead."

He ordered nachos and I ordered fajitas, because it was the most expensive thing on the menu. I watched this big hulk of a man eat nachos like he was at the Ritz Carlton eating caviar. So precise. Every chip had to have an equal amount of toppings on it. It was exhausting.

"So what was going on at the Blue Banana when I got there?" Monte asked, spooning *pico de gallo* onto a precariously loaded chip by (I swear) counting the tiny cubes.

"Nothing interesting," I said before shoving a third of an overloaded fajita into my mouth. Hey, it was about to leak.

"Looked pretty interesting," he said. "You and the mayor having problems?"

What the hell was with that? "The mayor and I have no problems," I mumbled around my food. "We aren't married anymore."

"He sure looked like he was all up in your business," Monte said.

I tilted my head and finished chewing. "Nothing new there."

"And the carnie guy?"

I blinked and gave him my best hard stare. *Monte* knew? "How do you know about the carnie guy?" I shook my head. "How would you even know he *was* the carnie guy?"

Monte shrugged. "Everyone knows. And he just bought out the damn pond I live on, so of course I know who he is."

I dropped my mangled fajita. "Sully bought the whole area? He bought out y'all's land?"

Monte shook his head and laughed like he'd just told a fart joke. "No, I'm exaggerating, but he bought everything from the levee to about a mile into the woods."

The woods. "The—"

"—caves," we said in unison.

Of course he did. He didn't own a house yet, but he owned our caves.

The caves.

Not ours.

Shit.

"So what was he doing?" Monte asked.

I frowned. "Talking." *Making Dean angry. Giving me heart palpitations.*

I took another giant bite to dissuade further questions that were none of his business and chewed as slowly as I could, but he waited me out.

"What are we going to do about my robbers?" he asked finally.

How sad was it that I was glad he was back on that topic?

"They aren't robbers, Monte," I said.

"You think that's normal activity in the middle of the night?" he blustered.

"No, probably not," I said. "But so far, it's not illegal either."

"So I have to wait till they kill me?"

I rolled my eyes. "Now they're homicidal, too? Do you have a good alarm system?"

He pouted. "Yes."

"Then you're good," I said. "And if they try something, the police will be there."

"What about you?"

"You don't need a lawyer at a robbery, Monte. And I'm about to be on vacation."

"Yeah?" he asked. "For how long?"

"Longer by the day."

Chapter Four

I glanced at the digital numbers on the bottom right of my computer screen. Four o'clock. Not late, but I wanted to head out in time to run by the vet's office for Ralph's special dog food (Lanie had truly lost her damn mind) and city hall to pay my water bill (because I waited too long to mail it and they were too stubborn to get on the internet) and change my clothes before I had to report to my mother's carpentry boot camp.

I'd been hitting the trailer park's books pretty hard since after Rojo's, even through the Mexican food coma. Not counting the respite I took to pull up the permits and sales records on the Lucky Charm entertainment complex.

Because yes, I was being *that girl*. The sappy one who couldn't stop poking the ant pile. Sully's name was everywhere. His loopy signature could have been an autograph from a movie star.

Sullivan Hart.

Liar.

Breaker of hearts.

Crusher of dreams.

And wow, was I being just a tad melodramatic?

I was too old for this. I started to click out of the documents when familiar handwriting caught my eye. I scrolled down till I saw it again. The other signature. The one I'd been staring at for years. I flipped a page in the dog-eared ledger in front of me, and there it was.

Larry Landell.

Why was Larry's signature on a lease cancellation for the trailer park? There was another one—Albert Bailey—the eccentric old man that no one ever saw who owned all the land on the northwest side of town, which included the pond, the developed wealthy residential section above it, and part of the woods. And the land containing the trailer park, but Larry said that that section wasn't part of the Bailey sale. He told my mother that they were fine. But if he cancelled the lease on the land, then where was he taking the park?

She couldn't possibly know this. Well, she shouldn't have known about Sully, but I needed to let that go. This was important. She would have said something. *Hey baby, I might need to come live with you* would have been a key conversation, and I was pretty sure I'd remember it. Larry lied. He—

"He sold out," I said, hearing my voice crack.

Hell, it might not have been much of a childhood home, but it was mine. It was Allie's. It was still home to my mom, and to Allie's dad, and to twenty-something other families.

And Sully knew that.

My blood ran hot. I shut down my computer, grabbed my wallet and keys, and headed out the door. Ralph was still good on food for another day; the vet could wait. I rushed out and into my car.

Damn it, the water bill couldn't wait. That was okay, though. That was a quick two minutes in and out, and then I could storm the trailer park office and kick Larry in the nuts.

How dare he do this on the sly. How dare he screw my mother over. She was the woman he'd fawned over for as long as I could remember. How could he treat her like this?

At city hall, I pulled into the parking lot and stopped my car crookedly next to a big black Chevy truck. There'd better not be a line. I had a bone to pick with Mr. Larry Landell, and I was ready to burst out of my skin to go tell old *Lar* what he could do with that fucking ledger.

"Frosty!"

"Fuck, fuck, fuck," I muttered under my breath, looking straight ahead as I walked up the sidewalk. Maybe he'd give up. Maybe I'd vanish after so many steps. Maybe a bee would sting Alan Bowman on the tongue, and he wouldn't be able to talk anymore.

No such luck.

I turned and walked backward, hoping he would get that I was in a big hurry. Alan held up his hands and smiled like we had all the time in the world to shoot the shit, which was interesting considering just last month he'd basically called me a stranger-fucking whore.

"Sorry, Alan, I'm on my way to about five different places," I said, turning forward again as I all-but-lunged for the door.

Unfortunately, he jogged the last bit to catch up, and held the door open for me. Damn.

"Haven't seen you since—"

"—since Lanie's house became Lanie's house?" I finished for him as we breezed in. The old building always smelled like bleach and mildewed paper. Today there was a hint of a cinnamon candle burning. "Yeah, I remember. Good times."

Alan's already reddened skin glowed under his spiky blond hair. Last month had been a banner time for him, as he'd teamed up with Lanie's asshole cousin to try to schmooze her inheritance. He and his obnoxious flirt-a-holic wife, Katrina, had stayed kind of under the radar ever since, thank God.

"Yes, yes, I know," Alan said. "We don't need to revisit all that."

I grabbed a pen from a stand with a peeling Formica top.

"Don't we?" Alan would never resist the opportunity to bring up—

"Hot damn, if it's not your old boy-toy," he said, a grin stretching his face.

"What?"

I followed the direction of his gaze, and had to stifle a groan at the sight of the man standing at the counter who was evidently *everywhere*. I felt it in the fucking soles of my feet. But for once, that was okay, because after Larry, he was next on my list to chew up. I wasn't picky about the order.

"Have y'all gotten to catch up yet?" Alan's voice buzzed like an annoying fly.

"Not just yet," I said, mostly to myself.

"Well, my buddy Dean—"

"Bye, Alan" I walked away.

I was done with sentences that included the words *Dean, ex, mayor, boyfriend,* um—most recently *boy-toy*. Oh, and *Frosty*. My name was Carmen Frost. If people couldn't manage those two words, don't fucking bother me.

I might have been a little on edge.

I heard Sully's voice as I joined the line at the counter, standing a few feet behind him. It was reasonable; I was going to the same damn counter. I could be in that line. I could be in four other ones, as well, but this one was feasible. I just had to keep my anger focused and not let that deep, honeyed, lazy-sexy tone of his settle into my bones.

"Five twenty-three Maple," he told the clerk. "I don't have a statement yet. It's only been two weeks since I had the utilities turned on."

Five twenty-three Maple. *Crap.* I couldn't unhear that. Now that address was permanently seared into my brain. Did Kia live there with him? Did their toothbrushes hang out together? Did they watch TV on the couch with his head in her lap?

Ugh. I pushed my thoughts into other places. Places not Sully-touched. I needed to get Lanie my spare car key, so she and Nick could pick up my car at the rental office after I exchanged it for the convertible. And call Wyatt, a boy down the road from me, about mowing the grass while I was gone. I might need to clear all the junk out of my spare bedroom *for my mother to come live with me.*

And I was back, but in a good way.

"Thank you," Sully said. He turned around and stopped short. Because I wasn't backing up. "Shit."

"Hi."

Sully stared at me in surprise, his eyes showing a multitude of things before he could shut it all back down. One of them was pain.

It disarmed me. For about three whole world-tumbling, which-way-is-up seconds, I lost my focus. I lost my thoughts. Sully felt pain as he looked at me? Something about me hurt *him*? *What the living hell?*

"What?" he said.

I pulled myself back together.

"You took the trailer park," I said in a low voice.

He blinked and I watched him catch up. Watched the recognition flicker across his face as he realized where I was coming from. It wasn't a long trip.

"I didn't take anything," he said in an equally low voice.

"Don't play me," I said. "I saw the records. You bought out Larry for the trailer park."

"I bought the land from Bailey," Sully said, glancing around and lowering his voice even more. "I wasn't even interested in that section, but Bailey wanted to unload it, so he made me a good deal with the rest."

"And Larry?"

Sully squared his jaw. "Go outside," he said through gritted teeth. "I'm really tired of being yelled at in public today."

"I'm not yelling," I growled.

He ignored me and walked out the door. He didn't even hold it open, letting it slam in my face as I followed him. That man.

I shoved the door open and walked out, standing with my arms crossed. "We're outside," I said. "Proceed."

"Larry Landell didn't have to do a damn thing," he said. "He was leasing the space from Bailey; he could have kept on with me. He chose to end the lease."

I blinked. "That doesn't make any sense."

Sully held his arms wide. "Take it up with him."

I shook my head. "So why did no one tell me this? Hell, you've clearly known for a while, why didn't *you*?"

He looked at me like I was crazy. "Excuse me?"

"My mother still lives there, Sully," I said. "Other people live there. Some don't even own the trailers. My mom doesn't. I don't think they've even been notified."

"That's Larry's job, not mine," he said defensively.

"This is *me*," I yelled. Okay, I yelled that time. "You knew where I used to live. You couldn't give me a little heads-up? You come sliding into town, trading in your free spirit for a ball and chain, and everyone in this whole fucking town knows but me. No one says a damn word, and you can't even let me know that my mother's about to be evicted?"

Sully took a step toward me. I took one back.

"When exactly was I supposed to do this, Carmen?" he said, his upper lip twitching. "At Brewster's as you ran away? Or the Blue Banana this afternoon when you did the same?"

I backed into a railing, halting my retreat, and he kept coming, inching closer. My heart sped up twice as fast, and my fingers tingled as he got close enough to touch.

Sully pointed at the ground. "Because right here is the longest conversation you've stuck around for."

Speak. Don't lose your shit. I focused on getting the words in my head to form on my tongue.

"I'm here now," I managed. "Astound me."

He was too close. Entirely too close, as his eyes dropped to my lips. My mouth parted of its own volition, and everything inside me got dizzy hot. Once upon a time that look would have accompanied a *hello, love* and a kiss that would have started slow and then rocked my world. His gaze went heavy for a half-second, as if he too forgot his bearings for a moment. Then he shut his eyes and backed up. I grabbed the railing and squeezed until my knuckles turned white.

What the hell was that? I was mad at him. *Remember that.* He—okay, maybe he didn't purposely screw over Larry and my mother, but there was still the rest. There was Kia he was all but flaunting at me—which meant he had *no* business rocking my world or thinking about it or making *me* think about it. We were in the past. And speaking of the past, there was enough shoved down and buried anger there to fuel a village, so that was plenty. There were no more *hello loves* in our near or distant future.

"How was I supposed to know your mother still lived there?" he said, running both hands over his face. "This wasn't personal."

I laughed out loud. "Bullshit." I stepped forward that time, pushing the boundary. "You can feed me a lot of lines, Sully Hart. And Lord knows you have—"

"No, I didn't."

"Bullshit again." Being the one to move forward and make him back up filled me with adrenaline. "You did well. Said all the right things, all the pretty words."

Sully stopped moving and became a wall. "Don't."

"And I believed it all," I said. "But to tell me that moving here after all these years wasn't personal?" Something took over my brain. Something brave. Or stupid. I laid my palm against his chest, feeling the heat through his shirt. The muscles in his face twitched before his hand closed over mine like a reflex. "You could have chosen any town, anywhere. You chose mine. That's fucking personal."

Liquid fire burned behind my eyes as I pulled my hand free and marched back into the building. At least I had the snap about me to remember I'd come there for a reason. Granted, I didn't know what it was—my hands shook, and the one he'd held felt cold without his touch, but hey, I'd walked the right direction.

"Are you okay?" the girl asked when I made it to the window.

"What is this line for?" I whispered, my voice tremulous.

She looked at me with concern. "Utilities."

I nodded and pulled an envelope out of my bag, swiping at my eyes. "Water bill."

The girl smiled and nodded like she totally got it, that she had to deal with women having mental breakdowns every day.

I glanced around, hoping at least that maybe Alan hadn't witnessed any of it. I didn't have the mental fortitude after that little showdown. Oh my God, I'd touched him on purpose; I brought up the things I had no business mentioning, and there for one non-breathing second I wanted to kiss him. All in the span of about ten seconds. In public. While angry.

What the crap would I have done with time, privacy, and a good mood?

Larry. I needed to get to Larry.

* * *

"He's gone for the day," my mother said, sitting all high and mighty in her office chair, her hair twisted up in a messy bun. She had her pen stuck in it, which I might not have noticed if she hadn't made a show of pulling it out to write a note. "Actually, he never came in. Said he had some personal things to do. Which was fine, because I pretty much handle things here anyway."

My gut twisted. If Larry had been there, I would have kicked him right in the nuts.

Gerry Frost was never one to stick to things. Jobs, projects, men—everything had an expiration date. It generally came down to boredom. She passed that itchy nature onto me, then fought me over for most of my life. My itch was never about boredom, though. Mine was about seeing more, doing more, experiencing life outside the same old boundaries.

Mom's was about hearing the same guy snore for too long.

Jobs were the same way. She'd get antsy, start taking too many days off and get fired, or she'd hear about the next great work-at-home whatever and sink a bunch of money into it, only to have it go belly-up two months later. She always did enough to get us by, but it was always tight. And I ate a lot of meals at Lanie's house.

Now she was actually doing something she was proud of. Something she might stick with, because a long-time friend needed her. And he was screwing her over.

"I'm sure you do, Mom," I said. "Do you know if he'll be in tomorrow?"

I could wait till tomorrow. I could also go to his house. I'd been there for five hundred barbecues in my lifetime and could find it with my eyes closed, but something put a hand out and held me down. This was big and this was messed up, but I didn't need to go storming his front door to find out why he was doing this, and listen to him lie about it. Maybe a little reconnaissance was a better plan.

"I never know, sweetheart. He does his own thing," she said. "Usually he's in first thing in the morning for coffee and donuts. Why?"

I picked up a paperweight I'd made for her at a summer recreational program when I was about eight. It had fake colored feathers under a glass dome, on top of a green felt backing. The pink and the purple feathers were faded, and the yellow one was sliding around loose. I felt like that yellow feather, lying to my mother. Sliding around, no footing and no grip. Not that I never lied to her, but not about anything big, not in a long time. And she had that mom thing that lie detectors had no hope of competing with. I needed more practice before attempting something of this magnitude.

"Just need to clarify some things," I said, staring into the paperweight.

"On the ledger?" she asked. "Because that one was before my time. This year's, now, it's going to be pristine."

I smiled up at her. "Yeah, I'll catch up with him later."

"You okay?" she asked, narrowing those eyes. "You look a little off. You run into *him* again?"

"Oh, he's everywhere," I said. "So I'm getting used to it."

See, now there was a little lie right there. I was already getting some practice in.

"Well, you aren't getting enough sleep or something then," she said. "You look pale. And stressed."

"I'll have a glass of wine tonight and buy some self-tanner," I said with a wink. "Gotta run. Have to change before you make me get all sweaty."

"I'm not buying it," she said, cutting a look my way as I shut the door.

"I know, Mom," I whispered on the way to the car. "Me neither."

Chapter Five

It was like being in high school again. Walking across the park to approach a milling, chatting group of people, many of whom I *did* go to school with, the anxiety washed over me like teenaged sweat.

Without Lanie to be my buffer, my wing-woman, I felt very exposed and solo. People liked Lanie. You couldn't help but like her.

I never had that gift.

In school, I was the one with the inappropriate, smart-aleck retorts. I pissed off the girls and intimidated the guys. I was pretty enough to attract attention, but as soon as someone found out I lived in the trailer park, my address explained everything about me. I didn't give a rat's ass about trend or fashion, so it had to be because I lived in a double-wide. I didn't pierce my cartilage or learn how to do the perfect smoky eye or giggle over boys because my house was on cinder blocks. It was like living in a trailer became an identity trait, the explanation for my mouth or my restless spirit or for any number of things that people wanted to pick apart about me.

With Lanie, I could fake it. As her sidekick, I could blend in with the crowd. As an adult, I'd learned to tone down and blend on my own, but like my mom was always so quick to point out, I could be harsh. This was a good thing in line of work. It got the job done for my clients. For the most part, though, I was still just an older version of my high school self, and walking up to that crowd brought back a million uncomfortable memories.

I scanned the crowd for Bash, the one person I knew would be a friendly face, but I didn't see him. Where the hell was *his* town spirit?

I didn't see Alan either, thank God, but there was his wife. Katrina Bowman had red hair pulled up in a perky ponytail, giant boobs that poked out of her too-tight tank top, and shorts flossing her ass. She was talking to my ex with her hand on his arm and giggling every ten seconds. Poor Dean looked equally stressed out and turned on, which probably stressed him out more.

There was Mr. Masoneaux, the candy man. Mrs. Boudreaux, who ran the feed store. Miss Mavis, who liked to ride her three-wheeled bike up and down Main Street to catch any juicy gossip. Charlie Nicholson, who would jack off in class just for entertainment and shock value, was there caressing a hammer. Go figure. Monte was there and looking around as well, so I ducked behind another big guy and hoped he didn't see me.

"Carmen!"

And my mother. Fantastic. Because every high school awkward moment needs to include your mom.

"Hey, Mom." I grabbed my phone and scrolled down the screen, pretending to read urgent messages from people who were so much more important than this crowd. I nodded toward a bubble-shaped, old, silver travel-trailer near the water. "What's with nineteen fifty-seven?"

She glanced over her shoulder, shrugged, and turned back to me. "I don't know. Did you bring any tools?" Her eyes panned over me in my worn-out blue-jean shorts (that were not flossing, thank you very much) and tank top. A top that would not flash the world when I bent over, because responsible grown women check these things.

"Did you think I'd be wearing a carpenter's belt?" I asked. "I own exactly one broken screwdriver. I thought tools would be here."

"There will be some extra," she said, scanning the group like a drill sergeant. "But I'm asking everyone, so I get a tally of who needs tools."

I held up a hand. "Mark me. Lanie will too, when she gets back."

"Her husband doesn't have tools?"

"Really, Mom?" I said.

"Well a lot of the volunteers were prepared and brought their own," she said.

"Probably because they volunteered *themselves*," I whispered. "They weren't signed up by their mothers."

"Okay, everyone!" she called out, ignoring me, the useless daughter with no tools. "I'm gonna turn it over to Frank Coffey and get started. He will be running this event, and I'll handle any stragglers."

Frank Coffey, of Coffey's Coffee Shop, started talking. (How perfect to be born with your name basically telling you what to do. I guess I could have gotten a degree in refrigeration. Or become a superhero.) Frank wasn't a natural choice for the leader of something outdoors and laborious. He leaned toward the softer side, with a quiet voice and a passive manner. He was kind of funny when you got to know him, but you had to get past the nervous nerdy stuff to get there.

Frank read from a stack of stapled papers that had been highlighted and notated, and he kept pausing awkwardly to look up at us like someone told him to do that. Or maybe he'd checked YouTube for a tutorial on how to address a crowd.

We were special. We were awesome. We were the pride of Charmed, and we were going to build a place for future Charmed citizens to use for generations to come. A gazebo for gazing at the water or for holding outdoor weddings. A covered pavilion for events and bands and premium booth space during the Honey Festival. An outside contractor would build the boardwalk that would frame the water outside the shops, but the gazebo and pavilion would be our contribution.

Bash had snuck in during all the rah-rah-ness of it all. He nudged me with his arm like a school kid.

"So you're coming to be Mr. Town Spirit after all," I said under my breath.

Bash had not been awkward nor an outcast in school; he was the hot funny one. Cute and witty, with All-Star everything, he hid his family issues behind eyes that could melt clothing and a zany sense of humor. I wasn't in his orbit in school, but giving him legal advice on his business after he returned from the Marines had turned us into fast friends.

"Only if there's a crown," he said with a smirk. "Just figured I needed to come do my civic duty."

"Do you have tools?" I whispered. "Because my mother has become the tool Nazi."

He gave me a sideways glance. "I built every one of my hives."

I rolled my eyes. "Show off."

"So why are they doing these outside things now, before construction begins?" Bash asked as Frank flipped over a page and droned on. "It's all going to be in the way."

I nudged him. "Good question. Ask it."

"Nah, I'll wait," he said. "There's probably a reason."

"There's probably not," I said. "And you could put a temporary end to this madness."

"You don't want to play?" he asked, grinning down at me.

"Not with my mother being team captain," I said.

"Then raise your hand and ask," he said, nodding toward the front with a mischievous glint to his eyes. "Impress the captain."

"Oh hell no," I said. "It's *your* question. I'm not drawing any more attention to myself."

"I'm sorry." My mother's voice cut over Frank's drone. He looked up in a panic and put a finger on the paper so he wouldn't lose his place. "Carmen, did you have something to share?"

I frowned at her and glanced at the faces as all heads turned to me. "Seriously?" I said.

"Well, you and Bash seem to have more important things to bring up than what Frank is saying," she said, her mom tone in full force. "So feel free."

Bash laughed behind his hand.

"You're such a shit ball," I whispered, jabbing him in the ribs.

"Quit, or she'll make you go put your nose on that tree," he whispered back.

I huffed out a breath. "Okay," I said. "So shouldn't this wait until they are done?"

Frank blinked a bunch of times and smiled. "I'm sorry?"

I pointed at the land along the pond. It was flat and muddy on our side, lifting to rocky ledges on the other side where the nice houses were. "With all the construction that's going to go on out here, it's going to be a mess. Big trucks in and out. Concrete trucks, bulldozers. Won't the gazebo and pavilion be in the way? Wouldn't it be better to wait and add our contribution to this… wonderful thing that will be out here, instead of building it in front of nothing and then it's in their way?"

"Yes."

The voice came from my left before Frank could open his mouth. I knew whom it belonged to without looking over, or at my mother's mortified expression.

The crowd turned collectively and the whispers started as Sully Hart walked out of the vintage trailer, the metal door banging shut behind him. He strode up in his worn jeans, work boots, and dark blue T-shirt. And the Ray-Bans. God help me. A ragged tool belt swung from his right hand; he clutched a box in the other.

"Shit," I muttered under my breath.

"I don't see you on the sign-up list," my mother said, holding up her ever-present clipboard. "Mr. Hart?" The acid in her tone was unmistakable.

"The more the merrier, right?" he answered, flashing her a brilliant smile as he set down his loads. "And yes to your question, Carmen," he said, looking right at me. My fingertips went numb. "It would be better, but the powers that be decided that this was the most important thing to do—right now. So we're doing it *right now*."

"Now who's showing off?" Bash muttered, nudging me with his elbow again.

I didn't have the concentration to spare to give Bash a dirty look. I had to focus on not looking like all the blood drained out of my head.

"But you can't be a part of this," Katrina said. Clearly, she and Alan were in Dean's freaky little band. "You are the company for the development. This is for Charmed residents."

Sully grinned slowly as he pushed up his sunglasses. "I'm a resident," he said.

"You're living in that trailer?" my mother asked.

He shook his head, glancing over his shoulder. "That's my office. And this project will be the first thing people see when they drive up to the Lucky Charm. The first impression they'll get. I want to make sure this is done right."

"Excuse me?" Dean stepped forward.

"This *should* be done afterward," Sully said, ignoring him. "Carmen's right. But it's not going to be, so I'm here to make sure it's portable."

"I'm sorry, portable?" Frank finally spoke up.

"Able to be broken down and moved," Sully clarified. "In my business—"

"Here we go," Dean muttered, turning around as if he had something else to do or somewhere to be. "He's gonna give us carnie wisdom."

Sully only gave him a second's pause. "Okay then, in *carnie wisdom*, everything has moving parts. Everything has a blueprint and a plan for assembly and disassembly, because when the event is up for that town, we generally have less than a day to be packed up and gone." His eyes landed on mine. "We have to disappear like we were never there."

I couldn't blink as three seconds stretched into forever. He pulled his shades back down and kept going. I tried to remember what inhaling was about.

"Every machine we have, every prop we build, every stage we put up—like the grandstand stage for the esteemed mayor to give his welcome speech—" Sully pointed at Dean. "They are in pieces. Each piece is marked, and they have slots, locks, and levers that work seamlessly into a finished product that is about as genius as it gets. It's sturdy, it's hardy, and it can be broken down and stored in an hour." He gave a smile that didn't reach his eyes. "Which in *carnie time*, since we're such an uneducated lot, is really just thirty minutes."

Dean scoffed loudly, and I glanced at Bash, who was shaking his head like he wanted to thump him in the back of the head. I wished he would.

"And you want to make our gazebo and pavilion this way?" Frank asked, looking disappointed.

"Yes sir," he said.

Frank stood a little taller, as though no one had ever called him 'sir' in his life. I had a feeling Sully had won one over.

"That way, it can be there for the media, for the ground-breaking, for whatever the city council needs it for," Sully said. "And then when the real work begins, it can be moved out of the way."

It was reasonable. It was logical. It made sense. I hated that, and felt a weird pride at the same time. What was that about?

"What do you think?" I asked under my breath as I looked up at a pensive Bash.

He chuckled. "I think it's brilliant."

I sighed. Great. Brilliant.

"Won't that require new plans?" my mother said, the chill in her voice apparent. "Frank already acquired instructions on how to build these."

"Trust me," Sully said.

"*Trust* you?" Mom sputtered, spurring me to leap forward before she said something I might never live down or forget.

"Let's just get started, shall we?" I said. "What do we need to do?"

The trailer door opened again, and Kia stepped out, looking like a carpenter's pinup poster. Of course she was there. Where else would she be but up Sully's ass?

"Who is *that*?" Bash asked.

"Sully's—" My throat fought the word. "Girlfriend, I guess. They grew up together on the carnival."

"Damn," he said, eyes glued to her.

"Really?" I shoved him. "You can't throw me a bone and tell me she's nothing special?"

He smiled and squeezed my shoulder.

"You're much hotter," he said, making his eyes all innocent.

"You don't lie very well."

He laughed shortly. "You'd be surprised." The spark returned to his eyes as she approached. "Oh yeah, she's hideous," he said in a whisper.

"I hate you," I whispered back.

"You can help me dole out the action items," she said, walking up to us. "Since you know everyone."

"Bash Anderson," Bash said, holding out a hand.

Her perfect eyebrows moved just a fraction of an inch. "Bash?"

"Sebastian," he amended.

The hint of a smile touched her lips. "Sebastian," she repeated. "Better. I'm Kia."

And I'm invisible. "I'm Carmen," I said. "It's been a long time, I don't know if you remember meeting me."

Her dark eyes fell on me. "I remember."

Okay.

Swallow your pride. Work with his new bang.

I licked my lips and smiled. "What do you need?"

My mother left in a huff about a half hour in, but the rest of us got to work. With Sully in charge, volunteers took down measurements. He distributed action items and a budget for people to go buy wood, nails, screws, and extra hammers. A few others said they had cordless drills at home, and Sully said he'd take care of the odd things like the levers and other tools I'd never heard of.

It was surreal.

Seeing him talking and walking among us like he'd always been there. Except that now he was mature and responsible and knew things about things, and had a sexy female sidekick. With the exception of two seemingly angry phone calls he had to take, he was on top of what everyone was doing. I felt a little sorry for Frank and his one chance to be team captain, but Sully was making it happen and quickly. With Frank in charge, we'd have still been there talking it to death after the whole theme park was done.

I was hot, and not in a good way. Definitely not in a Kia way. I was sweaty and smeared with dirt, and my knees were bruised from crawling around on the ground. Kia was sweaty and dirty, but she looked like she'd been doing the nasty in the dirt and loving it. Great. Good for her. Good for Sully. They'd make beautiful babies.

I ignored whatever crawled on my neck as I stretched string and tied it to sticks shoved into the ground marking areas that needed to be leveled. I was halfway done making indentions in the dirt with a shovel, when I felt Sully behind me.

"What are you doing?" he asked.

"Playing in the dirt," I said. "You?"

"Why?"

"I'm marking where the string is so we can pick it up," I said.

"We don't need to pick it up," he said as I turned around. "We leave it here till we have the wood to take its place."

"Great," I said. "Someone told me to do this."

"Someone probably wanted to watch you do that," he said, chuckling as his eyes scanning me. Before I could make a scathing remark about his once-over, he continued. "Speaking of, it'll be easier on your knees to wear jeans. You'll be kneeling a lot. And work gloves would be good, too."

I nodded toward the dream girl, stretching in the sun like a cat and laughing at something Bash was saying. "Kia has shorts on."

"She's used to things like this."

"And I'm a sissy weakling?" I said.

He held up his hands. "Fine. Wear whatever you want. I was just trying to help."

I blew out a breath. *Dial back the hormonal jealousy, Carmen. You are above this.*

"I may not be out here every day, anyway," I said. "I may be working late."

He nodded. "Because of me?"

I scoffed and scratched my cheek, realizing too late that I'd added more dirt to my face.

"No," I said indignantly. "Because I may have to *work late*." I forced a laugh. "Not everything I have to do pertains to you. And I'm leaving in a couple of weeks anyway."

"Leaving?"

"On vacation," I said.

"The work'll still be here when you get back," he said with a small smile. "You won't be gone forever."

"I wouldn't count on that," I said, surprising myself. The thought had been playing with me, but it was the first time I'd said it out loud. Damn it, the things he made me do. I shrugged. "I work for myself. I'm licensed to practice anywhere in Texas and there's no end date. And nothing keeping me here."

I watched the words land on him, expecting him to step back and go distant. To get pissed off and be a jerk. That's what I wanted. It's what I needed. I needed for him to stop being everywhere I breathed air, and just go play house with his sex goddess. Preferably in another town, in case I did end up back here.

There was no jerk, however. No distant jaw twitching. Instead, he reached out and then let his hand drop, lifting it again as if it had a mind of its own. He swiped the dirt from my cheek with one finger, and I almost lost my knees. My bruised dirt-covered knees. *Shit-damn-hell.*

"Sorry," he said, frowning at his hand as if it betrayed him and backing up a step.

I had to channel that surge of *what-the-fuck* into something, so I shoved the shovel into the dirt, letting it stick up like I knew what I was doing.

"I have to go," I said. "I—I'm housesitting for Lanie and I need to feed her dog, so…"

Jesus Christ. *I'm a big unlovable loser* wasn't taken, so that was the sentence I went with.

"Yeah," he said.

Thankfully, I didn't trip and break the string as I turned around. Unthankfully, I caught Dean's eye. He stood across the field watching me with his arms crossed like a jilted woman.

It was the final knot in my rope for the day. My heart pounded like I'd swum the perimeter of the pond; I was filthy, and I'd spent entirely too much time today way too close to Sully Hart. I was done with this day and these people. I wanted a shower, a book, and maybe Ralph snoring in my lap. And one more thing.

"Ice cream," I muttered. "Chocolate fucking ice cream."

* * *

Lanie and Nick were on their way home from their honeymoon, and I was thankful for about a billion reasons. Namely, that a relatively sane person I trusted could look me in the eye and remind me that I was a grown independent woman with no logical reason to need anything from Sully Hart. Answers, mouth-to-mouth, monkey sex in a cave….

None of it.

Not that any of those things were on my mind the last two days since crawling in the dirt or the one-on-one outside City Hall. At all. Or that I'd been obsessing over every word, every look, every inch he'd closed between us, or the way his hand had automatically closed over mine one day and had to touch me the next. Or that I was thinking of him or Kia— or him *and* Kia—or *any* of it while I drove home from the last-minute trip to the vet's office for Ralph's food (I promise; he didn't starve), fully aware that Maple Street was just four measly little blocks off of Main.

Because I was an adult. A responsible, non-flaky adult. Hitting my blinker. Turning down Eighth Avenue. To Maple.

I shook my head all the way down the road, unable to believe what

I was doing. This was the kind of thing I lectured my divorcing clients about. Obsessing over their exes.

I'm not obsessing. I'm just curious. Curious over what could make someone so untethered and beautifully free want to fence themselves in. Yep, that was all.

I didn't have long to find out. I turned left on Maple toward the five-hundred block and my palms started to sweat. My pulse raced. Even before I saw the house number, I knew it had to be the one with the big black Chevy out front. The Chevy I'd parked next to at city hall the other day. Of course I had.

The house itself was ordinary. Brick and wood, one story, non-descript with no real landscaping. Some of the flower beds had been marked off with stakes, but that was about it. I rolled slowly past, my mouth completely dry.

"This is crazy," I muttered.

And then he walked around the side of the house. I hunched over and gunned it at the same time, parking around the corner where I could still see him but he wouldn't notice me.

"How pathetic am I?" I whispered.

My phone screamed through the speakers. I yelped and then clapped a hand over my mouth as I hit the button.

"Hello?" I whispered, not caring who was on the other end of the line.

Because he was there. In a tight, ratty tank top, old jeans, and a backward baseball cap, he drove a shovel into the ground, arm muscles rippling. Now *that* was how to sink a shovel. Sweet Jesus.

"We're at the airport," Lanie said. Nick muttered something in the background. "So we should be home in a couple of hours. After they find our other suitcase, anyway."

"Awesome," I hissed, watching Sully turn over dirt, one shovelful after another. "Drive safe."

"Awesome?" she said. "They lost our suitcase."

"Oh, sorry," I said. "Hope they find it quickly."

"Why are you whispering?" Lanie whispered.

Because I'm hiding around the corner from Sully Hart's house, of all things, watching him play in the dirt and get sweaty.

Completely logical.

"Um, I'm in a building," I said, just as a truck pulling a squeaky trailer drove around me.

"You sound like you're outside."

"We have things to talk about when you get home," I said. "So plan on some ice-cream-on-the-couch girl time tonight after you get unpacked. Nick and Ralph can go somewhere and bond."

Lanie laughed. "I'll let him know. See you soon. And Carmen?"

"Yeah?"

"No Sully."

See? That's what I needed. But in person, with a leash or a stun gun. Or a box of imported chocolate. I dropped the phone in my lap and watched as my tattoo—*his* tattoo—moved with him. He had more of them now, but the one on his left bicep that matched the tiny one inside my left breast tugged at me. An infinity sign.

I love you, Carmen. Forever.

It was supposed to signify that. Something we'd done together the day before he left me. Forever. I guess it was significant after all.

The old pain stabbed through me like it was coming straight from that fifteen-year-old ink, and I welcomed it. Yes, *remember that.* Remember how that felt to stand there alone, waiting at the stadium, where he said he'd pick me up. Remember the confusion and pain as I left Charmed to drive hours to the last carnival stop, thinking maybe I just misunderstood.

Remember that.

He left you.

And now he was back.

Another person appeared from the side, her cute figure sporting a bandeau top and gym shorts, her long dark hair pulled up in a high ponytail. She carried a little spade, perfect for tending flowerbeds.

My stomach lurched at the domestic sight they made. Yeah, he left me, all right.

For her.

But something was off. Something like... awareness. That energy between couples that links them together and says they're a unit without doing a single couple-ish thing.

They didn't have it.

No. I wasn't going to sit here and analyze them. I refused. Fuck him.

I put the car in drive and coasted till I was out of sight, then hit the gas back to Lanie's house. Back to people who didn't ditch their loved ones.

* * *

"Aunt Ruby would have been so proud of us," Lanie said, flopping onto the couch and sitting cross-legged. "We actually went to a toga party at Caesar's Palace."

"No way," I said.

"Yep," she said. "I have pictures." She pointed at me. "Real pictures, too, not manufactured ones."

Lanie's Aunt Ruby had been an eccentric breed of woman who definitely marched to her own drummer. In all the times I spent in that house growing up, we did some crazy things. Waking up at midnight for a picnic under the stars. Blanket forts with twinkle lights. Wrapping ourselves in sheets for Julius Caesar's birthday. Baked cinnamon apple treats to mark special occasions, like a 'C' on a test or a particularly good hair day.

Aunt Ruby raised Lanie after her dad left and her mom died, and although there was always talk and speculation about the inexplicable and "special" things that happened in that house, there was never any question about the love there. Both ways. When Aunt Ruby hired me to do her will, she made sure to set Lanie up to succeed, even though Lanie had shown her fake pictures of a happy life. Now, possibly due to her aunt's interference, she had the real deal.

I wouldn't lie. The nights I spent there dog-sitting Ralph, I threw a few thoughts out to the cosmos. It wouldn't have hurt my feelings to have Aunt Ruby interfere a bit like that in my life.

"So tell me what's going on," Lanie said, as Nick dropped a drive-by kiss on her head. "Spill it all."

I gave her the low-down on everything since she'd left. Good lord, had that only been two weeks? It felt like two months. The big secrets that weren't secrets. Bailey. Larry. My mother. Sully.

"Holy shit," she said finally.

"Right?" I said, holding up a spoonful of double Dutch chocolate. This conversation needed the heavy armory. "It's like everything fell apart when you left."

"We knew about the permanent carnival thing coming," Lanie said. "But Lucky Hart doing that really didn't cross my mind."

"If it were just a rides thing it might have," I said. "But the boardwalk and shops and everything he's doing…I have to be impressed." I held up my spoon again, along with my other hand. "I don't want to be, but damn the guy has to have some heavy backing to pull this off."

"Not the rebellious hot carnie boy I remember," Lanie said.

My skin got hot. "He's so much that and more," I said. I thought it was to myself. But the look in Lanie's widened eyes told me it was out loud.

"Really, now?"

I ran a hand over my face. "I tell myself every day that he's still the asshole that crushed me and never looked back."

Lanie nodded. "And? But?"

I blinked and looked away. "And I don't know. That's easy to do from a distance." I stared down into my ice cream and shook my head. "I saw him and Kia at the Blue Banana. And then today, at—" I stopped. Foot in mouth.

"At where?" she asked. "At the site?"

"Yeah." I was lying to my best friend now? *Guilty, counselor.* "But, I don't know. Something doesn't fit."

Lanie furrowed her brow. . "What do you mean?"

I rolled my head. "Looks. A feeling. No, it's the looks," I reiterated. "The way he looks at me just—"

"Cher says that's just his eyes," Lanie said, spooning butter pecan into her mouth.

"Then his eyes are fucking killing me," I said, the witty charade fading as my own lame-ass words settled over me. "I don't know what to think," I said softly, blowing out a breath that wasn't all that steady. "Or why I'm thinking anything. And I can't stand that; you know I can't stand that. I'm always on top of everything. But..." But what? The way his eyes would burn into me every time? The way he'd fought the need to touch me? To be close? *The way I fucking liked it?* Damn it, that was the worst part of it all. "When he looks at me," I whispered to myself, staring at the pillow.

"Carmen."

I jumped at her tone and jerked my head up to see the old Lanie glaring at me.

"Don't you get lost in him again," she said in a low voice. "Don't let him break you."

The words hit me like ice pellets in the face. My eyes grew hot with unbidden tears.

"I'm trying," I said, hearing the tremble in my voice and hating it. "But every time he gets close it's like—"

"He gets close?" Lanie asked, leaning forward. "How, dear, is he doing that?"

"Because I'm a moron and can't seem to escape the magnetic pull," I said, swiping the tears off my cheeks as they fell. "I don't know. He's just friggin' everywhere. I don't go looking for him." *Except for today. But we'll keep that to ourselves.*

She leaned further forward and gave me a stern look. "You need to remember that he doesn't deserve you."

"Can you record that so I can play it on a loop?" I asked. "Now that Bailey sold him everything, it's like there's nothing he doesn't touch.

Including that thing my mother signed us up for. You are coming with me the next time."

"Which would have been today?"

"Okay, tomorrow."

Nick walked in, plopping into their oversized chair like the world had worn him clean out. "Vegas is exhausting,"

I blew out a breath and swiped under my eyes, grateful for the change in subject.

"Good exhausting, but I think I've walked around the planet twice in the last two weeks." He frowned at me and gave his wife a double-take. "Are you okay? Did I interrupt something?"

"Not at all," I said with a smile.

"Do I need to kick somebody's ass?" he asked, making me laugh out loud. "Because I'm on it."

"No," I said, kicking at his foot. "But thank you for offering. And you run every morning like a freak. How can walking tire you out?"

Nick shook his head. "Slow walking. Shopping walking. Strolling walking. Give me a hard fast run any damn day over that."

"Love you," Lanie sang.

Ralph jumped up on the couch next to her. He rolled onto his back with his head in her lap, tongue lolling out as she rubbed his belly. Oh, to be a dog.

"Love you too, babe," Nick said, saluting her. "Just let's look at a beach vacation next year, okay?"

"How about a cruise?"

Nick gave a thumbs-up. "Even better." He nodded my way. "So, back to the story. Sorry, this house is like an echo chamber. Who's Bailey?"

"He's kind of a mystery, as not too many people ever see him," Lanie said. "I think my aunt was friends with him when they were kids. But he owns like a third of the town, and he sold all the land around the pond for that entertainment area Alan was talking about last month."

"Alan," Nick said under his breath, like one might say *bed sores* or *pond scum*.

"I know," Lanie said with a grimace. "Sorry. Oh, Carmen, I had an e-mail that there's a town meeting tomorrow, so maybe they aren't working on the pavilion. You going?"

I looked at her. "The one driven by my ex-husband?" I asked. "Are you really asking me that question?"

"It's about the project."

I groaned. "Do you know how tired I am of that? And of people giving me the side-eye because they can't move into this century?"

"Which would give you a chance to look like a grown-up at a meeting with both men," Lanie said.

I sucked ice cream off my spoon. "Didn't make much difference the other day But maybe repetition might dispel some of my pariah status with those who still think I wronged Saint Dean in some way."

"It's a thought," Lanie said. "We can meet so you won't be by yourself. In case Kia is there, too. And in case you feel the need to speak up, you'll have the chance."

"I won't."

"But still."

I smiled. "So Mr. Bailey. He's supposed to be psychic or something."

Lanie tilted her head. "Really?"

"Yeah," I said. "Sully's dad knew him. When Sully and I were... dating..." My tongue tripped on the word. Was three weeks dating? Sounded lame now, but it sure felt like the moon and the sun at the time. "He told me that his dad was a big believer in that stuff, and was a stickler about only hiring the real thing for the carnival attractions. He'd rather pay for the real thing than have the fakes that other companies did. And somehow through the years he met Old Man Bailey and they got to be friends."

"So you think that's why he sold to Sully?" Lanie asked.

"Bigger question—two, actually," I said, sitting up as the curiosity bounced around in my veins. "Is what is Larry doing?" I held up a finger. "I mean, is he moving it? To where? Or selling it? And why the hell hasn't he said anything? And how the hell do I bring this up with my mother?"

"All those go with one finger?" Nick asked.

I slid him a look. "Yes."

"Keep up, babe," Lanie said, winking at him.

"And two," I said, holding up the second for Nick. "Is..." My throat closed on the question. I shouldn't care. But it was there. "Why would someone who had the world at their disposal and freedom to go wherever he chose want to move to Charmed, Texas and plant rosebushes?"

Lanie lifted an eyebrow. "He bought?"

"Leasing to own."

"With *her*?"

My heart fluttered. "It appears so."

"Hmm," she said, eyeing me. "Let's focus on that one."

I sighed. "I figured you would."

"First, counselor, why is it important?" she asked. *Boom.*

"Oh, we're playing that, are we?"

"Karma's a bitch, isn't it?" she asked, grinning.

"Am I missing something?" Nick asked.

I chuckled. "More than you know. Okay. Let's go." I cracked my knuckles. "Why is it important?" I echoed. "Because…because…it feels like something is off. Like…who is this person? The guy I fell in love with a hundred years ago was this vibrant rebel with a drive to see the world. Like me," I added as my heart pounded harder. "How do I reconcile that person with this businessman setting up utility bills for a house on Maple Street?"

"I'm not going to ask how you know he lives on Maple Street," Lanie said.

Busted. "That's a good plan."

"But Carmen, people change," she said. "The guy you fell for was a twenty-year-old travelling carnie. He's thirty-five now and just lost his dad. A dad he saw do nothing but run a carnival his whole life. Probably never had a house. He's probably checking his own mortality and figuring if he's going to change his course, he needs to do it now."

"But—"

"But you feel let down, because even though he hurt you and you swore never to feel that again, in your heart you preserved him as that wild soul that got away," Lanie said.

I stared at her. "Yes."

"And now he's back, but he's normal and not wild, playing house with flexi-girl, and you feel betrayed again," she said.

"Shit." She was good at this. Too good.

"So now we're back to my original question, counselor," Lanie said. "Why does it matter? Why is Sully Hart even on your radar after what he did?"

"And I have one," Nick said, raising his hand.

"You don't have to raise your hand, honey," Lanie said.

"I didn't know the rules," he said.

"Proceed," I said, still reeling from Lanie's questions. I wanted to put my head between my legs and do some counted breathing.

"Back in the day," Nick said. "You said he was this vibrant… something or other."

"Rebel," Lanie and I said in unison.

He pointed at me. "So, my question is… did you fall for the guy or the lifestyle?"

I blinked. "What?"

Nick shrugged. "Was it what he did or who he was that grabbed you?" he asked. "Because we all grow up. We change what we do. But whether he's travelling the country or planting bushes, he's the same guy."

"Who left her without a word, without a note, and just vanished into thin air," Lanie said.

"Okay," Nick said, looking back at me like he was waiting for something. "And?"

I raised my eyebrows. "And what?"

"Have you asked him why?"

Chapter Six

The sky looked ominous. Was that a sign that I should turn around and go home? Get the hell out of the very spot where I hit rock bottom? I pulled into the school parking lot the same time Lanie did. The big black Chevy wasn't there. The irony hit me like a wrecking ball to the groin. If that metaphor works.

Sully left me in that very parking lot. Two, actually, if you count the other one I then drove halfway across the state to stand in alone—again. This one had history, though. Our first kiss was behind the concession stand, forever linking lust to the smell of hot dogs and pretzels. Our first time was under the bleachers in the pouring rain, leaning against a beam with my leg wrapped around his waist and him slow-driving me till we both cried out into the thunder, our limbs shaking with exertion.

I'd changed my top four times before I left, settling on a red V-neck mid-sleeve shirt that always made my boobs look good, with just the tiniest peek of creamy cleavage. Not that I remembered how he was a die-hard boob man and couldn't keep his hands off mine. Because that would be teasing and messing with things that shouldn't be messed with.

Dear God, I was a head-case.

He would be here. I wondered if those memories would cross his mind when he drove up, or if guys even did that whole tortured memory-lane thing. I knew Dean did. He remembered far more than any woman I knew, and would bring up the smallest detail if it helped him win an argument.

I got out and fell into step beside Lanie as we approached the gymnasium doors.

"You okay?" she asked.

"Yeah."

"You're wearing your good boob shirt," she pointed out.

"Am I?" I said, feigning ignorance as I looked down. "Huh."

"Yeah," she said, laughing as she looped an arm through mine. "You are."

Have you asked him why?

I'd been thinking about Nick's question all day. No, I hadn't asked. Why not? Because maybe I didn't want to know. Or maybe part of me thought I shouldn't have to ask. Maybe he should know he owed me an explanation.

Or maybe I was just a big chicken shit wanting to keep my head in the sand rather than learn the truth.

When we walked into the gym, there were a whopping four people sitting in the bleachers, spread out so they didn't have to talk to each other. Not really the crowd I was hoping to make an impression on in one fell swoop.

"I hope this thing is quick," I said. "Before Armageddon hits out there."

"Radar said we have about an hour," Lanie said, peering out the open door. "According to Nick, who checks it religiously every day."

"Why?"

"It evidently tells him whether customers are going to venture out," she said. "So he's become the rain whisperer. Where do you want to sit?"

I gave her a look as we stood in front of nearly empty bleachers. "I think we pretty much have the run," I said. "It's ridiculous that he books the gym for this, like the whole town is going to come out in droves. They could have used the Blue Banana."

"True. Then we could at least eat."

"And have coffee."

"And dessert," she said. "Although Nick's cooking us a romantic dinner tonight with some kind of flaming dessert, so I'll stay hungry."

"I wanted to sit in the back," I said, my already limited patience with this event wearing thin. I looked around. "There is no back. Just up. God, I hated coming in here for pep rallies."

"The back wouldn't matter," Lanie said, walking up two steps and plopping down. "Do you really think neither of them would notice you?"

"Them?" I said, staring down at her. Yes, I was there to prove a point to people about both of them, but that was me. I wanted past the *Carmen and the Carnie* jokes I'd heard for the past decade. *They*—as in my ex and my whatever-the-hell-he-was—were not here for me. They had their own agendas. "There is no *them,* Lanie. Hell, there is no *one.* There's nothing. They aren't here about me."

"No, but their common denominator is you," she said. "As soon as they see each other, they'll look for you, and so will everyone else. Then you will have your moment to show how stupid they all are."

"Is this a pep talk?" I asked, starting to sweat. "God, this was a bad idea. I'm leaving." I turned to hightail it out of there before someone pulled out a megaphone. Or before Sully arrived, taking all my good sense.

"Ladies, I'm glad you could make it," Dean's voice echoed through the room as he walked up. He was smiling, a definite improvement over the sulking. "There's coffee on that table over there."

"Thank God," I muttered. "Is there rum, too?"

"I should have put BYOB on the invite," Dean said, smirking at me.

Hmm. He was trying to make nice. Joke. Be a normal person. Interesting tactic. Not enough to keep me there, though. My palms itched at the thought of Sully being there, schmoozing the crowd, talking to people, being part of the town the way he had the other day.

Was that it? Was I jealous about sharing him with everyone when he'd always just been mine?

That was a sobering thought.

"Might have gotten better attendance," I said, glancing around. "What's the real point of this meeting, Dean? Doesn't everyone already know about this? From what I've heard, Sully's had a mock-up over at the library for a while."

"I want people to be able to speak their mind," Dean said, smiling at old Miss Mavis, who had probably just come in to get off her tricycle before the rain hit. "Say their piece if they haven't had a chance. Tell Hart what they think of this whole thing. It affects everyone."

He had on his politician face, which meant there was no talking logic with him.

"Whatever," I said. "I'm not staying. Good luck tonight." I pointed as more people filed in. They were all business owners. Of course, they would be the only ones who cared about this shit. "Look, it's getting better."

"Carmen, come on," he begged. "You need to stay and be a part of things."

Geez. It was like being married to the man again.

"I have been a part of things."

"You haven't been back to the build."

"The… build?" I asked. "That's what it's called now?"

"Was it too much to be out there with *him*?" Dean asked, looking wounded.

Just shoot me. "I've just been busy," I said. "And tonight—I wasn't thinking. I came with Lanie but I… have a thing I need to do. Prepare for tomorrow."

"Tomorrow's Saturday."

"It'll take all weekend," I lied. "And the weather's about to get nasty, so…"

Go. Just go.

I went. Waving quickly at Lanie, I turned to head out the door before anyone else could stop me.

Sully walked in.

Oh, fuck balls.

We both stopped, and my insides went fifteen degrees warmer. A gray-and-navy pullover shirt clung to him like paint, over worn soft-looking jeans and his leather work boots. His hair—that's where my jaw dropped. Dear God, he'd cut his hair. He'd never cut his hair. I mean, he wasn't Samson, but he loved it long. But there it was—not short-short; it still swung a little in the front, but it was definitely above-the-collar respectable, and sweet Jesus it was even sexier than before.

No, it wasn't about sharing him. That was abundantly clear by the vise that gripped my chest as his gaze soaked me in. It was about sharing air *with* him. With the only man that ever broke me.

Have you asked him why?

I didn't speak. I just turned around and walked back in, straight to Lanie, and sat down.

"You're gray, Carmen," Lanie said. "You need to breathe. Look, there's your mom."

She pointed toward the door, where my mother walked in with Larry, and waved. *Larry.* My head pounded with yet another rush of adrenaline, but it wasn't the time. Not in front of her.

I cleared my throat of the gravel. "I'm fine," I said. All my muscles felt like they had gone on strike. *Keep it together. You aren't eighteen anymore.*

"Sully cut his hair," she said.

"Sully cut his hair," I echoed.

"It looks good," she said. "Wow. He's… he's grown up well."

I laced my fingers together and watched him walk across the gym floor, shaking a few hands and looking totally at ease in his skin. My skin wasn't easy at all. My skin was staging a coup.

"Yeah."

* * *

The weather knew what it was doing. From the moment Sullivan Hart introduced himself, every tense sentence, every ridiculous question clearly preplanned and planted by Dean, was punctuated with increasingly closer rumbles of thunder. Then the rain hit, banging off the metal gym roof at a deafening level. At that point, everyone slumped and relaxed into it. No point hurrying anything along when we were all obviously stuck there.

Sully held his own. Answered everything with that calm and soothing tone of his that drove me mad, but at least I could just sit back and watch him talk and move in relative anonymity. He wasn't talking to me, so I didn't have to focus on breathing or comebacks or body language or hiding my reactions.

Except maybe from Lanie, who kept sliding me looks every time he'd laugh or say something charming. Which was a lot. He was winning over the crowd—mostly. With the exception of Dean, whose dark cloud rivaled any outside, and a handful of his groupies. And my mother, whose glare could be seen in Canada.

And then it got fun.

Mom stood up during a lull, and I felt the impending doom crash over me like a wave.

"Shit," I mouthed.

"I think we all know you aren't new to Charmed," my mother said, crossing her arms.

"Oh, no," I said under my breath.

Lanie clapped a hand down on my knee.

Sully looked at my mother with a weird expression on his face. Not weird in the sense that I was just freaking out and probably holding my breath and getting lightheaded kind of weird, but in a familiar *I know you and don't like you* kind of weird. I didn't have time to think that out.

"No ma'am," he said. "I've come here every summer for many years."

"Ruining my daughter in the process," she said.

"Make it stop," I whispered.

"Stole the mayor's wife," someone said over to the far right, causing snickers.

"Excuse me?" I said, the words coming out of my mouth before I could stop them. Somebody said to be quiet and I think that was in my head, but—

"No, she was still underage," someone else said. "And he was a dirty carnie back then, not all glossy like he is now. What do you expect?"

"Hey!" Lanie stood up like she was someone to be reckoned with. "You don't know what you're talking about, and that's my friend you're bad-mouthing."

"Like you're any better," a buxom redhead said, standing to turn and face her. It was Katrina Bowman, Lanie's very slutty neighbor who'd put the moves on Nick when they first came to town. "You made up a husband just to screw everyone over."

Everyone started talking at once. Lanie climbed over people like a redneck monkey to get to Katrina. A big guy grabbed her before she could get her hands in that red hair. The ruckus was loud, the rain was louder, and Sully and my mother stood in absolute silence staring each other down.

I stood up.

"Excuse me!" I yelled. I put a finger and thumb in my mouth and let loose a piercing whistle, bringing an end to everything but the downpour on the tin. Dean turned his back as if he were embarrassed, but Sully's angry eyes rose to me. "For the record, you nosy assholes, I'm right here! I was not underage, nor was I married, *nor* was I even dating Dean Crestwell back then." Dean whirled around. "I was single. Nobody *stole* anyone. No one cheated on anyone." I glared at my mom. "Nobody *ruined* anyone. You've all dated people and broke up, right? There ya go. Sully Hart and I had a relationship, and then we didn't." I felt the burn behind my eyes as my volume went up. I couldn't stop. I'd had enough. For fifteen years, I'd had enough. "Then Dean and I got married after college, and now we're divorced. End of story. Not that any of it is anyone's fucking business, but I'm fucking tired of the comments!" I was breathing hard and something inside me was ringing warning bells and saying the trailer-park chick in me was rearing her ugly head, but I couldn't shut up. "I did nothing to your perfect mayor and if he'd be a man and grow a damn pair, he'd say that, too. Get a life!"

A flash of lightning hit something close, sounding like an explosion, and the lights went out. Shrieks filled the room.

I sank onto the bleacher seat and let the darkness absorb me as chaos took off like drunk ants in an anthill. Cell phone lights bounced around the room. People who had complained about the rain were suddenly willing to brave gale force winds to get to their cars. To get away from the crazy lady shouting obscenities. Dean got on his phone and left, schmoozing with whomever commented to him. Larry whisked my mother out the door, probably afraid of what I might say or do next, but the truth was I had no idea.

I sat in stunned silence as Lanie pulled herself together and sat next to me. Sully quietly thanked people for coming by.

What did I just do?

"Are you okay?" Lanie whispered, nudging my knee with hers.

"I don't know," I whispered back.

She took one of my hands. "That was really good, what you said."

My eyes closed. "I don't even know what I said. It's like a blur of noise in my head, but I'm pretty sure I didn't get that *I'm a grown-up now* thing across."

"Yeah, I don't know that that was the message," she said.

"I remember a lot of f-bombs."

"There were one or two," she said. "But you probably saved me from killing Katrina, so there's that."

"True." I leaned forward, my face in my hands. "Jesus. My mother."

"I blame her," Lanie said. "She started it."

"I need to move to Wyoming," I mumbled into my hands. "Raise goats and make buttermilk."

"You won't touch honey, but you'll make sour milk?"

"Wyoming," I said. "Bigger picture."

She nudged me again. "You don't need Wyoming. You just need all the stupid people to go away. What's wrong with these morons?"

I nudged her back. My best friend, ready to go to the mat for me. Once upon a time, I'd been so envious of her life. Of course, I'd also thought she was married and successful in California, not single and living paycheck to paycheck in Louisiana. And now she was back, all that behind her, and there I was sort of envious again. Not because she was jet-setting or living an adventurous life, but because she was happy. She was loved.

"You need to get home to your hottie hubby," I said. "You don't want to be late for your date."

"I don't want to leave you like this," she said. "Come with me."

I shook my head. "Go on," I said, looking at Sully's form in the near darkness as he bid goodbye to some stragglers. "I have some unfinished business to deal with."

Lanie paused. "Are you sure?"

I blew out a slow breath, watching his movements. "No. But I need to do it anyway."

She left.

A few minutes later, it was down to me and Sully. He stood in the doorway watching the rain fall, his right arm propped on the door jamb. He was beautiful.

And dangerous.

He turned my direction and slowly walked toward me, climbing up the two rows and sitting down next to me.

"You okay?" he asked.

I shrugged. "Probably not my shiniest moment."

"I don't know," he said. "I thought it was pretty good."

"You don't have to live here," I said, before thinking. "I mean, yeah, I guess you do now. But I have to live and work with these people, and I've fought the gossip my whole life. I don't know if I made it better with that speech."

Sully looked around the gym, careful to avoid my eyes.

"So this is what high school was like," he said. "Pep rallies and shit."

"Yep. Can't you just feel the school spirit?"

"I can smell the sweaty feet," he said, making me chuckle. "Or maybe that's just the wet doormats."

"So you never went to public school at all?" I asked.

I already knew some of it, but I'd babble about anything to give me more time.

"My mom made me go through the fourth grade," he said. "Then when she left and Camilla came in with Aidan, my dad hired tutors to home-school us the carnie way. On the road."

What kind of mother left her kid? Especially to a carnival life. As much as my gypsy spirit coveted that back then, I was the first to say it wasn't for children.

"She couldn't handle the life," Sully said, as though reading my thoughts. "It's not for everyone."

It was the time to ask the question. Now. While we were both facing the empty gym and not looking at each other.

"It wasn't for you," he said softly.

My head whipped like it was on a remote. "What?"

"That's why."

I stared at his profile. He hadn't even let me ask the question. He stole my question, and gave me the—hell no, that wasn't it. It was him deciding what was good for me without giving me that choice.

My blood ran hot, flushing my skin so fast I felt like I matched my sweater. My lip started to quiver, but not from tears, and when the heat from my gaze made him turn my way, I barely felt the kick to my heart.

"Carmen," he began.

"How dare you," I said.

"You don't understand."

"Damn right, I don't," I breathed, getting up and stepping down to the floor. I needed stability under my feet. "You decided that for me? That I was so weak and unprepared for the *perils* of life on the road, you'd be better off ditching me—"

"I didn't ditch you."

"—without a word and moving on so you wouldn't have to think of me again? So you and Kia could fuck every night?" Angry tears burned my eyes as the jealousy bug reared up. Wow. I never planned on playing the Kia card, but evidently it was there. She was all over him in the years I went to the carnival with Dean, draping over him like a blanket, and now—I flexed my fingers and walked away a few feet. Damn it, I was acting like a spurned teenager.

Like the person he left. We never got to have this conversation then.

I whirled around as he stepped down to the floor, looking just as angry as I felt.

"Kia?" he spat, coming so close we could have bumped chests. "Have you lost your damn mind?"

"Didn't ditch me?" I responded in the same tone, head tilted. Letting the heat from my anger hold me up there in his face. "Did you think I was in your trunk?"

Anger flashed in his eyes, and he slowly breathed out, probably to keep from throttling me. That was okay, because for once, being near him wasn't sending me into a wanton frenzy. All I felt was fifteen levels of pissed off.

I shook my head as I glared up at him. To hell with needing answers. I didn't have time for these games or this drama.

"Screw this," I said under my breath.

"Fine."

I walked around him, straight out the door, straight through the rain to my car. I couldn't feel the rain on my skin, and it didn't matter. I drove home as steadily and carefully as I could with rain streaming across my windshield and tears streaming down my face.

It wasn't for you.

What a self-righteous, pompous son of a bitch. How had I missed that side of him? How had I ever fallen for him? Why did he have to come back here and torture me?

Between the trek to my car and then to my front door, I looked like I'd jumped in the pond with all my clothes on. I stripped off my clothes as I walked to my bedroom, making a nice soggy trail that I couldn't care less about. All I wanted to do was climb into my bed naked and be angry. Think about all the hateful words people had said out there, all the things that just would not die, and dwell on the ones that made my blood boil. This town was toxic, and getting out of it sounded better by the second.

I'd just made it under my covers, wet hair and all, when my doorbell rang.

"Oh for the love of God," I groaned.

I pulled the comforter over my head, hoping whomever it was would go away.

The doorbell rang again.

What if it were my elderly neighbor Mr. Harlan, who frequently locked himself out of the house? I couldn't leave him outside in the rain.

It rang again.

Damn it.

I had to put on clothes.

Grunting out of bed, I pulled on my go-to cut-off sweatpants shorts and a Billy Joel tank top that probably showed a little too much with no bra, but Mr. Harlan was almost legally blind. Hence, my need to crawl out of bed in the middle of my misery to save him.

"Hang on, Mr. Harlan," I called out as another loud clap of thunder shook the house. I padded across my living room to grab his extra key out of a mosaic bowl. "I've got your—"

The face looking back at me when I opened the door wasn't sweet little wrinkled Mr. Harlan. It was a hot, wet, and fuming Sully.

Chapter Seven

Sully.

Fuck balls.

Sully stood in the doorway, anger radiating off him. Holding my wallet, with words stalled on his lips as his gaze fell to my chest.

I sucked in a breath and found my tongue again. "What are you—"

"You left your wallet on the bleachers," he said. His eyes lifted slowly to meet mine. They were angry. Well, good for him. So was I. "And we have things to discuss."

"We have nothing to discuss," I said, crossing my arms and wishing I'd gone for a different shirt. Like a giant sweatshirt that covered me head-to-toe. "You said enough."

"I wasn't done." He walked past me, forcing me to step aside.

I scoffed. The fucking nerve!

"Well, come on in," I said, making a sweeping motion behind him and shutting the door.

He tossed my wallet on a table and turned to face me. In my house. Sully was in my house. Just maybe five feet away. Maybe ten, but it didn't matter because he was *in my house*. Standing by the couch where I watched TV and read books and did all the normal things that people do when their old first loves aren't standing in their living rooms taking away the normal.

I was far too undressed for this, but there was no way I could walk into my bedroom with him there. I would have a stroke just thinking of the possibilities.

"Okay, you have the floor," I said. "Say what you came to say."

He slicked back his wet hair, and my toes curled. God, I hated my body's reaction to him. He was an ass. He had no right to make a speech in my living room, and yet there he was. I had to keep my arms crossed so my nipples wouldn't get hard.

"That life isn't—"

"—for me," I finished. "Really? You're leading with that again?"

"It's not a dig, Carmen," he said. "That's not an insult. It's hard. It's miserable." He took a step closer. "It shouldn't be for anyone."

"Don't patronize me, Sully," I said. "I'm not that naïve girl anymore. The one you left in a parking lot." He closed his eyes as if he were seeing that. Good. He should. "I'm a grown woman, and I don't need this drama back in my life. I thought I wanted to know why, but if that's all you've got, then I'm good."

"You think I didn't want you. That I wanted *Kia*?" he said incredulously. Ugh, why did I say that? Jealousy was the worst defense ever.

"It doesn't matter," I said. "But for starters, she's here with you."

"For *starters*, Kia is like a sister to me," he countered. "So no. Never have and never will. She's my family. She just wants off the road too, so she came with me to help."

I narrowed my eyes. "She was all over you. Every year, I saw the two of you."

"Because you were all over *your husband*," he snarled. "In front of me. She's my friend. She knew what that did to me."

What that did to him? What the hell?

"Why would you care?" I said with a bitter laugh. "You left *me*, Sully." I pointed. "You."

"You think you weren't with me?" he said, stepping closer again. Close enough to touch. Too close. And yet my feet couldn't move.

"I'm pretty sure I wasn't," I said, hating the shake that my voice held.

"You're wrong," he said through his teeth. His expression looked raw as his eyes drifted downward. I knew what he was looking at, and it wasn't just my too-exposed boobs. It was what was inked inside one of them. I needed to inhale and couldn't. He lifted his shirt sleeve. "Every day."

"That's bullshit," I whispered. "More words from—"

"Every... single... day," he repeated, not blinking, holding my stare. "I woke up and did what I had to do, in fuck knows what crappy town, with wheels under my feet and fast food in my belly, rarely seeing green grass because most places we set up are nothing but gravel and mud. That's the life I was given, Carmen, and that's okay. I lived it." His breathing was ragged as he leaned into me. "But I thanked God you weren't there to have to."

I sucked in a breath and mentally fought back the burn that was imminent. I'd cry when he left. *Don't you dare cry.*

"You had everything in front of you, baby," he continued. "I couldn't take that away and put you in another trailer. And I had too much to do before I could offer you anything else."

My world spun. No. He couldn't come here fifteen years later and do this. Not now. I backed up a step.

"You don't get to call me *baby*," I said, turning for the door. "That was another time, with two different—"

"I loved you."

They slammed into me like dynamite. Those words. Those... those fucking unfair words.

By the time I turned back around, my eyes were on fire and my legs were shaking so badly I didn't know how they held me up.

"You don't get to say that to me either," I said, my voice tremulous and irritatingly whispery. I didn't want to cry. I wanted to throw something at his beautiful head, but damn it I didn't want to cry.

"Carmen."

"No!" I yelled, my voice cracking. "You didn't just leave, you deserted me. You left me in this hell hole to rot and didn't even have the balls to say goodbye! That's not love."

"Yes, it was love," he yelled back. "I grew up with nothing, do you hear me? Not a damn thing. No bike, very few toys; there was no room. We didn't have Christmas; we're in Branson for Christmas every year. My dad gave us a new jacket every year and some money to go hang out in town. Merry fucking Christmas. Do you think I wanted to bring you into that? Raise kids to live like I did? Hell no."

"So why play me?" I said. "Why tell me you wanted me with you? Why tell me anything?"

"Because when I looked at you, I did," he said.

"No," I repeated, spinning around blindly toward the door, my hand finding the knob through a haze of hot tears. "You need to go. Just le—"

His body was against my back instantly, holding us against the door as his face pressed into my hair. His right hand went around my waist as the left held my head against his mouth.

"I'm sorry," he said above my ear. "I am so, so sorry."

"Don't," I whispered, shutting my eyes tightly against his words, against the way he felt against me, trying not to melt back into him. Trying not to be eighteen again. Trying to keep my damn dignity.

"I might not have done it right, but I loved you," he said, his voice breaking, crushing my heart for a second time. "Maybe it was the stupidest thing I've ever done, but—"

"It *was*," I cried, spinning around, pushing him back. Tears poured from my eyes, and I'd never been a pretty crier. Dignity had left the building. "It was the stupidest thing you've ever done. You had me, you idiot. I would have woken up with you *anywhere*." I shoved at him again as my sobs made the words catch. "You *had* me!"

His scent filled my nose as he pulled me to him, and I found myself crushed into his chest, his arms holding me like I might disappear. I gasped and knew there were important, smarter thoughts fighting to be heard. Thoughts that said to back away—far, far away—and not to melt into the all-consuming sensations of his hands going into my hair or travelling my back. I cried into him, unable to stop. Anger at him, at myself, at every memory that had stayed with me all these years. At my infuriating reaction to him. My hands moved up his sides all on their own, grabbing his shirt in my fist. I couldn't help it. I didn't care that he was soaking wet. I wasn't aware of anything except the feel, the smell, the need, the screaming voice in my head telling me no, and the direction my face was headed in spite of it.

There were no more words. There was just the sound of my crying, our erratic breathing, and the gentle scrape of his scruff against my hair, my forehead, my cheeks, as he dragged his lips in slow kisses along my face. Until almost… almost… and then his mouth. It was on mine as his hands came up to hold my head. His lips searched against mine, kissing my top lip as I kissed his bottom one. We switched. We tasted. My fingers found the bottom of his shirt and skimmed underneath to the skin above his jeans, making him hiss in a breath as his mouth covered mine hungrily. There was a groan and a clenching of fingers and pulling in tighter and then our eyes opened and—oh my God, what was I doing?

My whole body tingled like I'd been lightly electrocuted, and I was kissing Sully Hart like a woman starved.

"No," I whispered against his lips.

I slid my hands back around, and moved up his chest, pushing him back gently. Putting some space between us as my eyes fell from the haunted look in his eyes to his mouth. My lips missed him instantly.

"I can't," I said, my voice sounding odd and scratchy. I cleared my throat and shook my head. "I can't do this again."

"Why?" he said, his voice gravelly. "I'm not going anywhere this time." His brows came together as something else crossed his face. Something

I instinctively knew I didn't want him to ask. "Or is that the problem?"

My heart physically hurt as I pulled out of his grip, like it was telling me it couldn't do that, either. It couldn't detach from him again. I pressed a hand to my mouth before the pain could manifest itself as more tears. I'd done that enough. He'd seen enough of that from me. And the look on his face was—sweet Jesus. I needed out of this town.

Sully rubbed at his eyes with a finger and thumb as if trying to clear the fog, and raked his fingers through his damp hair. "I—" he began, just as his phone rang from his pocket.

I took the opportunity to walk away and breathe as he answered, flexing my fingers to rid myself of the shakes. The *what-the-fuck-did-we-just-do* shakes.

"What?" Sully said into the phone, the alarm in his voice making me turn back around and give him a questioning look. Not that he saw it, because he was kind-of-sort-of avoiding looking at me, too. He blew out a breath and paced a few steps. "Yeah, let me know what you hear, and I'll keep a lookout too."

He looked so solid and warm and good over there. Like climbing back into his arms would be such a fabulous idea. Except that it wasn't. It was a horrible life-destructing idea that should be stabbed and shot and left to die.

"Your brother?" I asked when he hung up.

"No, Bash," he said. "Half of his hives have been stolen."

Chapter Eight

"What?"

"I have to go," he said, his expression already gone, already moved on.

That was something different about him. Once upon a time, he was the most intense and focused person I'd ever seen. Nothing ruffled him. Like at the Blue Banana when Dean got in his face. But now, he looked like a man with business problems, his head already past me and onto however Bash's hives affected him. Sully was never a man with business problems.

His phone dinged with a text, and his whole face tightened.

"Fuck, Aidan, figure it out," he muttered.

Now, the brother. More business problems.

Yeah. Definitely different.

"Sully."

"I have to go," he repeated, stalling in the doorway, finally meeting my eyes. "I'm sorry," he said, pain and anger and sadness in his voice. It felt like those two words were meant to cover a hell of a lot. Then he was gone.

I sank onto a barstool and ran my fingers over my lips, feeling where he'd been. I could still feel him there.

Don't you get lost in him again. Don't let him break you.

I swallowed hard.

I'm not going anywhere this time. Or is that the problem?

So many problems.

* * *

Lanie came with me out to the pavilion site the next day. My mother would have hunted her down like a dog if she hadn't but also for moral support. And possibly to give Sully the evil eye. I was pretty sure Lanie'd been waiting to do that for a really, really long time.

She didn't get the chance.

When we got there, chaos was everywhere. There were probably twelve people with homemade signs protesting in front of the pond. Their signs read, *Save our Buzz* and *No Honey, No Money.* One said *The Lucky Charm isn't Charming!*

I'd bet that Dean had planned out those slogans for a week.

Sully looked like he could chew up the nails in his bag. Every muscle in his shoulders and neck popped when he moved. And something seemed to be missing. Something seemed less crowded. Something—

"The wood is gone!" Monte said in a non-whispered whisper, hurrying over to us.

"The what?" I asked. "The wood—oh, holy shit."

That's what it was. The stack of wood Sully had brought in—even the sections that had already been started on the portable pavilion—was gone.

"I heard that Bash's bees were jacked," Monte said in a hushed tone. "It looks like our wood was, too."

"This is crazy," I said. I looked at Lanie. "I have to go talk to him," I said. "As a lawyer."

She gave me a knowing look. "Because a lawyer comes to a crime scene to work a burglary?"

I felt so fortunate that Monte happened to be standing there to hear my own words come back at me. It was a moment of utmost pride and joy.

"Okay then, as a friend," I said. "He was…" I hadn't told her about the kiss yet. Yeah, I was a coward. "He was at my house when he got the call about the hives, so it just makes sense to ask him about the wood."

Her eyes got wide at the word house, so as soon as the last word was out of my mouth, I made a little *go ahead* motion with my hand. I had it coming.

"He was at your house?"

I nodded, watching Sully and Kia talk to two officers next to the trailer. His body language was tense and spring-loaded, like he could drive a whole bag of nails with his bare hands.

"Yes, Mother," I said, glancing around to make sure my actual mother wasn't around. She was, of course, but on the other side of the group. "I left my wallet at the gym. He dropped it off."

Lanie put a hand on her hip and narrowed her eyes. "Uh huh."

"What, do you want a play-by-play?" I said, feigning nonchalance. "We talked about stuff."

"And?"

"Kia's like a sister, and they're just friends," I said.

Lanie nodded, studying me way too closely. I felt like I was back in high school, convincing my mom I hadn't had anything to drink. I looked back toward the trailer. Kia was heading inside as the policemen left.

My mother walked up, hair up in a cute blinged-out cap and the ever-present clipboard in her hand.

"Hi, Mom," I said. "Here's Lanie. I'll be right back."

I walked over to Sully, with my best friend's death stare burning a hole in the back of my head. I'd make it up to her later.

"They took the wood," Sully told me as I approached. He was loud enough that several people looked over.

"I heard," I said. "They just—"

"*Did* you just hear?" he said, the anger visibly seething just under the surface. "Or does it have something to do with you?"

Taken aback, I stopped short. "Excuse me?"

"Ever since I got here, it's been nothing but shit," he said. He paced, pointing at me every time he got close. "From this town, from every asshole who thinks they have a point to make. About me." His voice got louder. "From every know-it-all prick and princess who thinks they know me." He stopped and pointed again. "Because of you."

All my Spidey senses told me to stand down, that he was just frustrated and blowing off steam and it wasn't directed at me. But it sure as hell felt directed at me.

"You're... blaming me?"

"You told me it was personal—me coming here," he said, walking closer.

I held up my chin, refusing to be intimidated. "Yes."

The trailer door opened behind him and Kia's curious face appeared. As she looked from him, to me, and then to the crowd behind us, her expression went neutral.

"You're right, it *was* personal," he said. "Of all the crapfuck towns we stopped in, this one was the only one that felt like anything. That we connected to in any way." One more step, just inches away. "Even when it wasn't about you, it was still the closest thing I ever felt to having a hometown. So yes, choosing Charmed was personal."

I blinked. "Okay."

"And every day, it's a fight. I'm trying to build something new, and the damn place is divided on it because fifteen years ago I met *you*. How fucked up is that?"

His phone dinged with a text. Grimacing, he strode straight to the water's edge and, with a roar, hurled the phone as far as he could throw it as the protestors parted like the Red Sea.

"Holy shit," I whispered.

Walking back up, he stopped a few feet from me. I felt the reverent hush behind me, like I was taking one for the team.

"All the wood, the hives—someone's trying to drive me out of here." Every muscle in his face twitched. "Is that you?"

I backed up a step and scrunched my face into the nastiest look I could muster. A look that said he was a son of a bitch for even thinking that question.

"Are you serious?" I hissed.

"Couldn't be more," he said through gritted teeth.

I narrowed my eyes, unable to believe the toxicity that was flowing out of his.

"How could you ask me that?" I asked, hands on hips now. He'd better hurry and answer, because once my mom caught up to this conversation, his missing wood would be the least of his worries.

"Because you want me gone," he said. "What better way?"

Oh, he'd better friggin' believe I wanted him gone right that second. If I could have thrown him into the pond with his phone, I would have.

"You think I know how to steal bees?" I asked, my voice shaking with barely restrained rage. "That I have a way to jack whole pallets of wood?"

"Excuse me?" My mother was right behind me. I closed my eyes as I heard the rant about to ramp up. "You're accusing Carmen of—"

"I know that someone's pretty smart," he cut her off. "They know I need that honey industry to be thriving. But what someone doesn't understand," he yelled so everyone behind me could hear, "is that Bash's business is going to take a serious hit. You can't just move hives wherever you want. It throws the bees into reorientation. If they can reorient at all. You live in a beekeeping town, people. You should know this! You aren't just hurting me, you're messing with one of your own."

"Sully—" Kia said.

"I'm fine," he said, putting up a hand to stop her. His angry eyes burned into me. "They don't want me here because I left you," he growled. "And you don't want me here because I want to stay." He untied the canvas nail bag from his waist and threw it on the ground. "To hell with all of you."

I wanted to respond with the perfect retort, but my brain was frozen. Sully stormed off to his truck and drove away. I breathed in slowly, feeling all the eyes of Charmed on me. Waiting. Judging. And one pair of eyes in particular.

"Not now, Mom," I whispered without turning around, trying to hold it all in.

"I wasn't saying a thing," she said. I knew her arms were crossed by the tone of her voice.

Lanie walked up and took my hand. "C'mon. Nothing's happening here now. It's Saturday. Let's go spend some money or something. Get a pedicure."

I loved her for that. I knew she really wanted to go rip Sully a new one, and she was comforting me instead. Honestly though, I didn't need comforting. I needed a reckoning. I was damn tired of being called out in public. I turned to meet Kia's dark-eyed gaze, and for someone I'd never known, she seemed strangely in sync with me.

"Give him a minute," she said.

*   *   *

I gave him a minute. I gave him an hour. I took a raincheck from Lanie and promised her I wouldn't do anything crazy. Although if she'd known what really went down at my house last night, I doubt she would have taken my word. I wouldn't have.

The crowd had thinned; only the nosiest stuck around to talk to the protestors and wait for more excitement that never came. I didn't know what they thought would happen—maybe all the bees would come flying up in a blaze of glory, carrying the wood on their little backs buzzing *heave-ho!* in unison?

Dean hadn't come today, so he'd missed the show. I wondered if he was with Bash, looking for the hives, or if he was just laying low over his lack of support for the project. As the mayor, that would be the smartest move, and if we were still married, that's what I would have advised, but we weren't and it wasn't my business.

And Sully actually accused me? That blew me away. His drama wasn't my business either, but it sure was pulling at me, telling me it wanted to be. I was such a hypocrite.

Possibly a stupid one, I mused as I pulled onto Maple Street and parked behind the big black truck. What was I hoping to achieve, coming here to provoke an already angry man? I was like a kid poking an anthill with a stick, hoping not to get bitten, but I was a bit ticked myself. So, *poke.*

I rang the doorbell and looked around at the newly planted greenery. I didn't get it. I didn't get it at my house either, which was why it still looked as plain and unadorned as it did the day I moved in. The smell of fresh dirt and potting soil wasn't unpleasant, though. It reminded me of my childhood, as Lanie's aunt was always planting or digging up and moving things she felt needed a new aura. The aroma had a weirdly soothing, domestic feel to it.

I would never say that out loud to another living soul.

The door swung inward as the screen door swung outward.

"What are you doing here, Carmen?"

Another aroma hit my nose, something soft and sweet contrasting with the sharp edges in his tone. Chocolate. Nuts. But—definitely chocolate. Wasn't enough. I was still pissed.

"No, I didn't steal your damn wood, or move any bees," I said. "What the hell would I do with bees?"

He looked ready to chew on a few. "Whatever. I'm sorry," he forced out.

"Wow, you really have the welcoming thing down," I said.

"I'm not in the mood," he said.

"Aw, damn," I said. "And I'm so giddy after what you just did. I wasn't all about you barging into my house last night, but it didn't stop you."

"Be my guest." He walked away, leaving the inner door open as the screen door slammed shut.

I laughed rather than voice one of the not-so-nice comments that danced on my tongue. I'd save them for a more effective moment, like one with the person standing in front of me rather than a door.

Yanking the screen door open, I followed him in. Being in Sully's house felt weird. Like last night, everything flipped out of context. We never had houses before; we were lucky to have cars. I'd been inside his carnival trailer, but it was cramped and messy and crammed with three other people. It wasn't a home; it was a glorified tent. This was... odd. The furniture was sparse but decent. A couch and a recliner faced a flat-screen TV in the living room, which was open to a small dining area. A beautiful old wooden table stood there, with equally old chairs. I stopped to run my fingers along the scarred wood.

"It was my mother's."

I jumped, startled, and looked up to see him leaning in the kitchen doorway.

"It's beautiful."

He looked down at it for a moment, then shrugged and turned back to the kitchen.

"She saved some things in storage, and my dad took over the payments when she died," he said. "I didn't even know about it till after his funeral." I frowned and followed him, surprised at the large kitchen. There was even an island in the middle. "I didn't know your mother died, too," I said. "I'm sorry."

"Don't be," he said, pulling a glass baking dish from the fridge and moving it to a trivet on the counter. "I was ten when she left, and twenty when I got the news that she died, so I really didn't know her well."

"Wait," I said. "Twenty? That's the—"

"The year that ruined everyone's lives?" he asked, yanking open a drawer. "Yeah, it was. Let's just leave it at that."

Something in me softened. What he'd said last night about not wanting that life for me, about raising kids there... I wondered if there had been a flip side to that worry. About being left again.

"Okay, let's stick to the current day then," I said, remembering the dressing down he'd given me in the park.

"Yeah, let's do that," he said, acid still dripping from his words. He pulled out a serving spatula and cut into a piece of whatever was in that pan that smelled amazing. "Grab a bowl from that cabinet, will you?"

I opened a door that revealed mismatched bowls and plates and glasses. Real glass ones, still with the stickers on the bottom. I grabbed a blue bowl and handed it to him as he fished for spoons. As normal as that sounded, it wasn't. It was like someone had pushed a button and amped up the energy in the room, and Sully had received the lightning-bolt portion. He was almost vibrating with it.

"Where's Kia?" I asked. "Isn't she living here, too?"

"She's still at the trailer, I guess," he said. "She's doing some office work for me there." He glanced my way. "I figured setting up a trailer on site to take care of business would be more efficient, and Kia's good at that stuff. She likes structure."

"She should go back to school for it," I said. "Get a—"

Sully snorted. "There's no *back* to school," he said. "We were home schooled. What she learned outside of that, she picked up on her own and she likes it, but college isn't in our world."

"You both left that world, so I'd say it's a choice," I said.

"Whatever."

Oh, *whatever*. But I quickly forgave him, since he was serving up something that made my mouth water.

Graham cracker crust, chocolate pudding maybe? Then vanilla. Then—chocolate again. With whipped cream and shaved chocolate on top and I thought I saw a layer of nuts in there too. Dear God, it was like the mother ship had sent an offering, served up by Thor.

"Can we talk about what—"

A spoonful of heaven went into my mouth, stopping all sound except for the moan of delight that escaped my throat.

"Jesus," Sully said, the tone in his voice making my eyes pop open. I didn't even know they'd closed. His expression had gone from enraged to lustful in under a second. "Do that again."

Men.

"Sorry," I said, around the explosion of flavor on my tongue. "God, that's good. What is it?"

"Sex in a Pan," he said.

"Seriously."

"I didn't make it up," he said. "But it fits."

"It—" My eyes landed on something on the far wall. "Please tell me you don't wear that."

He followed my gaze to the black apron hanging on a hook, and his face closed up. It was back to nasty Sully.

"If I'm cooking something messy, I do," he said. "Is that a problem?"

I grabbed the spoon and took another bite, refusing to look in the direction of anything apron-ish. All of this—*all of it*—was making me crazy and more of the sex chocolate was necessary.

"Oh holy orgasms, this is to die for," I mumbled, grabbing the island. When I looked back at him, he was looking at me like I was in that pan. "What?"

"You're killing me."

"You're due."

"And what's wrong with the apron?" he asked.

I held up a hand. "Don't spoil it."

He held up two. "What spoils it?"

I dropped the spoon and gestured around me. "This, Martha Stewart! Who are you?"

He dropped his spoon, too, and gave me a look. "You did not just call me that."

"How can you be so damn domestic now?" I blurted. "I mean, don't get me wrong, you can feed me this all day long, but—"

"As long as someone else cooks it or you don't see it happening, right?" he said, that anger flashing to the surface again. Yep, the anthill.

"I'm sorry. I just can't put the Sully I knew in an apron," I said.

"I'm not the Sully you knew!" he yelled. He took a deep breath as I stepped back. "The *Carmen* I knew would have never settled for a white picket fence married to a guy she didn't love, either," he said in a lower tone. "But life fucking happens, doesn't it?"

I gasped as his words hit home.

"That guy was a stupid kid with rainbows in his head who listened to everyone else but himself and ended up alone." He looked ready to punch something, and I wanted to throw myself in front of the dessert. "I watched my father live for the life and die alone. My mother *escaped* the life and still died alone. I came here to find something real and solid, and yes, I put things in the ground and I cook when I'm angry because I never had those things before and they give me peace!"

The sorrow under his anger hit my heart, pulling at everything I kept trying to stamp down. Everything in me was warring between wanting to pull him into my arms and give him what he was missing—and wanting to run out that door and never look back.

"Now I'm in this fucked-up town that I thought could finally be a real home," he said, looking out the window over his sink. "And yet I can stand in the middle of fifty people and I'm still alone. I'll always be the outsider. The dirty carnie that never graduated high school. We lie, we steal, we embellish things. We tarnish the sweet little town's golden girl."

The boulder in my chest was immense.

"You didn't tarnish me," I said. "And I was far from golden."

His focus was still far away. I didn't even know if he'd heard me.

"Doesn't matter," he said softly.

"Ever wish you hadn't done all this?" I asked.

"Only every day," he said automatically, as if he'd asked the question himself and was simply verifying it. "Every morning when I wake up, it's huge. It's heavy. It's daunting." He turned his head, driving that intense gaze into me. "But that's okay. At least I'm living."

I gave him a questioning look. "You call digging your toes into the bee puke of Charmed *living*?"

Sully's mouth pulled into a lopsided grin. "Yes," he said. He walked closer, looming over me as he reached for a cabinet door and opened it. "See that?" he asked, pointing inside at the dishes and bowls and glasses. He looked in there too, and the look of pride on his face was astounding. "That's living."

As I looked up into his face, just inches from mine, I couldn't breathe. I couldn't blink. And every nerve ending was on full alert. That was living, too.

Shit, did I just think that?

Sully turned back to his dessert. I took the opportunity to draw a full breath. What the hell.

"Bailey knew I couldn't pass that up," he said. "That old man sees things that shouldn't be seen." Sully chuckled as he dropped chocolate shavings over the top. "He knows my weaknesses, and he caught me at a weak moment."

"Of?"

Why did I ask that? I had no right to ask that.

Sully paused. "Of needing to get away from my brother before I walked away from the whole damn thing."

I remembered what Dean had blustered about.

"It's that bad?" I asked.

He nodded slightly. "It's that bad. He's toxic. He's dependent. I can't—" He shook his head. "I just can't anymore."

I didn't know what to say to that, so I just stood there, watching him fiddle with things. I could leave, but in some weird, messed-up sense, it felt comforting. Like he wanted me there. *I* wanted me there. And that right there should have been enough to shove me out the door.

"Bailey used to tell me I was a broken bird waiting for a little bird," he said. "He'd say I had wings but was too messed up to know how to use them."

I raised an eyebrow. "That sounds helpful."

He shrugged. "Yeah, he's a little whacked, but he's got a good heart."

"You told me once that he was psychic or something," I said.

Sully cut me a sideways glance. "Or something. I don't buy all that. My dad did, and he swore by him, but…" He stopped and ran a finger and thumb over his eyes. He looked exhausted and wired at the same time. "Still, I never let him get a read on me—just in case."

I smirked, and let my finger trace a pattern in the tiled countertop. "Yeah, heaven forbid someone figure you out."

I felt the weight of his stare and looked up.

"I'm easy," he said. "So are you."

I tilted my head, taken a little off-guard. "Really, now?"

"All you ever wanted was out of here."

My throat burned. "Yes."

"And all I've ever wanted was a house with no wheels that can't be broken down and moved in an hour… or less." He gripped the edge of the island and leaned on it, his arms spread wide. "I'm easy."

"And now—"

"Now I finally have that in my grasp, and it's being taken away."

The silence rang in my ears. "Because of me," I said, hearing the shake in my voice.

Sully stood up straight and picked up my spoon, filling it full of the decadent dessert.

"What are you doing?" I asked.

"Feeding you."

"Are you high?"

"No," he said, those eyes landing on me and sending my stomach into a fluttering frenzy. "I'm—" He stopped and clamped his jaw tight and shook his head. "It doesn't matter what I am," he said. "But listening to you moan as you eat this is what's going to get me through the rest of this day."

Everything in me went warm.

"You want me to moan on command? That won't work," I said.

"We'll see," he said. He brought the spoon to my mouth, only to tease me by smearing my lips with whipped cream instead of giving me the bite.

I darted out my tongue to lick them and went lightheaded as his eyes dropped to watch me do that. They went an impossibly dark shade of lust, and all systems loaded south. I was suddenly hyperaware of every air molecule touching my skin.

"Fuck," he whispered.

"Give me the chocolate," I whispered back, my words slow and deliberate.

He pushed the spoon into my mouth and I wrapped my tongue around it, sucking it clean while Sully Hart stopped breathing. Nothing in my life had ever felt more powerful. More demanding. More hot.

The spoon clattered to the floor as my hands went up into his hair and his mouth landed on mine.

Chapter Nine

He tasted of chocolate and testosterone and if I could have climbed under his skin, it wouldn't have been close enough. It wasn't yesterday's loving kiss of longing, searching need. This was punishing, lip-crushing, raw desire. This was fifteen years of pent-up and buried want and hurt and anger, manifesting into carnal need at a primal level.

I wrapped my arms around his head as my feet left the floor, pulling him in deeper, kissing him harder as my legs went around his waist. Sully growled into my mouth, lighting me on fire as he pinned me against the counter.

He pushed against me, already rock hard as his hands slid along my thighs, fingers splayed, needing. His hands were calloused and rough on my skin as they slid under my shirt, his fingertips digging into me as they shoved inside the back of my jeans, pulling me harder against him.

"Jesus, God," I moaned as he ground himself between my legs, dragging his lips down my neck as his hands pushed my breasts up to meet them. It had been too long. Too damn long. Somewhere deep down I knew that this was a bad idea on about a hundred and ten different levels, but oh my God his mouth felt glorious on my skin.

"So—fucking—sweet," Sully mumbled, licking and tasting along the neckline of my shirt, his scruff scratching me.

My fingers were wound in his hair, pulling him in. I needed more. I needed his shirt off. I needed—

He lifted his head at the same moment, like we shared the same thought. His face was in my hands and my breasts were in his, both of us breathing like we'd run a mile and back.

I closed my eyes as he leaned his forehead against mine. I wanted him so badly. I missed every nuance of him. But I couldn't need him. *I couldn't need him.*

That was off the table—so to speak. There was too much history, too much pain, regardless of the what-ifs and reasons. There was too much everything in this man. And I was leaving and he was staying and the fact that I couldn't take my hands off his body meant nothing. Knowing that his touch and his smell would send me into an orbital mess of freakish proportions was good to file away for the future.

So that I could avoid this.

Sully took the first step, sliding his hands out from under my shirt and setting me back on my feet. I let my hands trail down his neck and chest. My eyes followed the path. I couldn't just let go.

"I'm sorry," he said, his voice husky.

I shook my head, still looking at my hands. "I believe I—it was me."

"No, I..." He blew out a breath that was more of a growl as he backed up. "I'm so mad, I don't know where to go with it, and... I shouldn't have done that."

He looked so serious and pissed off, and suddenly the heat of the last thirty seconds cooled. Sully raked a hand through his hair. Good God, I'd had my hands in that hair, caught it on my fingers.

Get it together, woman.

"Yeah, well, I shouldn't have either, but..." I nodded accusingly toward the pan. "You fed me chocolate. You get what you get."

A chuckle rolled from his throat, even though the rest of his body was still tight with anger. "I get what I get, huh?"

I shrugged as the feel-goods crept into the kitchen, already looking for the exits. How messed up was that? I was good with jumping his bones in a hard, unemotional, carnal frenzy, but put a smile and a tinge of affection in the mix and I was ready to bolt?

Sully came closer, looking down into my face. So close, I could have kissed him again if I'd wanted to. I wanted to. I wanted to so badly, my lips tingled.

Walk away.

"I'm sorry, love," he said softly. He reached up to play with a strand of my hair, and that with the word that fell out of his mouth was the catalyst pulling me out the door. His eyes darted to mine immediately. "I'm sorry."

It was random, and sweet, and intimate—and I couldn't do that. I couldn't feel this again.

"I have to go," I said, sliding toward the doorway. "I have to— I've got things."

Sully shook his head and laughed sarcastically, turning away.

I stopped. "What?"

"Of course you have to go," he said. "That's all you do."

Oh, good, we were back. Heat—and not the good kind—rose to the surface of my skin.

"Excuse me, that's all *I* do?" I asked.

"I left," he said, nodding and holding his arms up to the universe. "And you punished me every year for that, yet you're still hell bent on beating that horse. Every day, every place, every conversation— and there you go."

I headed through the doorway.

"I'm not going to listen to this from the man who left me in a parking lot," I said with a smile over my shoulder.

I could actually say that with a *smile over my shoulder*. Damn, how far I'd rallied.

He pointed. "Like I said."

"Yeah, just keep saying," I mumbled under my breath, pausing to circle back. I grabbed the blue bowl, scooped another very ungraceful portion of Sex in a Pan into it, and walked out. "See you later."

It would be necessary. After that escapade? It would be vital.

"Fridge," he called after me.

Fuck balls.

"Martha."

* * *

I couldn't get to sleep that night. My mind raced, and my body refused to shut off the Sully effect. I even took a cold shower, something I'd never done on purpose in my life, and I still couldn't calm down. I could still taste him. I'd eaten the sex dessert (which probably didn't help, and I'd never look at whipped cream the same way again), chased that with ice cream, and still couldn't lose the taste of his mouth and the feel of him all over my body. I also might have waited—a while—to change my clothes.

Shit, I was becoming that pathetic person that smells their sex clothes, and we hadn't even had sex yet!

Yet. I said *yet*. Not out loud, but that thought was as loud as it gets.

That thought lived with me all night. All the next morning. By the time I picked Lanie up that afternoon to drive back out to the site, I was an irritable mess.

"Fuck," I muttered as we sat at a red light.

"What?" Lanie said, looking alarmed from the passenger side.

I shook my head. "Nothing," I said. "Just realizing the full force of my *screwedness*."

"You do realize this is voluntary, right?" she asked pointedly, but smiling. "Meaning—"

"That we don't have to go there," I finished for her. "You forget about my mother. If we didn't show up, I'd hear it from her for the next year."

"She doesn't like Sully," Lanie said. "I bet we could get a reprieve."

"Never bet on things to make sense when it comes to Geraldine Frost," I said, knowing I was full of crap and Lanie probably knew it, too.

I needed to steer clear of Sully Hart. I needed to avoid his eyes, his voice, his hands, his mouth... especially that last one. Maybe the last two. I couldn't seem to make it five minutes around him without falling into his mouth or getting felt up.

That had to stop. We couldn't keep doing that. He was here to settle down, and I was gearing up to move on. Apples and oranges. Oil and water. Ice cream and grits.

Certain things just didn't belong together.

So why did I keep trying to change that?

New wood had been purchased and delivered, and while the protestors—led by none other than Katrina Bowman, who'd been out there *with* us just last week—took up their pacing in front of the water, Sully appeared calmer than yesterday.

I wasn't about to claim responsibility for that. If his night were anything like mine, it would make him more frustrated, not less.

He was already working on the frame for—something needing a frame, lining up people to knock it out faster. He and a partner nailed together two-by-fours at the top. As Lanie and I walked up, Sully turned toward us. I tried not to look for something meaningful in his expression, but of course I did. I had smelled my damn almost-sex clothes, for God's sake; naturally, I searched his eyes like a lost puppy. Did he smell his clothes looking for me? Did he lay awake all night thinking about it, or did guys even do that?

"We need two more screwing at the middle and the bottom while we nail you," he said, meeting my eyes with bemusement. "Y'all up for it?"

"Charming," Lanie uttered with a smirk. "What are you, twelve?"

"Hi, Lanie," he said, the grin that pulled at his mouth disarmed me.

I was getting weak and ridiculous in my old age.

"Sully," she said. "Hand me a drill. I'll screw anything that needs it."

He laughed. I was envious. Why couldn't I have a witty comeback like that? Normally, I was the queen of snarky wit. I wasn't the queen of anything right now, though. Sully drove in a nail above my head, and his bicep rippled and contracted. I was lost in the memory of hands and tongue and all things carnal.

"Carmen?"

"Yes?" I said a little too loudly, jolting back to the present as he hovered over me.

"Screws are right there," he said, pointing with his chin. "You can use my drill."

I was too close for this conversation.

Spinning around and nearly taking out Lanie in the process, I grabbed his drill and a handful of screws. I stared at the boards in front of me.

"Okay," I said.

"Do you know how to do this?" he asked from behind me.

"Of course," I lied. "Just tell me where you want it."

Mm-hmm, two could play that game.

Lanie snorted below me, handling the drill with expertise.

"Where'd you learn to do that?" I asked her.

"Aunt Ruby," she said. "She was always wanting to build something, fix something." Lanie positioned another screw, lined up her drill bit, and *schwoop* there it went. "That usually meant *me* building or fixing. Unless it was plumbing. I know nothing about plumbing."

"I know," I said. "Your shower sucks."

"Two on the bottom, two in the middle where it intersects," Sully said, pointing, his body brushing up against my back. "You see?"

He was talking right above my ear and my skin was on fire, so no, I didn't see much of anything.

I cleared my throat. "Sure," I said.

"How was dessert?" he asked.

I blinked and opened my mouth as Lanie craned her neck backwards to look up at me.

Dessert? she mouthed.

"Screw," I said waggling a finger toward her boards.

Sully backed up and strolled along the line of people working, and I instantly missed his body close by and his voice hovering over my ear making me ape-shit crazy. *My screwedness.*

"We're making eight of these walls, but not attaching them together," he said to the group. "That's where the levers will come in, but that takes some finesse to get everything lined up. I'd like to get these done in the next hour."

Lanie was on her knees, already six screws in. I might not have finesse, but I could do this. I had a cordless screwdriver; this was just bigger and I was attaching things, not just putting a screw in the wall to hang a picture.

I lined up my screw, hit the trigger, and sent it flying off over Lanie's head.

"You have to put some weight behind it," Sully's partner said. "Otherwise it's just gonna flop all over the place."

"I've got it," I said. "I'm just rusty."

I pulled out another screw and lined the drill bit up into the grooves, pushing in a little. I hit the trigger again and luckily moved my other hand, because the drill jumped the screw and started drilling a hole in the wood, right where my hand had been two seconds earlier.

"Well, shit," I muttered.

"How's it going over there?" Sully asked from two "walls" over.

"Dandy," I said.

"Sounds it."

"Yeah, bite me," I mumbled.

"Need help?" said a female voice.

I turned to see Kia standing next to Sully, looking up where the slats were joined, shielding her eyes from the sun. She had on heavy work gloves, but a tank top and shorts. Because she was *used to it*.

"Those need to be flush," she said, pointing. "But that's hard to do from down here. Do you have a stepladder?"

"No," Sully said. "Put that on the shopping list."

"Then stoop down," she said. "I'll hold it."

I didn't know what that meant—I didn't know if anyone else knew what that meant—but Sully knelt without question and didn't blink when tank-top-and-shorts wrapped her legs around his neck and tapped his shoulder to tell him to rise.

It was like the circus act where the pretty lady mounts an elephant to ride around the arena. I stopped screwing. Or attempting to, since I hadn't actually sunk one yet. Lanie did, too, sitting back on her heels to watch.

Sully rose easily, holding Kia's right calf, and she reached out to grab the wood in question as he and his partner backed out two screws and redid them. They moved around to two other places before Sully knelt for her to dismount.

Lanie looked up at me.

"Sister," I whispered.

"Weird," she whispered back.

"Carnies," I mouthed, focusing back on my screwing, thinking that kind of covered it. They really were their own kind of family, culture, and village. They had their own way of doing things, driven by limited resources and time.

It didn't change the bolt of jealousy that shot through me like I was sixteen.

I'm a grown woman. I'm a lawyer. I am not a hormonal teenager.

"How's that coming," Sully asked, literally against my ear that time. I dropped the screw and damn near broke his nose with the drill.

"Shit, Sully," I gasped.

"Sorry."

"Is this hour of yours real or in carnie time?" I asked. "Because if you keep doing shit like that, I'm gonna be here for double that."

Sully laughed and moved on. Again.

Okay, I *was* a hormonal teenager.

"Hey guys, can I get you to listen up for a quick second?" Sully called out. Conversations died down as everyone turned to see what today's drama would entail. "I just wanted to apologize for yesterday," he said in a low voice. "I kind of hit the wall, and I behaved badly, and I'm sorry. That's not the kind of leadership I want to provide." He frowned and looked down at his hands. "That was my dad's way, actually. And not something I ever want to be, so... I hope you'll forget you ever saw me act like such a fool." He smiled, but his eyes weren't quite back yet.

"Leadership?" quipped a familiar voice. It made me want to hide behind one of those walls.

Dean stood with his hands in the pockets of his slacks, the sleeves of his dress shirt rolled up to show off his fancy new watch. He was shaved and clean cut and definitely not dressed to work or slosh through the muddy pond bank with the protestors. So, why was he here?

"I thought the *leadership* was Frank Coffey," Dean said. "Frank, weren't you the one to kick off this little project?"

Poor Frank turned four shades of neon. "Well, Mr. Hart had the skills to—"

"Mr. Hart has no authority here," Dean said.

"Neither does Frank," Lanie whispered. I nodded, watching Sully's good intentions and improved mood sink back into someplace dark. Dean was a dick.

"His *skills* lie in running a traveling carnival, not a waterfront entertainment and retail area," Dean said. "But he didn't even stick around for that. He pawned it off on his alcoholic little brother so that he could come play white picket fence with his old flame."

"Dean!" I hissed.

Dean turned as if he hadn't seen me, his hands still in his pockets. "Oh good, you're here, Carmen. I'd hate for you to miss this." He pulled a piece of paper from his pocket and unfolded it. Sully stood there like he was before a firing squad. "There's all kinds of interesting information out there when you start making phone calls," Dean said with a satisfied grin. I knew that grin, and I knew that nothing good ever came of it.

Sully crossed his arms. "I have nothing to hide, Crestwell," he said. "You're the one making a scene right now, and I'm kind of busy catching up after losing an entire load of wood. Heard anything about that? Or about Bash's hives?"

"Nope," Dean said. "And let's just see what you have to hide," he added, chuckling as he held the paper out at arm's length.

Sully leaned against a sawhorse like he might need to brace himself.

"It appears that our esteemed Sullivan Hart had quite the colorful life on the road," Dean said. "Bailing out family right and left." He squinted at the paper as if he hadn't memorized the damn thing. "Daddy filed bankruptcy a few years back? Little brother had one—no, *two* DUI's and a public indecency charge?"

I watched the glaze come over Sully's face.

"Yeah, we've had some challenges," Sully said. "My family's not perfect. If yours is, feel blessed."

"It's not," I said, walking forward. Sully's expression was a mix of gratitude and old-school male ego hit. He fought his own battles and didn't want me defending him; I got that. But Dean's self-righteousness was enough to choke a horse.

"Stay out of this, Carmen," Dean warned.

"Oh no, you very much included me with the 'I'd hate for you to miss this comment,'" I said, putting my hands on my hips. "So if you're into throwing stones, then let's look at your house."

"You don't have to do this," Sully said under his breath.

"Your sister humps a pole for a living, Dean," I said. Snickers rippled through the crowd. A few people probably knew that, but he definitely kept a lid on it. "Do you advertise that? What about Uncle Bobby and his secret swill in the shed?"

"How dare you," Dean said through his teeth, hands out of the pockets now, the carefree look gone. "They were once *your* family."

"And not one has said boo to me in six years," I said. "So not so much." I turned to the crowd. "Any of you have gems to share from your closets?" I met my mother's wary look. "I, for one, never knew my dad. And my mom has this weird fondness for overly red hair color."

My mother smirked and chuckled as Mr. Mercer from the drugstore patted her on the head.

"My aunt had magic powers," Lanie said, raising her hand, bringing chuckles from the crowd. Everyone knew about Lanie's Aunt Ruby. It was just a measure of whether they believed or not.

"My cousin is a transvestite," said Mr. Masoneaux, from the candy store. Everyone stopped and gaped on that one.

I held out a hand toward him and kept a neutral face. "So see? Mayberry doesn't exist, not even in sweet little honey-soaked Charmed. And Sully's family drama isn't any different from some of ours, so—"

"Really?" Dean said, looking really put out that his little witch hunt hadn't brought out the torches. "So you wouldn't be interested to know that he got a coworker pregnant and then paid for the abortion?"

The words didn't process in my head right away. It was like the word 'pregnant' stalled everything, putting the world in slow motion, and I had to circle the wagons to catch up. Pregnant meant sex. Sully had sex with someone. Of course Sully had sex with someone; did I think he was celibate for fifteen years? But the gasp to my left brought my gaze to Kia, who turned a sickly shade of gray with eyes full of tears.

Kia.

The *like-a-sister* girl.

Then I saw Lanie's eyebrows go up, and the world sped up to real time.

"What the hell is your problem, man?" Sully said, coming off the sawhorse like he'd been shot in the ass. "I keep trying to coexist with you here, and you have such a twisted vendetta against me that you'll hurt other people just to get to me?"

He stopped just a foot from Dean, and my whole body tensed. My brain was spinning and my heart hurt, but the very real possibility of a brawl made me shove my feelings aside. It was the lawyer thing, ranking the priorities. I'd kick Sully in the nuts later for lying to me. Right now—

"Why, Mayor?" Sully said in a low voice, staring at Dean. "Because she loved me? Were you so insecure that you couldn't handle not being her one-and-only?"

"Get out of my face," Dean said, drawing out each word.

"She married *you*," Sully said. "Get over it."

"And never got over *you*," Dean spat. "Try marrying that."

It was like watching an episode of *This Is Your Life*, but without the sweet video playbacks and happy moments. It was horrifying. Absolutely horrifying. I tore my eyes away from the two of them to scan the faces watching the show. The shocked faces. The fascinated faces. The really fucking nosy faces. I worked very hard to keep my private life private, in spite of the fact that everyone knew my story. This was like being stripped naked in the middle of the football field during halftime. Even the Kia sideshow was a dim flicker compared to watching these two men talk about me like I wasn't even there.

My mother was at my side; I hadn't even seen her walk up. She linked her arm in mine. It was nice. Solidarity and all that. In a minute, I'd ask her to hold my hair so I could puke behind some shrubs.

Dean saw us, and did a double take, pulling his attention away from Sully. For a fleeting second, I thought that was going to be a good thing.

"Since you're all so tight, Carmen," Dean said. "I'm sure one of them has told you the truth by now."

I blinked in confusion as my mother's arm tensed beneath mine. Sully shook his head.

"What?"

"Don't," Sully said. There's a moment of clarity right before the wrecking ball smashes into your life, when everything is crystal clear and logical. It was that moment. And without knowing the details, I knew without question what it was.

I turned to look her in the eyes. Her very frightened eyes.

"What did you do?" I asked.

Chapter Ten

"Tell her, Sully," Dean said. "Tell her how you bailed on her because her mom paid you off."

I jolted like I'd been struck by lightning. No way my mother would have—

"What?" my mom said, letting go of me, her attention fully on my ex-husband. "There was no money."

"You're full of shit," Sully said to Dean. "Her mother never gave me a dime."

My mouth opened, but no words came out. There was nothing. How—why—nothing. All I was, was more naked, if that was possible. I'd always been under a spotlight in this town, and now I was more bare, more stripped, more everything, because the people I thought I knew had kept something life-altering from me.

"Right," Dean said. "Because you'd just leave a girl like Carmen behind without something to make it worthwhile. Just because her mother asked you to."

My mind reeled. *The life wasn't for you.*

"Yes, actually," Sully said. "That's exactly what I did."

He turned and what looked like him pulling gravity out of the ground to do it, looked at me, a million apologies in his eyes.

"Where on earth would you think I would get money to pay off some boy?" my mom was asking—screeching—yelling. "Honestly!"

Sully held out a hand to quiet down, but she was Gerry Frost. She was having none of being outed, insulted, and shushed in one sitting.

"Put your hand down," she said. "I'm not a child. I'm a grown woman and a mother, and if any of you ever have kids one day, I hope you never have to make a decision like that. But you do what you have to do to protect them."

Several older people in the crowd nodded in agreement. It was surreal.

"You!" she said, pointing at Sully. "She would have followed you to the ends of the earth and jumped off with you, to hell with anything else." Her voice cracked at the end and she stopped to gain her composure. "She was eighteen. And maybe it broke her heart and maybe I was wrong, but she was too young to make that kind of choice. To live that hard of a life."

"I know," Sully said. His eyes glazed over.

Her shoulders drooped. "I know you do," she said, grabbing his hand.

It was like I was dreaming. Or dead. And watching it all on some afterlife rerun. Lanie stood next to me and took my hand.

"Honey, you're shaking," she whispered, squeezing my hand.

"Please tell me you don't have a secret, too," I whispered back, my voice trembling.

"You know all my secrets."

"And you!" Mom said, letting go of Sully to point at Dean. "You sorry excuse for a human being." I straightened up. Even though I felt gutted a hundred different ways, I didn't want to miss this. "How convenient that you throw everyone under the bus but yourself, Mayor Crestwell."

"I don't know what you're talking about," Dean said.

"Of course you don't," she said. "You're a politician. And a bad one, by the way. You talk too much and think your petty little underlings don't pay attention."

"You're babbling," he sneered.

"We'll get back to that," she said, putting both hands firmly on her hips and stepping up into his space. "First, since you are all about sharing today, be sure to mention how I even found out that they were planning to leave town together. Because it sure didn't come from *my daughter*," she said, turning around to give me the eyebrow.

Like she had any right to give me the eyebrow.

When I didn't respond, some of her cockiness drained, and she turned back to Dean with an angry expression.

"You came whining to me like a little boy, crying 'I love her' and 'I can't live without her,' and begging me to do something to stop them from leaving," she said, turning back to me. "He heard your plan from following you around."

My mouth fell open.

"Oh my God," Lanie said under her breath, grabbing my arm. "Breathe."

"Oh, I'm breathing," I said, stepping free of her, of everyone. Of everything. I was shaking from anger and pain and embarrassment and sadness, and none of it mattered. The only person I could trust in my entire life to be there for me and never leave—was me.

"This is absurd," Dean said, shaking his head, but his face was as red as a beet. "I'm not staying here for this."

"Oh and back to my babbling and your lousiness?" my mother said, turning to Dean's red face as he backed up. "I left a message with Bash's secretary. Anonymously, because I didn't want to make a stir, but now I don't care. I know you took the bees."

A gasp went through the crowd, through me, and even Sully stepped back.

"I did no such thing," he blustered.

Oh, Dean. This was too much. Even for you.

"Your bragging and arrogance get the best of you, Mayor," she said. "You go on and on about what you get away with, about hiring people to do your dirty work." She leaned into him. "You love the sound of your own voice. And people listen."

"And my lumber?" Sully steamed.

"If I had to guess…" Mom said, shrugging. "Don't have proof on that one, but I heard the hives are in the caves."

"You son of a bitch," Sully breathed.

"You people don't know what you're talking about," Dean said, backing up. I recognized the panic on his face. He was guilty as hell.

"Stop!" I yelled. Everyone turned around, as if they'd forgotten I was there. Me—Carmen Frost—the common denominator in all of these cluster fucks. I was still here. I was shaking like a leaf and tears were rolling down my cheeks, but I was still here. And boiling mad.

I pointed at Dean, taking a cue from my mother as I approached him. "Don't ever, *ever* talk to me again," I said, my voice not sounding like mine. "If you see me in town, walk the other way."

He narrowed his eyes at me. "You were my wife."

"And Bash was your *friend*," I said. "Clearly your agendas are more important than either of those things. Go away."

I dismissed him with a look and let my watery gaze land on my mother. "You—" I swallowed hard, the emotion slamming into me. Her betrayal hurt more. I shook my head. "You kept it all from me. All these years. You—let me believe that he just—"

"Carmen," she said, her eyes filling, too.

"No," I said, pushing her hands away as she reached for me. "You let me marry a stalker, even? I don't know you!"

"Carmen!" she cried, as I turned to walk blindly toward my little stack of belongings. I passed whispers and averted looks, and I didn't care. I was almost there when Kia stepped into my path.

I sucked in a breath. "I'm really not in the—"

"It wasn't his," she whispered, fresh tears welling in her eyes.

"What?"

"Of all the things, don't blame him for that. He covered for someone else," she finished, the tears breaking in her voice. "He's my friend."

I watched the pain work in her face, and I knew she was telling the truth.

"His brother," I said.

She swiped at her face and blinked back more tears, but I saw the hurt break through the pride before she brought the walls up. I nodded and touched her arm as I kept going.

"Are we leaving?" Lanie said, appearing at my side as I reached our stuff.

"We're so leaving."

People were going back to their stations, working on whatever, or milling in little groups to gossip about what they'd just witnessed. It was mortifying. And as we walked by them all, there was one constant.

Sully hadn't moved. He stood in the exact same place, arms crossed, alone again now that Dean and my mother had bolted. I had to pass him. I had to look at him. Or—I didn't have to, but I was damn well going to.

I paused as he looked at me. Looked at me hard, with everything we'd both ever felt. There were too many things, too many hurts, too many lies. I shook my head. There weren't words.

I kept walking.

* * *

I took Lanie home. She tried to get me to come in, to talk, to wind down, but I wasn't interested in winding down. I didn't want to put it behind me or find my center. I wanted to be pissed.

I felt betrayed and embarrassed. My husband and my mother had lied to me for years. The man who'd left me behind, whom I thought just didn't love me, had done it because my mother told him to. And as long as he'd been back in town, and as many times as we'd beaten this "horse" as he called it, he'd never sold her out. Okay, that was honorable, I guess. It was. But I was still…I don't know. He could have told me. I just felt so damn stupid and blindsided.

Speaking of blindsided, I was pretty sure Dean was headed straight to Bash to do damage control before the damage, so I made a bee line. No pun intended.

Just as I expected, Dean's sleek little car was parked in front of the main office for Anderson's Apiary. He was probably spinning something about being framed, or conspiracies, or maybe even owning up to it with a twist that it was supposed to be a good thing that went wrong. That was typical poor, mistreated, misunderstood Dean.

He wasn't going to pawn off any of this on anyone else. Not this time. Not if I could help it. Dean Crestwell was going to live with this one. I opened the door to the lobby to see Erin Joffries, a woman I'd helped with a law suit over a faulty boob job two years ago, running from the hallway with panicked eyes and a very white face.

"He's got a gun!" she cried in a squeaky whisper. "He's got a—"

The words disappeared as she ran out the front door.

"He's—Dean?" I cried out, my voice hitting a weird octave. A gun? Oh my God. Dean never even used to own a mousetrap, much less a gun. "Shit," I muttered, reaching for my phone as I ran down the hall Erin had vacated. The phone that was still in my car. I blew out a frustrated breath as I reached Bash's office door. "Damn it, damn it, damn it, Dean, don't be ridic—"

I pushed open the door to see Dean, sweating profusely and holding—a flare gun. Not toward Bash, who stood behind a desk. Not toward himself. Toward a window that looked out onto a field of hive boxes. Or, more specifically, the few hive boxes that were left.

"Dean!"

He swung around, flare gun in hand, and all I heard was a *fwump* as I hit the ground. A bright ball of red hurtled over my head, through the door, and exploded in flame as it slammed into the hallway wall. My mouth dropped open as the circle of fire burned through the wall, forming a black rim into the sheetrock. I turned back in shock.

"Carmen!" Dean cried. "Oh my God."

"Shit, are you okay?" Bash asked, nearly vaulting over his desk to snatch the gun from Dean. "Give me that, you idiot," he said. "I should knock you out with this thing."

Warily, I pushed myself to my feet. "That—would—have—been—*me*," I said, pointing to the charred circle behind me. "My head, to be exact!"

"You startled me!" Dean said, sinking onto a chair with a look of shock. "Shit, Carmen, you know me! You know I'd never hurt you!"

"I knew you'd never kidnap a bunch of bees, either," I said. "What the hell are you doing with a flare gun?"

"I keep it in my car," he said, burying his face in his hands. "For emergencies."

"And brought it in here, why?" Bash asked. "To shoot me after confessing?"

"No, I was just going to threaten to knock out all the rest of the hives if you tried to turn me in," Dean said miserably into his hands.

Bash looked at me and then down at Dean like he was crazy.

"Who *are* you?" he said.

"I don't know," Dean moaned.

"How could you do—"

"I don't know!" Dean repeated, sitting up. "I'm messed up! I'm a broken man."

"Broken from what?" I asked. "You're the mayor of Charmed! You have this town wrapped around your little finger. It's what you always wanted."

"I don't have you," he blurted.

Oh, holy hell.

"Dean—"

"Don't *Dean* me," he said. "Don't use your lawyer voice on me."

"We tried," I said. "For years. It just didn't work."

"Like hell you tried," he said. "It didn't work because half of you left with—"

"Carmen!" A husky, panicked male voice yelled from down the hall.

"What the—" I began, turning toward the door to see Sully and Allie burst through, Sully sliding in like Tom Cruise in *Risky Business*. Okay maybe not exactly that. Maybe with a little more blunder and a lot less cool, especially with an equally panicked woman tumbling in after him.

"Carmen—" Sully repeated, scanning me up and down. "Jesus, you're okay," he said in one breath. He shoved Allie aside like she was a bean bag and pulled me into his arms.

"I—*oompf.*"

My face was buried in Sully's chest as his hands cradled my head and back, pinning my arms to my sides. I wanted to say something. Something like that I was fine, or something bad ass like, "Get your damn hands off me, you big fat liar." But my nose was full of Sully, and that rendered me speechless.

"I rest my case," Dean said.

"Are you okay?" Allie asked. She couldn't be talking to Dean; her tone was too breathy. I pulled back from Sully to see her wrap her arms around Bash's neck in a full-on tackle. "We heard there was a gun, and—"

She kissed him. Holy shit, it was a day.

His face was in her hands and she was in his, and he wasn't arguing.

"It's all good," Bash said finally, leaning his forehead against hers. "I'm okay, Al." He didn't seem in a big hurry to let her go. I knew the feeling. "Dean was just…showing me his new flare gun."

Sully whirled around. "In the hallway?" He stared down a beaten-looking Dean. "You could have killed someone."

"It was an accident," I said, backing a step away from Sully before all my neurons reached out for more of him.

"Jesus," Sully said, rubbing his face and grabbing the door frame like he might need it to hold him up. "Lady was yelling that there was a gun, and that you were here, and…." He closed his eyes and shook his head.

"And you came running," I said softly. It wasn't meant to be out loud. It wasn't even meant to be a full-fledged thought. It was just there. And clearly verbalized.

"I don't even remember driving here," he said under his breath. He glanced at Allie, who'd finally let go of Bash, looking flushed. "Or picking up a passenger. Where did you sit?"

"In the back like a ten-year-old," Allie said. "You drive like a lunatic, by the way."

"Am I… are you…" Dean began, giving Bash a pleading look.

Bash took a deep breath, looking more distracted by Allie's kiss and tackle than he did about having a flare gun pulled on him and finding out that his old friend had stolen his bee hives.

"No," he said. "But get your shit together, man. And my hives better be back here *tonight*. Packed right and with not one bee missing, disoriented, or harmed."

"I'll make sure of it," Dean said. "No matter what it costs, buddy."

"It cost plenty already," Bash said. "Honey production stopped the day they were moved, and with reorientation time, it could be weeks before they're back on track again." He sat on the front of his desk. "Moving hives takes a plan and a schedule and knowing what the fuck you're doing. I don't know who you got to do this, but you screwed me. *Buddy*."

Dean leaned over his knees, raking his fingers through his hair.

"I got some guys from another apiary—not anyone from around here—to do it in the middle of the night," he said.

"The stupidest time to move bees," Bash said.

"They did it over the water, just in case," Dean said.

Middle of the night, over the pond, headed to the caves. Monte's stalkers. I sighed, knowing I'd have to give him the disappointing news that no one was after him.

"I'm sorry," Dean said to the floor. "I just lost it. Hart—"

"*Hart* has every right to string your ass up," Bash said. I glanced over to where Sully sat on a high stool. He looked a million miles away. "Especially since he now owns the very land you have my bees stashed on. He could sue your ass. So you'd be best to leave him out of this."

"Bash is right," I said. "He likes you. I don't think Sully does."

"And I don't even like you all that much right now," Bash said. "Damn it, Dean, this is going to be a cluster."

I walked over and gave Bash a quick hug. "Sorry," I said. "Indirectly, this is because of me, and I'm sorry about that."

He winked at me. "Don't suppose you'll cart him out of here for me?"

"I'm not a dog," Dean said, sitting up. "And I have a car, thank you very much."

"No," I said. "But Allie and I can get out of your way."

Passing Sully on the way out—again—was harder this time. I wanted to stop and do something. Hug him. Kiss him. Squeeze his hand. All of the things I had no business doing. I was still mad. I was still leaving. But him coming to save me… good God almighty, that was sexy as hell.

I walked past him, feeling every microscopic magnetic particle tugging on me as I did. I was close enough that he could have reached out to me. He didn't.

"I'm impressed," Allie said in a low voice as we walked down the hall. The hall with the black hole in the wall right at the level of my head.

"At what?" I asked.

"I thought you'd cave," she said. "Touch him or something on the way out. Damn, I would have."

"We talking about me and Sully, or that lip-lock you just did with Bash?" I asked.

She swallowed hard but glared at me sideways. "I have no idea what you're talking about."

I thought of Sully still sitting back there, and how he'd rushed in like Rambo to save me.

"Yeah, me neither."

* * *

I was ready to get the hell out of Dodge. Or Charmed, as it were. Whether it was just a vacation, or… or something a little longer. After today, it was maybe time to plan for the *little longer*.

I made a list of things to take care of and turn off, things I needed to buy, and people to notify. Sully would be one of them. I would not do to him what he did to me.

I dug out my suitcase and my duffel bag. Pulled some favorite winter clothes out of the closet and laid them on my bed, because there was suddenly a very good chance I'd need them. I included an old jean jacket of my mom's that she loved and I stole because it was worn and comfortable and pissed her off when I wore it. And I made one other very important executive decision.

Right before my doorbell rang.

I glanced out the side window and shook my head. No. I wasn't ready to—

"Carmen, I saw you look out the window," my mother said. "Open the door."

"Screw that," I muttered, going back to my organizing.

She banged on it three times. "I can stand here and do this all day!" she called out.

"Knock yourself out," I said quietly. To my list.

"Oh, hi, Mr. Harlan!" she sang out. "No, I'm fine. Carmen just won't let me in."

"Jesus," I hissed, storming to the door and yanking it open. "Seriously, how old are you?"

She walked by me smiling like we were going to have coffee.

"It worked," she said, dropping her keys on the side table and turning to face me. "You do what you have to do."

"I'm really not interested in having this conversation with you right now," I said. "I've had enough of this psycho day. Let me cool off and—"

"And leave?" she said. "For God knows how long?" She tilted her head. "You think I don't know that? No. We aren't leaving it like that."

I couldn't believe her. "You are a piece of work," I said. "You have no right to tell me how we're leaving it. You blew that." I pointed at her and headed back to my bedroom to finish packing. "*You.*"

She followed me. "Do you remember what I said when I walked in?"

"No." I yanked my sweaters off my closet shelves and threw them on the bed. "You ramble a lot, so I don't commit it to memory."

She stepped in front of me, blocking my path to the closet.

"I said, you do what you have to do."

Her eyes were red and free of makeup, but the stare-down she gave me wasn't distraught or wanting to make it up to me. It said Mama Tiger was fired up.

That was fine, because the tiger cub was pretty fired up, too. I'd just been lied to, betrayed, and shot at. I was done.

I turned to my dresser and opened the top drawer. I rummaged through my old scarves, needing something to do. Looking at her just—

"You have to talk to me sometime, Carmen," she said. "You can't just keep running away."

"Running—" I whirled around, holding a tattered blue scarf. "Running away? Seriously? That's hilarious coming from you."

She crossed her arms. "What does that mean?"

"It means that you run from everything," I said. "Anything that gets boring, or hard, or complicated... you will find any justification under the sun to bail. Jobs, people—"

"If you're putting yourself on that list, I will cross this floor and slap your face," she said, her voice shaking with anger.

For a moment, I was taken off-guard, my own anger blown out. It wasn't often that I'd seen my mother angry to the point of shaking. That was my m.o.

"I may be flighty and undependable in a lot of ways," she said, walking toward me. "I know that. I know what you think of me." Her eyes filled with tears, but her tone remained fiery. "But I have always—*always*—been there for you. Never once in your life have I bailed on you. I made *damn* sure of it."

"I never said you bailed on me," I said. "But that day..." My breath left me in a rush and I had to back away from her.

"I made the tough decision."

"You crossed a line!" I cried. "You played God and messed with my life, Mom. That wasn't being there for me, that was... that was taking away my dreams and setting me up for a life of mediocrity. And then you lied about it for over a decade." I couldn't stop. The plug had been pulled and the words rushed out like sand from a jar. "You trashed Sully all these years, about how he *ruined me and left me distraught*, and how Dean was this rock, the best, most stable thing for me, and all along it was you. You made him leave and let me think he didn't love me."

She closed her eye, and crossed her arms again, soaking in my words as she rocked on her heels.

"I didn't make him do anything, Carmen," she said, her voice gone quiet and introspective. It was a little eerie, as it was very unlike her. "I simply pointed out what you had ahead of you, and asked him to think about that." Her gaze focused hard on mine. "He told me he loved you more than anything."

I gasped, and swallowed it before it could take root. My hands went to my stomach, the scarf fluttering to the floor.

"So I told him to think about what that love meant," she said. "And if he really loved you unselfishly, then to do what was right for you."

I blinked my tears free. "What was right for me," I echoed. Pretty much the same words he'd said. He just never said they'd come from my mother.

"He did the honorable thing," she said. "Or so I thought. Now I hear he got that girl he's with pregnant—"

"No, his brother did," I said, wiping my face. "Sully just covered for him and helped her out."

My mother covered her mouth and took two long breaths. "Then like I said, he's honorable. I was wrong to bad-mouth him all this time. He was a good guy. I think it just made it easier after a while to think otherwise."

"He *was* a good guy. Sully was the love of my life," I said, the words going to a whisper, catching at the end.

My mom nodded as she dropped her hands and frowned against her own new tears. "I know."

"Really? Then how could you keep this from me?" I asked. "How would you feel if someone did this to you? If your entire life was decided by someone else?"

"It was," my mother said, crossing her arms so tightly she almost hugged herself. "Your grandmother did exactly that. With the love of *my* life. With your father."

Chapter Eleven

My father. When I was growing up, my father was never mentioned. He was the one not spoken of. As if my mom had been blessed by an angel like the Virgin Mary.

I'd always assumed he had knocked her up and either didn't know or didn't care and moved on. Now, the way my mother was shifting from foot to foot like she'd just released the Kraken, I felt I might need to sit.

I sank onto the foot of my bed.

"Aren't you just full of revelations today?"

She closed her eyes like it hurt. "I didn't want to be," she said. "God, I never wanted to be."

I narrowed my eyes. "Please tell me that Larry isn't my father."

"No," she said, a blustery chuckle breaking the doom and gloom around her before she went serious again. It was a little disconcerting, seeing her like that. All messed up and bothered over something. Over a man. *The love of her life.*

Shit, she looked like me.

"The carnival came through here back then, too," she said.

My stomach went sour. "Please tell me Sully's *dad* isn't my father!"

"No!" she said. "He wasn't from here, and he…went away." Her eyes took on a faraway look as she stared at a stone vase on my dresser. "My mother sent him packing, before I even knew about you."

"Why?" I asked.

Mom shrugged. "I was sixteen. He'd just graduated high school and was on his way to California from Florida on a motorcycle. He stopped here at the *carnival* to get something to eat." She shook her head slightly. "Damn carnival."

I raised my eyebrows. No kidding.

"The point is, my mother was right," she said. "He was a drifter and always would be. He wouldn't have stayed anyway." She sat down on the bed next to me. "That doesn't mean I wasn't crushed."

"So then how could you do it?" I asked. "Look me in the eyes and do the same thing to me?"

"Because I was afraid," she said, her voice a whisper. "You have a double dose of wanderlust in your blood, sweetheart. I saw you leaving forever in that young man." She drew in a shaky breath. "I saw me. I'm sorry."

I rubbed my eyes. "Okay, well, I have a lot to do, so…"

"Carmen, I'm trying to talk to you," she said.

"And you did!" I cried. "You told me. I heard you. Now I have to start getting ready."

Maybe I wouldn't even wait the couple of weeks. What was stopping me? Nothing, really. I could go anytime. I could handle a few straggler clients remotely.

Nothing was holding me here.

"And what about Sully?" she asked, as if reading my mind.

I stared at her.

"Now you're worried about me leaving Sully?" I said. "The man you talked into leaving me? That's rich."

"No, I'm worried about you, you dipshit," she said, pushing my arm. "For your sanity, when you realize he was here for the taking and you had to go on a road trip."

"Here for the taking," I echoed.

"Shit, Carmen, I'm sorry." Her tears were more angry now than sad. At me or at herself, I wasn't sure. "I'm sorry. I screwed up. Haven't you ever screwed up and couldn't undo it?"

I leaned over and picked up the scarf.

"You could have undone it," I said. "You could have said something at any point in time during the past fifteen years. Why didn't you ever tell me any of this?"

A bitter laugh escaped her throat. "It's a little hard to bring up in casual conversation."

I looked at her. Really looked at her. At the too-red hair, the soft sag her skin was starting to show, the lines that appeared more prominent around her eyes than they did yesterday. I could stay mad. Or I could let it go.

"What was his name?" Her bottom lip drew between her teeth, and I knew the quick steps her brain was doing. "My dad—what was his name?"

"John."

I tilted my head. "Mom."

"On my life," she said, tracing a cross over her heart. "His name was John."

"Last name?"

"I don't remember."

I scoffed. "I don't believe you."

"I don't care," she said, without skipping a beat.

"You just don't want to tell me," I said. "Because you know I'll look him up."

My mother patted my leg. "Some things are left better to themselves, Carmen."

"Then tell me something about him," I said.

She looked away—as if that might break every rule in the world—and took a deep breath.

"That old blue jean jacket over there that you don't think I know you took?" she said. "It was his."

All the air left my body. How many times had I wrapped it around me? Felt safe and cozy in its warmth and size.

"Jesus."

"And he hated honey, too," she added.

I got up and walked in a circle, feeling like the crazy had landed right on my house. I stopped and pulled my hair up off my neck, letting my gaze drop to her hand. The hand that had never sported a wedding ring.

"You never married anyone," I said. "I remember a lot of men, but you've never—"

I stopped when I met her eyes and saw the new tears there as she shook her head. She didn't have to explain that. For once, I understood where she was coming from. She might be flighty, she might not stick with a relationship, but that wasn't because she never found the right one. It was because she did.

I did something impulsive. Something I rarely did. I hugged her. For a long moment. We rocked back and forth until there were no more moments to milk, and then I pulled back, purposely not looking her in the eye.

"So, are there any other big secrets?" I asked. "Because this seems to be the time."

She took a deep breath and wiped face.

"Just that I'm buying the trailer park."

Chapter Twelve

A whole week went by. I didn't go back out to the site. I didn't go by his house. I didn't go to the Blue Banana or Rojo's or the bank or either grocery store, or anywhere that I could possibly run into Sully. It just didn't seem like a good idea. It was time to steer clear. Time to make the break and get ready to go. Because I was going. Tomorrow.

And sharing air with Sully… that was not conducive to that goal.

I spent some time with my mom and found out what she was up to. Saving a shit-ton of money was what she'd been up to. Saving enough to buy out Larry and stay there doing the only thing she'd ever done well. Run the trailer park. She was majorly pissed off at old man Bailey for selling to Sully, because that was a twist she didn't plan on. Leasing from the man she'd secretly begged to leave her daughter, never expecting him to return. Yeah, life has a way of laughing at you sometimes.

Today, I had bigger fish to fry. Lanie called and was bringing lunch to the office so we could have a coffee-table picnic, and I knew there was going to be a conversation. I'd already boxed up most of the personal items in my office. I wasn't giving up the space completely, but I was subletting it out to a lawyer friend. Just temporarily. No big deal.

Lanie wasn't going to see it that way. To be honest, I was okay with all of it, except the part that involved telling her. I took a deep breath.

She and I had just found our friendship again. We'd gone in different directions: She'd lived in Louisiana for a while, then returned to Charmed and found love, and then had to find her way back to the small-town life. She was happy again. My "different direction" held me here like a bungee cord—it let me go for college and law school, but then snapped me back. While I was thrilled to have my friend back, I was sick to death of Charmed. Maybe that was too harsh, but I needed to stretch, to see something more than the same four exits off the highway.

I needed out.

My vacation was supposed to help out in that regard. Then Sully arrived. And suddenly an already small town got infinitely smaller. I knew what I had to do; I just wasn't sure how to tell certain people.

One of them walked in.

"I hope you're hungry, because I got double cheeseburgers," Lanie said. She carried two bags in her hands, two bottled waters in the crook of her elbow. Something smelled suspiciously like apple pie. How do you leave someone who brings apple pie for lunch? "Did you hear about Mayor Dean resigning?" she asked breathlessly, kicking off her shoes. "Of course you did."

"Not from him," I said. "But my mother has her ever-present ear to the wall of City Hall, so she gave me the scoop. He's so melodramatic."

"That he is. So are you all packed for your trip? Oops, shit, grab the waters before I drop—" She stopped and wrinkled her nose. "Are you moving offices?"

"Here." I grabbed a bag and a water, wanting to have my food safely in my possession before she figured things out. "Grab some floor." I set the bag on the coffee table as we sat cross-legged.

"So are you?" she repeated, opening her water. "Moving offices?"

"No, I'm just moving my stuff out of the way while I sublet out this office." I turned on the most nonchalant expression I could summon. "You know, just while I'm gone. My electricity and water will be turned off at home by the end of the week, so nothing to worry about there. Luckily, I don't have any pesky plants to complicate things," I added with a laugh.

With nothing to soak up the sound, the laugh echoed off my empty walls and floor. Lanie dropped her water bottle back on the table, and went quiet. I unwrapped my hamburger with as much noise as I could.

"Where did you say the rental place was?" she asked, her tone going to that funny place where last chance confessions go to die. "Where Nick and I need to pick up your car?"

I shook my head and took a quick bite of my cheeseburger. It might be the only one I'd get.

"I decided to skip the rental," I said around my mouthful of food, reaching for my water so she couldn't throw it at me. "Just taking mine, it'll be eas—"

"You aren't coming back," Lanie said under her breath. Scrambling to her feet like ants bit her ass, she put her hands on her hips. "Carmen-fucking-Frost, you're leaving for good, aren't you?"

Any time my middle name became "fucking," it was probably going to be bad. I set down my burger and pushed to my feet, trying to come up with just the right words on the way up.

"No," I said. "Obviously I have to come back at some point. I mean—"

"Don't," she said, shaking her head. "Don't play games with me. I'm not Sully or Dean or your mother. You asked me the other day if *I* had any secrets? Put on your big-girl panties and be straight to my face, or I'm taking your lunch and leaving."

I closed my eyes and cracked my neck. This was Lanie and she deserved better than my chicken ass beating around the bush for her.

"Okay, fine, I'm… maybe staying gone for a while," I said.

"Forever."

"Not forever," I said. "I just… don't want to box it in with a time stamp."

Lanie blinked and looked at me funny, then grabbed her purse and hunted for her shoes.

"Where are you going?" I asked.

"Back to work," she said flatly. "Keep the food. Nick said enjoy the pie."

"Lanie!"

"No," she said, stumbling into one of her shoes and then turning to face me with tears in her eyes. "You weren't going to tell me."

"I was."

"You leave tomorrow."

"And… that's what I'm doing now," I said, knowing full well that things were going a horrible shade of bad.

"You were too big of a coward to tell me," she said. "To share your plans, your excitement with me. I would have been excited for you, Carmen," she said, wiping under her eyes. "I might have given you a little shit about it, but I'd have been happy for you. Instead, you made me insignificant. You can bitch to me about Sully, but you were going to do the exact same thing to me, and I'm not some man who comes and goes. I'm your friend." She opened my door without looking back. "Have a good trip. Drive safe."

And she was gone.

Tears clogged my throat as her words hit home.

"Shit."

* * *

I was done. I was packed. Everything was scheduled that needed scheduling, turned off that needed offing, and I was left looking around my house. Alone.

The alone part was my fault. I'd done that with my assholeness, and I needed to fix it before I hit the road tomorrow. I couldn't go with Lanie on my conscience. To really enjoy this adventure, I needed a clear mind. So I'd go see her tonight, and Sully—I'd run by the trailer on my way out. Just to check that box. Not that I needed to see him, but I wouldn't leave without saying goodbye. I wouldn't do what he did to me. Not to anyone.

Tomorrow. He was on tomorrow's agenda. Because if I went to his house tonight, well, he might have another dessert that would do me in.

I grabbed the plastic grocery bag with today's untouched burgers and pie and headed out the door. But I didn't drive to Lanie's house. Or Sully's. I went to the pond.

No cars—or black Chevy trucks—were parked at the trailer, thank God. I think. I didn't want him to be there, but then again I wasn't sure why I was there if not to see him. I had hit some special flavor of screwed up.

I took it as a sign, though. I was there, it was turning out to be a nice night—dusk was settling without humidity or mosquitoes—and it could be the beginning of my introspective adventure. I headed to the water to say goodbye to my past. I never wondered if there would be any boats. Promise. With all the protesting lately, it was unlikely there would be.

Except that there were.

Damn it.

I stared at the two little rowboats floating down there, looking all innocent and sweet and *come float around in me*. I was going to go float around in one. At night, like an idiot. Not like I hadn't done it a million times before, but now it just seemed—silly. A grown woman rowing a boat alone at night to say goodbye to water. In a boat that had been dry rotting on that water for over twenty years. If I were still married to Dean, he would have told me to get my ass back in the car. Which was why I wasn't still married to him.

I did the obligatory checks before I untied and pushed off. No creatures hunkering in. My phone in my pocket. An old flashlight was clipped to the side, and I checked it. The light was dim, but it would be a great weapon to beat the crap out of anything that tried to climb in with me. It was enough to attract attention if I dropped my paddle and couldn't get back. Although to be honest, I'd probably just jump in and swim. Bailey's Pond wasn't exactly the Gulf of Mexico.

Pushing off, I looked around at the darker gray settling on the far banks, into the private little nooks and coves that were hidden from view from the pond's bank. It looked creepy, but the pond had never scared me at night. Maybe because I'd spent two summers there, mostly the second, mostly in the dark. Mostly naked. It was more romantic than scary.

I knew exactly where I was going.

The place I'd avoided for the last fifteen years. The last time I'd been out there was right after Sully left, when I was craving something that felt like him. I'd lain on the stone dock spread-eagle and cried the cry that only others who had been gutted and left to die would understand.

I might have been a tad overly dramatic back then. Eighteen and a bit hormonal. Regardless, it was all there, rushing back to me like voices whispering in my ears as I moved across the water. It had been a long time, but as I approached our spot, it felt like yesterday.

The pond was quiet, the only sounds coming from my paddle slicing through the dark water and the crickets that were beginning to wake up. Nothing had changed except for the big houses to the right, lighting up the surface like fairy lights. Everyone was inside, eating dinner, done with their day, not paying attention to the crazy woman paddling through their backyard.

I rounded the point that designated our cove and took a deep breath. The cove actually belonged to Sully now. That was weird. I'd bet when we were out here doing the wild thing, he'd never dreamed that someday he'd own that space.

The bottom of the row boat slid onto grass next to the old stone dock, and I turned to look at it. I could still see that girl, sobbing alone on the stones, but I chose to look away. I wasn't her anymore. I hadn't been her in a very long time, and not even the great Sully Hart's return could completely remove the armor I'd built around myself over the years. I threw out the rope and kicked off my shoes to step out on the spongy land. Grabbing the flashlight, I aimed it around. It had been many years, but I was pretty sure "trampled" didn't describe it before. The traffic that had been in and out of there with the Great 2016 Bee Heist had taken its toll. I tied the boat to a tree, then took a deep breath and headed up the rocks. Anxiety sunk into me the closer I got to the caves.

The closer I got to history.

I climbed the rocks, amazed that people carrying beehives had managed this without pissing off any of the little shits. Huffing around a bend, I aimed my flashlight toward the caves.

To my right, something snapped.

"Carmen?"

I yelped, spun, and threw the flashlight. *Smack!*

"Ow!"

"Sully?" I exclaimed. "What are you doing out here?"

I dug my phone out of my pocket and turned on the flashlight app, which was a million times brighter than that real flashlight had been.

"I could ask you the same question," he said. "What the hell are you doing rowing out here after dark?"

"I'm... just..." Shit, there was no good way to answer this. "I asked you first."

I shined my light in his face. He grimaced. "Do you mind?"

"Sorry." I lowered it to his body, which was clad in a white T-shirt and jeans.

"I was coming to see Bailey, and walked down here first," he said.

"Bailey?"

"Old man Bailey?" he said. "We've had this conversation."

"Not that he lives here," I said.

"Yeah, right up this path," Sully said, turning to point at the dirt path he'd come down. "You have to drive down that crappy road through the woods the long way, but as long as it hasn't rained recently—"

"Yeah, yada yada yada crappy road," I said, waving my hand even though he probably couldn't see. "*Bailey* lives here?"

Sully paused. "Yeah."

"Did he live here when we..." I gestured toward the caves.

He laughed and stepped closer, making my heart go a little faster. *No. No faster heart. Remember that you're mad. Remember that you're leaving.*

"When we made love in there?" he asked, his voice going lower. "When we sexed up every inch of that dock over there? When I went down—"

"Yes," I said, digging my nails into my palms to stave off the imagery. *He remembered all that.* "All of that, and you're telling me he was right up that road?"

Sully shrugged. "I didn't find out exactly where till the next year, but yeah."

"Oh my God," I said, covering my face.

"So what? You said you never met him."

"That doesn't make it less mortifying," I said. "Did he hear us?"

He laughed. "I never asked. Do you want me to?"

"No, thank you." I turned back to the boat.

"Where are you going?" he asked.

"Back."

"Why?"

"Because this was a dumb idea," I said, nearly tripping on a tree limb.

"Seriously, Carmen." Sully came up behind me and grabbed my arm. "What was your idea?"

I looked up at him. I didn't need the flashlight anymore; my eyes had adjusted to the low light from the moon. Being with him there was the weirdest kind of déjà vu, and yet incredibly different at the same time. And I needed to tell him that I was leaving. It had gone *so* well with Lanie, I couldn't imagine what my hesitation was about... but regardless of our issues, I needed to tell him goodbye.

And that last thought nearly buckled my knees.

"I leave tomorrow," I said.

"The vacation," he said, nodding.

I licked my lips and looked back at the boat. It was calling to me. I really didn't want to get fussed at again.

"I'm *leaving*," I said. "Tomorrow."

A million crickets sang in that pause, as Sully looked at me, soaking in my meaning, not blinking. Then he looked past me to the water.

"So tonight is your last night here," he said softly.

I couldn't open my mouth to speak. It hurt. It physically hurt to think of saying it out loud. I nodded slightly. He might not have even seen it.

He exhaled slowly as he walked past me, down the rocks; the moonlight shining on him as he pulled off his shirt and tossed it on the dock.

"What are you doing?" I asked

I could see the tattoos, the outline of the muscles in his back, and when he turned, his jeans were unzipped.

"Going for a swim," he said as his jeans hit the ground. "Coming?"

Chapter Thirteen

He was beautiful in the moonlight. Carved from marble, his hair just long enough to swing around his face and into his eyes. Muscles rippling, and an ass that—oh my God, I needed to walk away. Float away. Get in the boat and row away, now.

Except he was standing between me and the boat.

"I—" I laughed to cut the tension. "I can't."

"Because?"

It would have been better if he'd gotten mad and yelled at me. I was getting to be an expert on angry people. This was uncharted territory. Or not uncharted. I'd been here before. And it was scary as hell.

"Because I…I'm going to Lanie's after this?" Why did I pose it as a question? "Because I'm not eighteen."

"I wasn't eighteen," he countered.

"No, you were old enough to know better," I said.

"I always know better," he said, walking into the water. "That doesn't change anything."

"Sully—"

"Scared?" he said, turning just enough for me to see everything I remembered. "Can't handle it?"

"I'm an adult, Sully," I said. "I don't go skinny-dipping in the pond with houses nearby."

"The Carmen I knew was fearless," he said, resting back in the water. He went under briefly. When he surfaced, his hair was slicked back with water.

Sweet Jesus.

I wasn't fearless now. I was absolutely terrified. What was I doing? I was a grown woman. A business woman. I had no sensible, logical, sane reason to do this.

I tossed my shoes onto the dock.

And unbuttoned my shorts, sliding them down slowly as he watched. *This is a bad idea.* I pulled my T-shirt over my head and threw my clothes on the dock, feeling like I was doing a strip tease. *Such a bad idea.*

"Turn around," I said.

"Yes ma'am." Chuckling, he swirled around to give me a view of his back.

"Dear God, I've lost my mind," I whispered, shimmying out of my underwear. I couldn't bring my phone in the water with me, so I followed the moonlight and picked my way down to the grass barefoot, praying I didn't step on something or do something that would require medical attention naked.

The water was warm from the hot day, and the bottom was muddy over the rocks. I slid in, and he turned around just as the water reached my breasts.

"That's cheating," I said, going lower.

"I don't always play fair," he said, pushing off and treading water.

There's something very intimate and vulnerable about skinny dipping. You can't bullshit, you can't lie, you are exposed and bare and everything feels more raw. More personal. More naked.

Watching him in the water was so familiar, like we had gone back in time. It took my breath away. My chest burned. I had to either keep it together or get out and leave.

I held my breath and went under. The crickets disappeared as the water closed in over my head and there was only the sound of bubbles drifting upward. Nothing in this world gave more clarity than being underwater. Things made sense there.

Sully's fingers intertwining with my left hand in that silent simple world made sense, too. If only I didn't need to breathe.

When I rose to the surface, still holding his hand, life got complicated again. He tried to pull me to him, but I kept my arm rigid.

"Not so fast," I said.

A small smile pulled at his lips. "I figured that."

"But you had to try," I said.

His fingers squeezed mine, the playfulness fading a little from his expression. "You're here. Two feet away and naked, holding my hand and talking to me. I'm thinking I've already beaten my odds tonight."

"What were you doing at the cave?" I asked.

"Same as you, probably," he said. "Seeing where they put the bees." He grinned. "Revisiting history. Been a long time since I've been there."

"Your last time was mine," I said.

He looked surprised. "Really?"

"I couldn't go back there," I said. "I couldn't even—I only came out here once afterward, and then never again."

I looked at our hands on the water's surface, fingers laced together like lovers. How many nights had we done this? Truthfully, not many—we'd only had three weeks—but it felt like so much more. How I could fall so hard in such a short time? So hard that I would never be the same. So hard that fifteen years later, those memories both warmed me and stabbed me in the heart, hurting so much I couldn't breathe.

"You okay?"

I swallowed the burn. "You should have told me," I said finally, my voice a whisper. "Then. Now. I shouldn't have heard it from my ex-husband."

"I know," he said. "I'm sorry."

"You were protecting my mom."

"No," he said. "I was protecting you. She's all you had. I didn't want to take that away."

Burn, burn, burn. Shit. I turned away as the tears came, unbidden, and let go of his hand. I ducked under the water to cool my head and wash away the tears as I treaded over to the dock, automatically landing in the spot where we used to lean against the rocks and make out and talk for hours.

"So what's going on with your brother?" I asked, wiping the water from my face.

"Subject change?" he asked, following me.

"Necessary."

He nodded and stopped very close, probably aware that I'd backed myself into a wall. Into *the* wall. I ignored the fact that all my sensations were traveling to one specific place.

"Aiden has problems," he said.

"So I gathered."

"Everything with him is about anger," he said, stretching his arms and somehow using every muscle in his body to do it. "About entitlement and being wronged in every possible way."

"You inheriting the business?"

"Oh yeah, that didn't help things," Sully said. "You'd think I orchestrated that on my own, to listen to him, but in all honesty, I never saw it coming."

I frowned. "Really? Who else would it be?"

"No one," Sully said bluntly. "It's been in the red for years. I thought it would shut down to pay everyone. My dad was an excellent carnie host. He was an entertainer. He was from the smoke-and-mirrors days where charm and a slick acting job got you by. Everyone loved him. But slick doesn't cut it anymore, and charm didn't pay the bills."

"Enter free spirit, Sully?"

"Exactly," Sully said. "That free spirit was great until we couldn't afford food. That'll change things. Then I became the one who'd stay up all night poring over the books to figure out which towns were usually profitable and which ones were a drain and should be skipped."

"Wow," I said. "And Aiden?"

"Drank every penny that landed in his pocket," he said. "And then started drinking the profits, too."

I took a deep breath. "And Kia?"

Sully's jaw tightened. "Kia was raised by her grandmother, who'd been with the company since before my dad, even. She's family. She—" Sully stopped and looked away, like he needed to catch his breath. "The carnie world tends to be a little freer with things. People walk around half naked all the time, no one thinks a thing of it. That being said, Kia does like sex." Sully held up his hands. "Not with me. I've never touched her that way. But just because you like it doesn't mean people should take advantage of it. And Kia isn't perfect; she is too blunt sometimes and pisses off the wrong people." Sully's eyes flashed in anger, something even the dark couldn't hide. "Aiden had a thing for her and she rebuffed him one too many times, so one night she was drinking and he put something in her beer and took what he thought was his right to take."

"Oh my God," I said. "Did she press charges?"

Sully shook his head. "Doesn't work that way in our world. You don't…you don't rat on your own."

"I would think you don't rape your own, either!"

"I know," he said, rubbing his eyes. "But she wouldn't tell anyone. She didn't even tell *me* until she ended up pregnant. She was afraid I'd kill him."

"And you helped her get an abortion," I said.

"We left right after."

"Wait, this is recently?"

"I couldn't look at him anymore," he said. "I didn't care about the carnival, I was so full of hate and rage I just needed out before I did something I'd regret. I needed something else. Something real and permanent and—"

"Here."

Sully's breath came faster. It was all I could do not to wrap myself around him and make it all better.

"Here," he echoed, his voice strained. "Then came Bailey."

"And all the calls from your brother?"

"He's flailing like a fish," Sully said. "The carnival's sinking; he's trying to play the big dog, and screaming at me one second and begging for help the next." He came up next to me, facing the rocks, his hands splayed on them like he'd push them all out of the way if he could. "I feel bad for our people. They don't deserve that. They don't deserve to go down with Aiden, but... I can't keep it afloat anymore. I'm fucking tired. I need something for myself."

I was moving before I let myself think about it. It was all I could do.

Ducking under his arm, I slid between him and the rocks, filling the space, our bodies pressed together. I took his face in my hands and leaned it down to rest on mine. It felt right. It felt more right than in any other place in the entire world. Then I kissed him.

Softly. Slowly. Giving him every ounce of comfort I could. I wanted this moment to be different. To be an emotional connection and not be a carnal frenzy. But at the same time I was hit to the core with exactly why it always became one.

Because this hurt.

This was... real. Every kiss, every touch, every stroke was a gut-checking reminder of what we had and lost and were losing again. This was it. My throat burned with tears. I refused to let them come as I buried my heart in him instead.

"I'm sorry," he said against my mouth. He sounded broken.

The tears won, spilling over my eyes and my heart, breaking me in so many places.

"I know," I mouthed against him, tasting the salt and closing my eyes to will it away.

"I need you," he said, kissing my cheeks and neck and burying his face in my shoulder as I wrapped my arms around his head. His arms went around my body, pulling me in tight, making us one.

"You have me," I whispered against his hair. "You've always had me."

"And you've always had me," he said against my neck, dragging his lips up along my jawline, back to my mouth. "God, I wasted so much time."

I shut my eyes tightly, breathing him in. "And now—tomorrow—"

"Shh," he said kissing my top lip and pressing his forehead to mine. "We aren't talking about tomorrow. Not right now. Tonight, you're not two feet away anymore." I laughed through my crying and he smiled. "Tonight you're here, in my arms. You're mine."

I kissed him with all I had, exploring his mouth, delving my fingers into his hair and roaming the tight lines of his shoulders as his hands travelled my body. I could feel him hard against my belly. It was all I could do not to wrap my legs around him and bring us to a primal place really damn fast, but I wanted it to go slowly. I wanted to stretch this out and remember this night forever.

Then he did *the thing.*

I couldn't remember slow anymore.

Sully lifted me out of the water so that my chest was in his face and my back against the rocks, his hands pulling my legs around him and sliding up to caress my breasts as his mouth made love to them.

God, I loved that. I'd forgotten how much I loved that. My fingers clenched in his wet hair as he drew a nipple between his teeth and sucked on it, taking more and more before deserting that one and sharing the love with the other.

Watching him, his head in my arms, his face in my chest, kissing my tattoo that was put there for him—it was surreal. Like some bizarre time warp that put us right back where we left off, but fifteen years older. I couldn't take my eyes off him, I couldn't stop touching him. It was like I'd opened a floodgate of everything I'd shut down.

Then he moved. Against me. And we both groaned.

"Carmen," he breathed against my skin. "God, baby, you feel good."

My thighs tightened around him, pulling him in, pushing me against everything I needed. And I needed. Oh my God, I needed. I had to keep moving. Nothing was more important than moving.

"Sully," I gasped, pulling back on his hair so I could get to his mouth again.

He let go of my breasts to grab my ass, water splashing around us as he dug his fingers into my flesh, guiding me as I moved against him. Because I had to move. I had to feel him or lose my fucking mind. And when he pulled me hard to him, I captured his growl in my mouth.

"*Fuck*, baby—" he began, sucking in a breath when I reached down to stroke him against me. "You keep doing that—"

"I need you," I said against his mouth, not recognizing my own voice, my own desperation. I'd never begged a man in my life. Not even *this* man. "Please, I need you, Sully."

Even in the dark, I saw the rawness in his eyes, heard the ragged expel of breath as he changed one angle and plunged into me. Pushing, driving, burying deep with no mercy.

The moan that came from him was primal, as pain and pleasure shattered me. I had no thoughts, no logic, no functional breathing, just muscles tightening and reacting around this man in my arms. We'd been here before, and yet nothing was like before. Nothing and no one had ever fit me so perfectly or known my body so instinctively. We moved like we'd been making love all our lives, touching, tasting, lifting my legs higher so he could drive impossibly deeper, harder, faster. My limbs were on fire with exertion and I didn't care.

"Carmen—"

"Oh God—"

"Are you—*fuck*—" he forced out like it was coming from his feet.

I couldn't answer. I couldn't breathe. My climax climbed upon me so tantalizingly slow and muscle-curling that I was shaking violently, clinging to him in another state of reality when it finally crested.

"Shit—Sully—*Jesus*—"

I broke. The sounds coming from me were nothing I recognized. Words that weren't even words tumbled from my mouth as wave after wave of body-rocking orgasm slammed into me. And then there was Sully.

Bowing up like a beast and roaring through his teeth, he pounded his climax into me, following me over each hill, water splashing in our faces, both of us with a death grip, shaking with adrenaline and exhaustion, unable to stop the rhythm that propelled us forward.

Gasping for air as we finally slowed, Sully collapsed against me and buried his face in my hair. I took every bit. I wrapped my arms all the way around his neck and latched my feet at the ankles, not willing to let it go yet. Not ready to—

Emotion washed over me like another orgasmic wave, except not nearly as pleasurable. Trembling that had nothing to do with sexual exertion took over and I held my breath to try to stem it. I wasn't this girl. I wasn't sappy. I wasn't a basket case who got weepy after sex. Even after astronomical sex. But my God, that wasn't even—it wasn't just sex. It was fucking mental. Damn it. I had to be delusional, but all I knew was that I couldn't let go. I couldn't let it be over yet. Because once it was….

I pressed my face into his shoulder, willing the burn to go away, hating the knowledge that I was the one walking away this time. This was on me. I was leaving this. I was leaving *him*.

Why?

The question was as loud as if a voice had spoken it in my ear, and I jumped.

"You okay?" he asked, actually against my ear.

His voice brought all the feelings blazing to the surface. I nodded against him as my head screamed the opposite.

"I'm good," I whispered, kissing his neck, his jaw, his chin, meeting his lips as he met mine. It was soft, lingering. Two people who just wanted to stay right there forever.

Sully leaned his head back a fraction to look at me. He brought a hand up out of the water to smooth back a strand of hair that had mostly dried and fallen into my face in the frenzy. He tucked it behind my ear and moved his finger along my cheek, down to my lips.

I didn't breathe. I closed my eyes but could feel his gaze as clearly as if I were looking back. This was why we shouldn't have done this. This was the moment of clarity that comes rushing in after the post-orgasmic bliss to slap the crap out of you.

"I don't want you to go," he said slowly, softly. He kissed my nose and then my forehead. "I'll never ask you not to. But God, I'll miss you."

Slap.

There were things. *Say something.* Hovering on the edges of my logical thoughts were important *things* I needed to say. Things that mattered right this minute, and the clock was running out. *My* clock was running out.

I swallowed hard and opened my mouth to speak, and then I heard the snap of twigs behind us on the bank. Sully's grip on me tightened.

"Who the hell is out there?" an old man crowed. "Whose clothes are all over my dock?"

Chapter Fourteen

I cringed, and Sully let his head fall.

"Damn it," he whispered.

"Really?" I whispered back. "*This* is how I meet Mr. Bailey?"

I was all too aware that not only were we naked and soaking wet, but we were still joined at the—

"I'm talking to you!" Bailey hollered, followed by a crack that sounded like a cane on stone. "More bee thieves trampling up my cove? Come out here!"

"You've got to be kidding me," I muttered, leaning my head back against the rock. "Think he'll go away?"

"Your boat is over there in *his* cove, and our clothes are all over *his* dock," he said, chuckling. "I doubt it."

"So how are you going to protect my honor here, Lancelot?" I asked.

"Well, for starters…" he began, pulling out of me with a crooked grin that tugged on my heart. "There's that." He dropped a kiss on my lips and backed away, out of my arms. I missed him instantly.

"Hey, old man," he said. "It's just me. You didn't see my truck?"

Bailey scoffed. "Your truck is black. How am I supposed to see that at night? And what are you doing down here in the middle of the night? Don't you know about all the trouble that went on out here?"

Sully laughed and swam out of my line of vision, so I turned and pulled up on the stones with my fingertips just enough to peek over the top. All I could see was a flashlight beam swinging around and the form of a skinny old man.

"It's not even eight o'clock yet," Sully said. "And don't act like you're so old you don't know what I'm doing. You know you did the same thing."

"Not in my thirties, I didn't," Bailey said. "I was an adult, raising kids. When you gonna learn how to adult, Sully?" Sully strode out of the water. "Jiminy Christmas, get some clothes on, boy. You made enough of a mess with them."

"My mess, my cove, my dock," Sully said, holding out his arms. "Your idea."

"If I'd known the whole world would be here every night, I might not have suggested it," he said.

"The bee thieves weren't me, and that won't happen again," Sully said. "How about you stroll on back up that path," he said, pointing. "So my lady friend can have some dignity getting out. I'll be up to the house shortly."

"If she had any dignity, she wouldn't be trolling with the likes of you," he said. "Again."

Again? I pulled up a little higher and frowned. He knew it was me?

"Just—"

"I'm going, I'm going," Bailey said, waving his cane as he turned to pick his way back up. "I'm not totally heartless. I'm not totally deaf, either," he called back over his shoulder.

"Oh my God," I said under my breath, pressing my face against the warm stone. "Kill me now. An old man heard me come."

"Bring her up to the house with you," he said. "I'd like to meet the woman that Sullivan Hart comes walking on water to defend."

* * *

I'd worn white. So shuffling up a gravel path pulling wet panties out of my ass, while struggling to stretch out tight white shorts and an equally clingy white T-shirt, with a bra that didn't want to play nice with anyone… well, I was just having all the fun. To be fair, I hadn't anticipated swimming tonight. If I had, I might have worn something a little less see-through. Or brought a towel.

I combed back my wet hair with my fingers. "God, we look like you're bringing home your girlfriend to meet the parents." I looked down. "Straight from a wet T-shirt contest."

Sully, on the other hand, looked mostly normal in his jeans and white T-shirt, with just a few damp spots here and there. His slicked-back hair was starting to dry and looked sexy as hell. Guys suck.

And he was looking at me with a grin in his eyes that wasn't necessarily on his face.

"What?"

"You called yourself my girlfriend," he said, the smile tugging at one corner of his lips.

Heat flooded my neck and face, and I cursed the timing.

"Well, it was just—I mean—I said it *looked* like that—" I snorted.

"You know what? After tonight's activities, I'm borrowing the term for the night. Because—it wasn't just—and I feel like I should sort of qualify—"

Sully grabbed my face and kissed me into silence.

"Anyone ever tell you that you babble when you're nervous," he said softly.

"Occasionally."

"Relax," he said, squeezing my hand and dropping another kiss on my lips. "He's all gripe, but he's a softie. And don't shake his hand."

"What? Why?"

The door opened, and the thin old man in front of me scoffed. "Get a room."

Great.

Sully blew out a breath. "Quit ball-busting me, Albert. Be nice."

The old man gave him a snarky look, turned around and walked back into the house. We followed him. Tucked into the woods, from the outside, the house was pretty nondescript. Bare stone met brick and wood, with few windows and mostly scrubby bushes and trees around it. From the front, it looked very small, but the sides disappeared into the trees. It was easy to see why I'd never noticed it before. It blended. This was a man who wanted to be unseen, and he'd pulled it off.

Inside, on the other hand, was something else. From the moment we stepped over the threshold, I was ensconced in warm light and honeyed earth tones that made it feel huge. Rich wood made it very much a man's domain, but candles, clocks, books, and buttery leather furniture softened up the feel. Books were everywhere—on built-in shelves and random nooks, stacked on end tables and used as props for bowls or lamps or pictures. The bowls held random things, like paper clips and keys, and I had to lean over to verify that another held eyeglasses. Maybe eight or nine pairs. Assorted framed pictures, including family photographs to one of an old-fashioned ship sailing on a rough ocean, kept the eye moving around the room. It was interesting. Beautiful in an odd sort of way, and very homey, but so busy I couldn't imagine relaxing in there.

Maybe why that was why he was so cranky.

"Have a seat," he said, perching over a recliner and falling into it with a sigh.

Sully landed on the couch, but I sank to my knees on the floor next to him. "My clothes are wet, so…" I explained. I gave Sully a look, waiting for him to introduce me, and then I rolled my eyes. "I'm Carmen—"

"Frost," he finished, nodding as he hooked his cane on the arm of his chair. "Yes, I know."

I tilted my head and looked again at Sully, who shrugged at me without surprise. Then again, I was a lawyer, I'd represented many Charmed residents over the years and there was a newspaper photo a while ago before I decided not to waste my money on ads.

"You have me at a disadvantage then, Mr. Bailey," I said. "Because I don't recall us meeting before."

He looked up at me, matter-of-fact. "We haven't," he said. "But your friend's aunt and I were close once—"

"You knew Aunt Ruby?" I asked.

"We grew up together," he said. "The best of friends." Something in his tone, though, said there was a story untold. "I've also met your mother a time or two. And you're the spitting image of your father."

* * *

I didn't remember getting to my feet, I was just there. Sully even sat forward in interest from his laid back sprawl. The question about Lanie's Aunt Ruby was forgotten with the mention of—

"My father."

"Yes ma'am."

"I don't have a father." I felt dizzy, thinking about how many times I'd used that word just this week, when I'd maybe said it twice my whole life.

"Everyone has a father," Bailey said, chuckling as he opened a small wooden box and pulled out a pipe. "Do you think you just hatched like a little bird? Even they have fathers."

I narrowed my eyes. "Mine doesn't live here, sir. You're mistaken." So much for being psychic.

"No, he doesn't," Bailey said. "He's probably on the west coast somewhere, if I had to guess."

My mouth went dry. But that could have just been a good hunch, too.

"Probably?" I asked. "I thought you were psychic."

Bailey looked up from fiddling with his pipe, and glanced over to Sully, eyebrows raised. "Quite the brazen one you have here." His eyes settled back on me as he packed his pipe. "Who told you that malarkey about being psychic?"

I crossed my arms, about two minutes away from walking out and back to my little boat.

"Come see," he said, holding out a hand. His knuckles were swollen.

"See what?"

He gestured again. I looked at Sully, who was being surprisingly silent and introspective, and shook my head. Men were useless. I walked over to Bailey, feeling like I was walking the plank. I stopped just short of his chair.

"I'm here."

"Give me your hand," he said.

Don't shake his hand.

"I'm good, thanks," I said.

"Miss Frost," he said quietly, watery blue eyes peering up at me. "Old isn't contagious. You'll get there on your own one day. I just need your hand for about five seconds."

I sighed, unfolding my arms and holding my hand out. "This is silly. This is—"

The second his cool dry skin touched mine, my whole body went tingly. Like getting goosebumps that don't go away. I could hear my breath in my ears and see everything the same around me, the room, the old man, I knew Sully was behind me on the couch, but it was like I was watching it from just a step away.

Thoughts—like memories but not memories; more like home movies or a video—swirled around my head.

A man on a motorcycle with dark blond hair. The same man talking on a bench. I couldn't hear the words and couldn't possibly know what he was saying, yet I did. I knew every word as if I had experienced them myself. Words about turmoil and indecision. A need to keep moving. Someone wanted him to go, but someone—there was someone wanting him to stay. Fingers through the hair and dark eyes looking around for something. Answers. Needing someone to tell him what to do. But God help him, he was already jacked up over this girl.

Answers swam like they lived on the air, sinking into the solid things. No one could tell him what to do, because he already knew. If it was real, if he truly loved her, there would be no decision to make. The fact that there was—he'd already made his choice. But Gerry—

I yanked my hand away, sucking in a breath like I'd been underwater for an hour. Sully was behind me, holding me up. When did he cross the room? Why were my legs not working?

"What the living fuck was that?" I said. My voice was weird and gravelly, and I had a headache from hell. "What did you do to me?"

"I told you not to shake his hand," Sully said.

"Seriously?" I said, trying to turn around but failing. "You sat there like a lump and let me walk over here and now you want to say that?"

Bailey looked unfazed, sitting there with his unlit pipe in his mouth like any other weird eccentric old man.

"What did you see?" he asked, as if I'd just peeked through a keyhole.

I stared back at him. "Who are you?"

"I'm Albert Bailey, Miss Frost," he said, holding out his other hand in greeting.

"Yeah, I'll pass," I said, feeling my feet come back. I took a deep breath and let it go, waving off Sully as the old man and I locked gazes. "I'm good."

I wasn't good. I was confused and bewildered and more than a little freaked out. Good had left the picture. That had been—I couldn't even put into words what that had been. I wasn't one to believe in the weird and unexplained, but that had definitely qualified.

"What did you see?" Bailey repeated, a quiet smile relaxing his face.

Emotion crept over me, blanketing me in something sad and unfair. A sense of loss that ached deep in my chest. The random memory of the days after Sully left, when all I could do was cry, and my mother quietly took care of me without question. I thought she was clueless, but she'd not only been fighting her own guilt over causing my heartbreak, she'd lived it herself. When my father made his choice.

"You know what I saw," I said in a shaky whisper.

"And what did it tell you, little bird?" he asked, glancing sideways at Sully.

Bailey used to tell me I was a broken bird waiting for a little bird...

No.

"I have to go," I said, backing up.

I couldn't be his bird. I couldn't be his anything. Yes, I got the damn message. Yes, I had a choice to make, but you know what? Damn it, he had a choice back then, too. And he might have done it for all the right reasons, but he still left. And now it was my turn. A turn that had been calling to me my whole life, and if I didn't take it now I might never get the chance again.

"Carmen, you okay?" Sully asked.

"Not really," I said, a breathy chuckle escaping my throat as I moved toward the door. "I just—nice to meet you. Don't move, stay here and visit with Yoda." I held up a hand when Sully moved to follow me. "I'll take the boat back. No biggie. Great night. All that—"

I turned and was out the door into the night air before I finished speaking. I couldn't get away fast enough, like gravity was pulling me back, like there wasn't enough oxygen in the air. Like I was clawing my way out of a hole that only I could see.

It was too much. I'd seen my father. I knew it was him. I knew it like I'd known him my entire life. Even though it was fuzzy and weird and not totally clear, it was like I'd been there having the conversation. But there was no explainable way for me to have seen him. Holding an old man's hand? Yeah, not my version of explainable. Aunt Ruby had had some interesting, possibly other-worldly things going on, but it damn sure was nothing like that.

"Carmen!" Sully called from behind me. I was speed-walking blindly up the path we'd come, not even using the flashlight on my phone. The moon was bright enough through the trees. Hell, for that matter, my state of mind was amped up so high it would probably light my way. "Hey, would you wait?"

"I told you to stay," I said, not slowing down. "I'm a big girl. I know how to row a boat back the direction I came."

Footsteps jogged up behind me, and Sully circled around in front of me, stopping me in my tracks. "I have no doubt you can row all over this damn pond," he said. "But if you think I'm gonna let you just float away tonight without—" He stopped, rubbing his jaw. "I'm taking you home."

My heart was still racing, so I took a slow breath. I needed to calm down and process. Process what, I had no idea. But something. I had to make sense of something. Tomorrow. While I was driving.

"My car's at your trailer," I said.

"Then I'm bringing you there."

"Okay," I said, gesturing toward the path. "Let's go."

We didn't talk the rest of the way, and after making sure the boat was secure, we headed toward his truck. It was odd, him bringing me home like two people on a normal date. We'd never had a normal date. Dinner out with a movie. Sex in a bed. A kiss goodnight.

We didn't talk as he maneuvered the twisty road out of the woods, or as we passed the houses that framed the east end, or when he pulled into the parking lot next to my car. The closer we got, the more my panic built. It was getting real. I wasn't ready. I was ready to be gone, just not to do the going. I didn't know how to do the going. My eyes filled with tears when he turned off the engine, everything going quiet as we sat and absorbed the silence. I wanted to leap over the console and bury myself in his arms. Kiss him two or three or a million more times. Memorize his smell and his taste and the way his hair felt when it fell against my face.

Who was I kidding? I'd done that fifteen years ago.

"If you hadn't run into me out there," he said softly. "Would you have said goodbye?"

"You mean like you did?" I asked.

He looked at me. "In spite of it."

"I was planning to stop and see you in the morning," I said, hearing how stupid that sounded now. So lame and impersonal. I whisked away a tear before he saw it. "I still can. I can come by. I want to." He shook his head, and my stomach clenched, like when you're falling or lose something important. "Or—we could stay together tonight. Either place—"

"No," he said softly.

"Sully, please," I said, taking his hand. It was so warm, and calloused, and perfect.

"I can't," he said. "Not after—" He shook his head. "I can't keep doing this." The park lights reflected in his eyes. "Saying goodbye to you. I feel like every time I see you, it's one more last time, and… if you're moving on, then it needs to just *be* the last time."

Moving on. My heart felt like it was turning inside out at those words. I saw the image of my father as a young man, moving on, tormented by it. Did my mother physically ask him to stay? Sully said he never would.

Ask me to stay.

"I'm sorry," I said quickly, shocked by the thought, by the words that echoed in my brain. My heart took off double-time.

"It's okay," he said. "I get it. But I want the real deal." Sully pulled his hand away and raked his fingers through his hair, staring forward into the darkness. Somewhere up ahead was the pond and across that was our cove and where we'd just done everything we should have never done. "After tonight, it's going to be all I can do to watch you get out of this truck. If you sleep in my arms tonight, I won't be able to watch you walk away."

Wham.

I looked at his profile, and memorized it. The one I'd carried with me was Sully as barely more than a boy. This man—I would never forget this man. I clapped a hand over my mouth, pressing hard against my lips to stem the full-out ugly cry I felt coming on. He didn't need to have that be his last memory of me.

He pulled my head to his lips and kissed my forehead, lingering there, and I touched his face. He didn't want to kiss me; I knew that instinctively.

He would break if he did, and he was too proud for that. If Sully Hart was going to lose his composure that way, no one would ever see it.

He pulled back and reached for my hand, squeezing it.

Don't let me go. Ask me to stay.

"Take care of yourself, love."

He didn't just say that.

Air rushed from my lungs, and I sucked it back in. *Don't show it. Walk away.*

Turning away, I opened the door, bathing us in light, and forced myself out of his truck on feet I couldn't feel.

Why am I leaving? Ask me!

I couldn't shut the door, standing there staring at it like it needed to move on its own. *Close the door. Walk away. Get in your car.*

"Carmen."

"Yes?" I said, my head jerking his direction, my heart slamming against my ribs.

I would. I knew in that very second of last hopes and dreams, that I would. If he asked me to stay in that crap town forever, I would. The realization of that nearly took me to the ground.

"What did you see?" he asked instead. "With Bailey. What did he make you see?"

The hope curled into a fetal position, withered up into a charred mess, and died. He would never ask me. Sully had told me that he didn't want me to go, and that was as close as he'd get. He'd never ask the question and make himself the reason I stayed, no more than I would ask him to give up his dream and come with me.

"History repeating itself," I said. I kissed my fingers and touched the seat I'd left vacant. "I love you, Sully Hart."

The look on his face would never leave me. Ever. If I lived to be three hundred and fifty-two years old, I'd see that pain searing through his eyes for the rest of my life.

I shut the door, sucking in several breaths as I kept my hand on the handle. As long as I didn't take my hand away, I could still take it back. Take it all back. Get back in and say those words again and again and again and bury myself in everything Sully. Silently, I stood there for the longest seconds of my life.

"Stop me," I whispered on a ragged breath, crying harder as the words stabbed my heart. "Please, Sully," I sobbed.

His engine starting made me jump. I let go.

I let go. It was done. Nodding in the dark, I turned to my car and dug for my keys with shaking fingers, managing to get in and drive away without hitting anything or passing out from hyperventilation, both of which were imminent. His truck never moved. I drove away and left the park in darkness, and he never moved.

I didn't even remember the drive to Lanie's house, or walking up to her porch. Suddenly I was just there, holding three bags and losing my shit completely.

When she opened the door, her face went from pissed to worry to alarm.

"What's the matter?" she said, rushing forward as my world caved in from all sides.

"I'm sorry," I sobbed. "I'm sorry I didn't—te-te-tell you," I hiccupped. "I couldn't and I wanted to b-b-but I didn't know how to—tell you goodb-b-bye."

Lanie's eyes filled with tears, and she took the bags from my hands.

"I know," she said, her voice wobbling. "I'm sorry, too. I'm just gonna miss you so much. We just—"

"Got this back—I know," I said, wiping at my face and hugging my arms around my waist. Sully's face swam across my vision, and I shut my eyes tightly. "But it won't b-b-be like before," I wailed. Yes, I wailed. I was that far gone.

She shook her head, tears flowing down her face. "No. We have cell phones now."

"And Skype," she added, transferring the bags to one hand so she could wipe her face. She sniffed one and frowned. "What did you give me?"

I covered my face, shaking from head to toe. "The hamburgers are p-p-probably garbage, but maybe the pie's still good?" I knew I could barely be understood but that she would get it. I needed her. "We—we—and I saw my father—*my father!* And—he did the same—and Sully—oh God his face—I said I loved him." I doubled over, unable to breathe. I'd hurt him. Telling him the most intimate thing in my heart had crushed him.

"What happened?" Nick said, walking up behind Lanie with a concerned look.

Her gaze landed on me, sharp, and she reached for me and pulled me inside, sniffling.

"She slept with Sully."

He lifted an eyebrow. "How did you get that?"

"I speak hysterical female," she said, walking me to the couch.

Chapter Fifteen

"Okay, talk to me," Lanie said as we settled in with leftover pie (still awesome when heated) and the ice cream that Nick added before bailing to the bedroom. I didn't blame him. I was usually the level-headed one, not the one snotting all over the place, unable to form complete sentences.

"I went… to the cove," I hiccuped.

"You drove over there?"

I shook my head. "Boat."

"Tonight? After dark?"

I nodded, the burn closing my throat again as I remembered the final scene.

"With Sully?"

"By myself, but he was there." I covered my face with the paper towel Nick had given me. He'd left me the entire roll. "Skinny dipping."

"Y'all went skinny dipping?" Lanie asked, raising her eyebrows.

"He dared me," I managed.

She shrugged and nodded, no further explanation necessary. That was why she was my best friend.

"So then—*that*."

"And—?"

"Amazing," I said, my voice cracking. I closed my eyes. "Not because of the sex, which—yeah, but—damn it."

"Crap." She shoved a spoonful of ice cream and pie into her mouth. "Take a bite."

I spooned some pie and ice cream and let the warm and cold sweetness work its magic on my tongue. Cool my mouth. Cool my blood.

"You said you told him—"

I nodded as my eyes filled again, making the bowl swim before me. "I did. Then shut his door and... the look on his face." I would never forget that. Ever.

She pointed to my bowl with her spoon. "Eat."

We ate in silence for a moment, our spoons clinking the glass bowls. Lanie took her final bite. "So now what?"

"I don't know." I swirled melted ice cream around the remains of my pie.

"You aren't disappearing off the face of the earth, right?" Lanie asked, setting her bowl down for Ralph to lick. "I mean, your mom's here, and—"

"And you're here," I continued. "And my house is here. Yes, obviously I'm coming back at some point, but... maybe just to visit." I met her eyes. "I don't know yet, and that's the whole point—I don't want to know yet. I want to know what that's like."

She nodded. "I get it."

"Do you?"

She chuckled and shook her head. "Not really, but I get that you do. And that's enough."

"Thank you," I whispered.

"Wait, what did you say about—your father?" she asked.

"Oh God," I said, setting my bowl down and giving Ralph a really good night. "I don't even know how to explain that one."

I went through it as best I could, starting with my mother's confession and then describing the experience with Albert Bailey. When I closed my eyes to picture the scene, it felt like a dream on steroids.

When I was done, Lanie sat there with wide eyes.

"Holy shit."

I nodded. "Holy shit."

"Do you... do you think that was real? That it really happened?" she asked.

"I don't know what else it would be," I said, pulling a pillow into my lap. "I mean, I've never been big into that stuff, but it sure as hell felt real. And then there's Aunt Ruby—oh, and he was friends with her!"

Lanie leaned forward. "Seriously?"

"He said they were close once," I said. "He already knew who we were because of her." I ran fingers through my now-dry pond-water hair. "I would have asked more on that, but then my father entered the picture and my brain exploded."

"Wow," she said. "Man, I wish she was around to ask."

"Hey," I said, reaching across for her hand. "Thank you."

She tilted her head in her very Lanie way. "For what?"

"For being there," I said. "For kicking my ass when I need it, and for always being my best friend."

"You've talked me down a time or two yourself," she said.

"True," I said. Ralph finished licking my bowl. He looked up at us as if expecting more. "Look out for Sully for me, okay?" I said. "This town is... this town. They can be merciless."

"You got it," she said. Her eyes went wet again, making mine do the same. She reached out to hug me. "Damn it, I've never cried this much over a woman."

"I've never cried this much, period," I said.

I couldn't imagine not having Lanie in my world. Someone I could tell anything. Anything except the one thing I couldn't voice out loud. The thought that had kept pinging in my mind. That when it came down to it, I wished he'd—

No. I wasn't even going to think about it anymore. It was a moot point. Sully didn't ask. He did what I said I wanted.

He let me go.

* * *

The next morning—as if it wasn't weird enough not getting ready to go to the office—I laid in bed till daylight, just listening. Listening to the sounds of my house. The thump-thump my air conditioner made every time it cranked on. The clink-clink my icemaker made dropping ice (because I forgot to turn that off). An acorn rolling down my roof. Two blue jays fighting a very territorial squirrel for squatters rights just outside my bedroom window. I'd listened all night, barely sleeping.

I was leaving this. And totally fucked-up confused about it. It was seriously like the fifth circle of hell, that now that I'd decided on a real departure, I was second-guessing everything and not completely wanting to go. I was fighting the very thing I'd always wanted to do, feeling sad because I *had* to go. I didn't *have* to go anywhere. No one was holding a gun to my head. But as soon as I started thinking like that, the travel genie swooped down and slapped me and said, "Yes, you do!"

So not cool. All of this was supposed to be exciting and giddy-making, and I wasn't feeling the giddy. I was feeling stressed that I wasn't going to remember to turn off the ice maker or that I'd forgotten to tell the woman subletting my office that the outlet by the door didn't work.

I got up and made a cup of coffee, emptying the water reservoir afterward. I checked my to-do list for the eightieth time. I went outside to sit on my porch—my very bare porch that never had plants because I didn't want that level of commitment (and I'd kill them). I wanted to be able to cut and run anytime, even though I never did. I sat in my boring chair that I'd bought years ago instead of the beautiful wooden rocker that I really wanted. I got the boring one so I could easily leave it behind. Looking around, my whole life was about the ability to disconnect.

That was kind of sad.

I had designed my entire life to lead up to this moment, so yes—I did have to do it. If I bailed now, not only would I always wonder *what if,* but everything up till now would have been for nothing.

Last night—

I couldn't dwell on last night. I'd done that for hours, and I had to quit. I told him good-bye. That's what I had planned to do today, anyway, minus the naked swimming, so I could check that off the list.

I love you, Sully Hart.

That hadn't been on the list.

Fuck.

Lanie had warned me not to get lost in him again. Not to let him get under my skin again. But in all honesty, there was no *again* to it. It had just been on hold, waiting. I'd never felt for Dean the way I did for Sully. I never felt love like that for *anyone.* It wasn't possible. Sully already had my heart. Everything and everyone after him was just going through the motions.

Now, here I was again. Motions. With brand-new updated images to go with them. Sitting in this ugly chair, drinking coffee, trying desperately to pretend I wasn't scouring the end of the street for signs of a black truck. Because the thought of him rushing over this morning to try to stop me like they do in the movies hadn't crossed my pathetic mind at *all.*

So the question was… how long was I going to sit here and wait and ponder before I got off my ass and did what I'd always planned to do?

How long, indeed. Enough was enough. I pushed myself up and out of that chair and forced my feet to carry me back inside.

Forty-five minutes later, I drove away from my life. I won't say that I didn't cry a little, or drive by Sully's street, or make a sweep through the park parking lot to see if his truck was there. I did. And it wasn't. He wasn't either place, and that was okay. Because neither was I.

Chapter Sixteen

The funny thing about driving without a destination, is driving without a destination. When do you ever do that? For me, never. When I get in my car, it's to get from point A to point B, so this driving aimlessly with no B in mind was a little surreal.

In my fantasies about this journey, I always went east or north. I don't know why, maybe because that was against history. Everyone always went west. "Go west young man" was instilled in us in textbooks. *The Beverly Hillbillies* loaded up the truck, strapped Granny on top with her rocking chair, and off they went. Lanie even made up going to California because it sounded better than her real life, and then ended up with a job offer there that teased her some more. My own father went there, supposedly.

So imagine my surprise when, four weeks in, I paid attention to the map I'd thrown in—yes, a real live paper map—and noticed an unexpected trend. I wanted to mark everywhere I went on my adventure. Somehow, unintentionally, while I was rolling merrily along northward, and saw a town or a landmark I wanted to check out, I was slowly migrating west. Currently, I was hovering over a quaint little town in northwest Utah, and had stopped stressing over it. So I'd hit the west coast—most likely Oregon, not California, and see what the Pacific was all about. No big deal. I could then chart a hard course east along all the northern states before winter hit.

Except that there was no charting in this trip. No plans allowed. Just me and my car and whatever the day wanted.

Just me and my car.

Sigh.

I'd never been one to spend a lot of time on the phone. Wasn't my thing. Since I'd left Charmed, however, the biggest highlight of my days were the evenings when I'd call Lanie or my mother and catch up. Tell them what I'd seen or done or explain the millions of photos that I'd take and send daily. I couldn't wait to tell them about the crazy you-had-to-be-there moments that were much more entertaining if you were actually there. Like the man-I-thought-was-a-woman, dressed like a clown in drag on a street in Denver. Or the guy that was hellbent on selling me beets in Oklahoma. Or some of the sunsets in Utah that pictures could never do justice. I wished every time that there was someone to share it with.

I stopped asking about Sully, and they stopped throwing it in there. It hurt to hear about how the build was going, or if Lanie saw him at the bank. And an actual conversation repeated for me just made me imagine the inflections in his voice or how his face looked when he laughed. I missed him possibly more than I had the first time. Maybe because I wasn't angry this time. Maybe because I'd done the leaving. All I knew was that the moments I didn't stay busy—that I let my mind drift back to a little cove in Charmed—it was crushing.

"Hey, J.T.," I called out to the fry cook at a diner I'd taken a fancy to in this blink-and-you-miss-it town.

It was a much smaller version of the Blue Banana, and I was the only person there younger than seventy. Possibly eighty. The food was phenomenal, though, and every time I tried a dish I made a note to tell Nick the next time I saw him.

Whenever that would be.

"Hey, yourself, Five," the older man said, not looking up from the waffles he had steaming in a giant waffle maker.

"Five?"

"How many mornings you've shown up for breakfast," he said. "Considering the first day you told me you were driving through."

True. But it was nice to be somewhere more than a day or so. I missed some cool details if I went too fast. And finding a laundromat was a plus.

"I might grow an ego if you keep showing up for my food like this."

"Your food is worth an ego." I slid up to the small counter and turned over a clean coffee cup from a stack, as was the custom here. "People would come here from every surrounding state if they knew about you."

"And where would I put these so-called hordes of people?" he asked, glancing up and adjusting his backward-facing baseball cap right back to the same position. Short gray hair flashed in the interim. "Out back with the dumpster?"

"You'd make more money," I said. "You could expand. Add on."

He looked up again and winked. "I'm fine just like I am, Five. I don't need more money."

J.T.'s wife Kat, the diner's waitress, came in from the back and grabbed a coffee pot.

"Here for my coffee again?" she asked, smiling

"She's here for my waffles, woman," he said gruffly, but with a twinkle.

"What day are we on?" she asked.

I laughed. "Evidently five."

"She says that customers will swarm here if they knew how good we were," J.T. said.

Kat chuckled as she filled my cup and put the creamer in front of me. "And where will we put these swarms?" she said. "On the roof?"

J.T. laughed heartily at his wife's unknowing echo and glanced at me. "And that, young lady, is why she's my soulmate."

I smiled and stirred creamer into my coffee as the two of them laughed and fussed and worked, and he swatted her behind with a towel. That was how it should be. That was what real-life love was about. Putting in the time, and knowing someone so well that your thoughts mingle.

"So I have a question I've been wanting to ask you," J.T. said a few minutes later, as he put down a plate of waffles and blueberries, along with a bowl of fresh butter and a steaming carafe of maple syrup.

"Why's a single woman like me traveling alone?" I said. I was getting accustomed to the question.

J.T. wiped his face on the sleeve of his worn-out plaid shirt, his dark eyes peering down at me. "Well, I was going to ask how you could stand to eat waffles every day, but sure, we can go with yours."

I nearly choked on my coffee.

"Good one."

"I still have it occasionally," he said with a grin. He grabbed a dispenser of honey and set that next to the syrup. "In case you like that. I can't stand it, but a lot of people like it."

"Me either," I said. "Nasty stuff."

"So I'm a stranger and you don't have to tell me, but you sure look lonely and I know a little bit about that. You okay?"

Wow. This guy was good.

"I... just always wanted to see more than the small town I've lived my whole life in," I said, trying to keep it at that and knowing instinctively that we'd already passed it.

"What do you do for a living?" he asked.

"I'm a lawyer."

His eyes widened with appreciation, as most people's usually did at my profession.

"That's not as glamorous as you might think."

"What I might think is that you're bored and antsy and looking for something you won't find driving for miles on end." He knocked his knuckles on the counter.

I paused in the middle of pouring the syrup. That was a little close to the vest. Something that sounded immensely personal on his end, too.

"Do tell," I said finally, finishing my pour. Because a breakfast this perfect wasn't going to be spoiled with life's little dramas.

"I'm just saying I've been where you are," he said. "Thinking I was missing something. Needing the next thing, the next place, the next person. Thinking that everything was stagnant and claustrophobic and all would just make more sense and line up if I could just keep moving and breathe different air."

Goosebumps covered my body. It was like talking to my own brain.

"And?" I asked.

He shrugged and looked around. "Air is air. None of it is any sweeter than the place before it. And even if it were, who's there to tell?"

Who's there to tell?

I thanked God every day that you didn't have to live like that.

It was like a kick to the gut.

I forked a mouthful of waffle and blueberries and shoveled it in, wanting to get lost in the wonder of the food and not in the thought process that J.T. had started.

"I'm just talking about me now," J.T. said, holding up a hand. "I don't know your story. But I crossed this country on a motorcycle once, thinking I was so worldly. And I found out that seeing the world alone didn't make me worldly. It just made me alone. The day my life started making sense was the day I met Kat."

I smiled. "She was perfect for you?"

"God, no," he said. "She drove me insane. Pissed me off every other day. We were like oil and water." He leaned forward. "And I knew I couldn't breathe another day without her." He winked and walked back to his bowl of waffle batter. "You find that, Five. You find the one that makes you want to beat your head against a wall every day and wake up looking forward to doing it again—" He pointed a finger my way without looking up. "And all that itchy blood of yours will settle right down and be happy making waffles for wandering strangers for the rest of your life."

I ate the rest, not really tasting it but not willing to waste what he'd made for me. My hands shook, my feet were numb, and for the first time that I could remember, I had perfect clarity. It's overwhelming when you realize at thirty-three years old that your whole life's plan had been wrong.

When Kat laid the check in front of me, I laid a fifty on it, and then my hand on hers when she reached for it.

"I don't need change," I said.

Her eyes widened. "Sweetheart, I know he's a good cook, but that's a bit overkill for a tip."

I laughed. "It's not for that. It's just—I just want to," I said. "Go out and do something special with your guy with it."

Her pretty blue eyes went all soft. "You are a blessing, you know that? Will we see you again tomorrow?"

I narrowed my eyes, swallowing against the words that were about to shock the hell out of me. "I don't think so," I said. "I think I'm leaving today."

"Well, you've been a joy and a boost to his ego, that's for sure," she said, looking behind her. "John, did you hear? She's about to leave us."

I froze. "Your name is John?"

He laughed as he closed the waffle iron and walked over. "Well, my mother didn't name me with initials."

Lots of men in the world were named John. Who hated honey. And rode motorcycles across the country with the same wanderlust that I had. With dark eyes like mine. Like I'd seen in—

No. That was ridiculous.

"This is a nutso question," I said. "But did you ever ride through Texas on that motorcycle back then?"

He nodded slowly. "I did. I rode through pretty much everything."

My stomach fluttered like a million butterflies. *Silly, so silly. Don't ask it.*

"Charmed, Texas?" My voice had a weird lilt.

Did I imagine the pause? The quick blink? The flash of recognition? Yes. Yes I did. Because I'd had a sentimental moment with a man who was the right age, and now I was a sentimental fool, seeing things just because I wanted to, with odds being about ten million to one.

Finally he shook his head.

"I don't think so," he said. "But that was a long, long time ago. I went through so many towns, I don't remember them all."

I nodded.

See? Not him.

Good lord, Carmen.

"Just a thought I had," I said. "Anyway, yes, I'm leaving, but thank you. For *everything*."

"More adventure ahead?" he asked, the grin back in his eyes.

I took a deep breath, unable to believe what I was about to say.

"Only what I hit up on the way back," I said. "I think I'm going home."

The look on his face was nothing short of proud. "Something special there?" he asked, draping an arm over Kat's shoulders.

I chuckled and shook my head. "Something infuriatingly head-banging."

His grin got so big it almost outgrew his face. "Good luck with that."

"Is there a secret language you two want to let me in on?" Kat said, looking back and forth between us.

He laughed and kissed her head. "Just an old wanderer giving a new one some tips," he said. "Be careful, Five. Drive safe."

"Carmen," I said, smiling. "My numbered days are over."

I walked out, got in my car, and drove past the big window. He stood at the counter, watching me drive away. J.T., John, whoever. Whether he was thinking of his old wanderlust days that a stranger reminded him of, or thinking how he helped a woman get her head straight, or possibly thinking about the fact that a teenaged fling back in a Texas town named Charmed might have produced a daughter he'd just fed for five days… It didn't matter. Weirdly, it just didn't. I glanced back at the jean jacket lying across my backseat.

Whoever he was, he'd given me exactly what I needed. And Bailey had been right, too. There was never a choice. For once, I had a destination and a plan. I knew exactly where I was going.

Chapter Seventeen

My nerves were everywhere: in my stomach, my fingers, my ears, shooting fireworks like never before. I'd never been anxious about returning to my own damn town, but this was intense. I'd been gone almost a month to the day. A month. The time had flown. I was busy and doing and seeing different things every day. Then I fell in love with a certain little diner, and time finally slowed down enough to let it catch up to me.

Driving through Charmed, I noticed nothing had changed. No projects had sped forward in my absence, or fallen apart without me. I thought everyone had known about my leaving, but no one looked surprised to see me driving around.

The universe had served me a giant slice of humble pie. I wasn't nearly as important as I thought I was.

I needed to go by Mom's. Lanie's. My house. I hadn't told anyone I was coming back—

I wanted to surprise them. But that was secondary to whom I needed to see first. Whom I needed to see and touch and look in the eye and tell that there was never really a choice; it just took me a minute.

My fingers had started itching as soon as I saw the "World Famous Honey" welcome sign. My mouth went dry, and my breathing sped up. I couldn't wait to see his face again. Once I knew I was coming home and would look into those gorgeous eyes again, it was all I could think about. Everything my best friend had told me not to do—the falling and getting lost and all that—I'd done in spades, sometimes twice, and wearing glitter.

"You told the man you loved him," I said out loud as I scanned the parking lots for a certain black truck. "What on earth made you think you could run away from that?"

I turned off of Main and headed toward Maple. I needed me some 523 Maple in a big way. In the form of a big hunky man with hazel eyes and a smile that could take me down. I could barely breathe as I turned onto his street, my hands shaking so badly I had to grip the wheel tighter. And then the wicked blow of disappointment sucked everything out of me like a giant vacuum cleaner. It wasn't there. His truck wasn't there.

Damn it.

Plan B was the trailer, but I was really hoping for a one-on-one conversation. No townspeople working, no Kia lingering, just me and Sully. I could barely control myself where Sully was concerned, and I was tired of embarrassing myself in front of whole town. And if Sully wasn't as excited to see me... yeah, I didn't want any witnesses for that, either. Charmed had witnessed enough humiliating moments of mine, thanks.

But that's why they call it Plan B.

So be it.

But first, I stopped by my house to shake off the nerves and use the bathroom. The stifling heat nearly knocked me out. I'd have to cool off back in my air-conditioned car. The first order of back-to-Charmed business was to get the power turned back on, but it was a Friday. Nothing would happen till Monday. Sully needed to be so happy to see me that I'd have a place to stay. Otherwise I'd die in a large Easy Bake Oven.

Surely he'll be happy, right?

All the way back across four states, I'd assumed he would be. I could see the look on his face as plain as day, happy and relieved and ecstatic and wanting to sweep me off my feet and begin our life together. Now that I was here, I realized I might have been channeling a little *Officer and a Gentleman*. Doubts bubbled up, making me second-guess my grand return.

Yes, I'd told him I loved him. *And then drove away.*

I took a deep breath at a red light. "How big a moron could I possibly be?" I whispered.

I didn't need to answer that, because he'd probably answer it for me. He was going to stand there looking at me like I'd lost my damn mind, and then proceed to tell me I truly did. Then he would point in the direction of the road, not the pond, because I would be banned from the pond as unworthy, and told to get back in my car and keep driving. He would suggest I go north this time. Like maybe to Canada. Or the Arctic Circle.

I paused at the turn into the parking lot. Was I ready for that possibility? Could I take it if he turned on me with the same anger and hurt pride that I'd had for him? Was I back for him, or for myself?

The driver behind me leaned on his horn. I pulled up my big girl panties and turned in just past the trees.

No black truck.

"Are you friggin' kidding me?"

No trucks at all. Lots of cars and SUV's; people beginning work on a new structure. It had to be the gazebo. But no Sully.

I slammed my hands on the steering wheel. My sails were seriously deflated. Concave and sucking wind. Yes, it was on me because I didn't call anyone, but still… can't a girl surprise someone?

Glancing around, I didn't see my mom's little Toyota, so I parked and got out. I wanted that reunion to be one-on-one, too. Walking nonchalantly past the worker bees, hoping no one noticed me, I knocked on the trailer door.

Kia opened it, blinking in surprise. "Hello."

"Hi," I said. "Sorry to bother you. Do you know where Sully is?"

"Where he—" Surprised, she stepped back. "Wow, he wasn't kidding."

"He—kidding?"

Kia licked her lips and pushed the door all the way open. "Come in."

I followed her in, confused. "So—"

"Hey, Carmen," said Bash. He stood up from the trailer's small couch, raking his fingers through his hair.

"Um… Bash," I said, raising an eyebrow.

He raised his in a snarky response, then winked and grinned as he scooted past Kia, giving her the once-over.

"See y'all later," he said, pushing open the door and leaving.

Kia looked at me.

"Okay then," I said. "Sorry if I—"

"Want a water?" she asked, pulling open a small fridge.

I nodded. We weren't going to be girlfriends. Cool; I could respect that.

"Yes, actually, that would be great," I said. She handed a bottle to me. "Thank you." I took a long swig. "So—"

"To be honest, I thought he was with you," she said.

I coughed and cleared my throat.

"Excuse me?"

"Sully left two weeks ago."

* * *

It was a grounding moment. Literally grounding, as I felt every ounce of blood, energy, and thought go straight to my feet.

"He—" I shook my head. "What… what do you mean, he left?"

Kia nodded and sat on a table, pulling up her legs and crossing them into each other without using her hands. I would have fallen off the damn table. As it was, I was close to falling down anyway.

"He said he had some things to do with his brother," she said casually. "He put a few people in charge of construction and took off."

"To—with his brother?" I asked, my voice a little too loud. I cleared my throat again. "Sorry. Do you know where?"

"Not a clue," she said. "His phone is turned off and I cut ties with all of those people. I don't have numbers anymore."

I stared at her as if my gaze could make her cough up the answers I needed. It didn't make sense.

"Sully despises his brother."

She raised her right eyebrow. "I'm aware."

I shook my head and hands free of the stupid.

"Oh God," I said, covering my face for a minute to get it together, then crossing my arms. "I'm sorry; I know you do. I just mean—why would he go there?"

"I don't know," she said, shrugging. "To be honest, I didn't believe him. I thought he was just saying that, and had gone to find you."

Blink. Goosebumps. Blink. *Find me?* Would he… would he do that?

"Why?" I asked.

Kia looked at me like I was an idiot. That wasn't exactly news to me. "Because drama and angst are the only things that seem to kick either of you in the ass."

"You have a point." I put my hands on my head, trying to make sense of everything.

Shit. What if Sully *did* go looking for me? Although that would be ludicrous, right? *I* didn't even know where I was going; how would he know where to look? No. He had to have done what he said he was doing. Gone to see his brother, for some insane reason.

"Well, he's not with me," I said, closing my eyes. "So he's—" My eyes popped open. "This project's still on, right?" I asked. "Nothing has changed? Or been cancelled?"

She laughed. "Yes, it's still on. He does have to come back at some point."

I rolled back my shoulders, getting rid of the tension.

"Unless he delegates it to someone else," Kia continued. "Construction isn't for another month."

Unrelaxed.

"He wouldn't do that, would he?" I asked. "I mean, he would—this is his baby. He would want to take charge of it, right?"

Kia tilted her head and pulled her knee into a position my body would never tolerate.

"Aren't you a big-shot attorney?" she asked.

Where did that come from?

"Attorney, yes," I said, picking up a stray folder to fan my suddenly flushed self. "Big shot, no. Why?"

"Because you never struck me as the weepy, go-limp-over-a-guy type," she said. "I thought you were tougher."

Hang on. Did she just—

I stopped fanning.

"Excuse me?"

She pointed at me, clearly missing my tone that communicated she'd been insulting and needed to dial it back. "Look at you. You're about to collapse into a puddle on the floor—"

"I am not."

"Over Sully not being here waiting for you." She leaned forward. "You left *him*."

"I know that," I said, feeling my hackles rise up. Whatever the hell hackles were. "I was there. There wasn't a fight, no sneaking off, we—we had—we said what we needed to say."

"Are you back for good, or just to mess with his head?" she asked.

"What?" I said, crossing my arms. *The nerve of this bitch.* "I'm not messing with anything."

"So then why are you here, with the same broken-puppy look he had, acting all distraught?" she asked.

"I'm—I'm not distraught, I'm just—"

"You are," she argued. "Because he's out there somewhere still thinking you left, not knowing you're back, and that's eating you up."

My mouth dropped open. This woman, whom I'd barely said hello to before today, was reaming me out better than any opposing counsel ever had, without changing expressions or even breaking a sweat. I should hire her to be my attack dog. Especially since she was right.

He looked like a broken puppy?

I could convince myself for the next month that telling him I loved him was something positive, but the look on his face was burned into my retinas. Gifting him with that hadn't been a gift at all, and now I couldn't tell him how much I wanted him to stop me. That I was madly in love for the second time in my life, with the same damn man, and how I didn't see the spotlight beam shining on what I should do till later. How I was stupid. How I needed him more than I needed air, and I would still return a million times even if he didn't love me back. That I wasn't going anywhere.

"I don't know you well enough to have this conversation," I said, turning to leave. "But assuming you were right—just so you know, I don't get weepy-limp over anyone. If Sully Hart has done that to me, then that should tell you something about—" I stopped and swallowed hard before *weepy-limp* made another appearance. "He's important." My bottom lip quivered, and I stood tall and held up my chin to make it stop. "He's everything."

I turned and opened the door, taking a step out into the sunshine.

"Good," she said behind me.

* * *

I stood behind four other people at the bank, waiting in Lanie's line. When she saw me, it made my heart feel a little better to see her jaw drop and toes bounce. At least my being back in town mattered to someone.

Maybe I was feeling a little sorry for myself. Justifiably—but still. I could probably only milk that a few more times.

By the time I got up to her teller booth, she was beaming.

"What are you doing?" she asked. "Did I miss a call or something?"

"No, I wanted to surprise everyone," I said.

"Aw," she said. "Is your mom excited? How long are you here?"

"I haven't seen her yet, she's next," I said. "And—I'm back."

Lanie's eyebrows rose slowly. "Be... cause you missed local raw honey?"

I nodded. "Exactly."

"Seriously, what triggered this change of heart?" She narrowed one eye. "Or who?"

"It's a long story," I said. "One that goes beyond standing in this line. But on that note, did you know Sully left?"

The surprise on her face couldn't have been faked.

"Like—*left* left?"

Please God, I hope not. "I don't think so." I tried to look more confident than I actually felt. "The pond project is still going on, so I doubt it. But no one knows for sure, not even Kia."

"Wow."

Yeah. Wow. I wished that's all I felt about it.

"So, we'll catch up later," I said. "Can I maybe crash at your house this weekend, till I get my utilities back on?"

"Of course," she said. "And Nick's making spinach alfredo tonight, so you picked a good night to swoop in."

I smiled. "Then consider me swooping."

I left, knowing I had another stop to make and trying to muster up the energy for it. I'd been so damn wound up when I got there, all my battery life drained at once when I found out about Sully. And as much as it irritated me, Kia had nailed it. Sully could travel the world doing whatever errands he needed to and I'd be fine with that. Envious, but fine. Knowing that he was out there believing I was still gone, however, was the worst kind of torture.

Chapter Eighteen

My mother was not a hugger. Never had been. Affectionate, yes, and hugs on special occasions were fine, but she wasn't one to tackle people in every greeting or farewell. So when she got up from her desk and hugged me for the sixth time, I knew my coming back was a big deal.

"So you'll stay in your old room till your A/C comes back on," she said, ignoring the ringing phone.

My teeny tiny room in the double-wide, versus the guest room with the queen-sized bed at Lanie's house? Plus Lanie. And ice cream. And Nick's cooking. Not a hard choice.

"Actually, Lanie already asked me to—" The crestfallen look on her face was just too much to let me to finish that sentence. What the hell happened to my unshakable mother? Somehow while I was gone, she developed a sentimental streak. "Or my room is good, too," I said. "But I'm having dinner over there tonight."

"Fair enough," Mom said, perking up like she was planning a sleepover. "I'll pick up some wine on the way home."

"On the way?" I said. "Is there a liquor store between this trailer and yours?"

"Ha ha," she said. "Okay, smartie, *you* pick up some wine on the way home from Lanie's."

"Will do," I said. I'd probably need it.

"Have you seen him yet?" she asked.

That answered my next question. And reminded me of another *him* that I'd never tell her about. It was a long shot and probably laughable, but even if it were the case, she didn't need to know. And there I went. Doing what she did. But what happened with Mr. Bailey—that wasn't going anywhere. I told Lanie because I was having a nervous breakdown at the time, but my mother didn't need to know.

"No, he's… not here right now," I said. I didn't have it in me to explain it again.

"I saw him a few weeks ago," she said. My ears perked up. "He was coming out of the Blue Banana when I was going in."

"Oh?" I said, acting like that was just mildly interesting.

My mother gave me a look that let me know she wasn't born yesterday. "Oh?" she mimicked. "Yes, *oh*. He said hello, and we talked about the rent for a minute, and then he had to go. Nothing exciting."

"Okay."

"Nothing about you," she added.

I shrugged. "Didn't think there would be."

"So what do you think about this girl, Kia?" she asked.

"I think she's banging Bash Anderson," I said. "What do you think?"

"Oh?" she said, sitting forward and taking off her glasses.

"Yes, *oh*," I said, all head-tilty and cocky. "More later. I gotta go take care of some things."

My "things" would take all of fifteen minutes, but my road trip had taught me to appreciate the power of aloneness. I needed some time by myself to process things. To go pick up wine (early), and snacks, and sit out on Lanie's patio and ponder what came next. Because this day and what was coming next wasn't what I anticipated it would be. What I had thought was a sure thing had been splintered into all these maybes wrapped in question marks. Good maybes—maybe—but question marks just the same.

I hugged her again as I left and noticed a little extra linger. My heart stung a little as I realized the toll her confession and my month-long walkabout had taken on her. It had scared her—the thought that I might stay gone forever. The thought of losing me. And I knew how that felt.

"So I'll see you after dinner," I said as I pulled back. "I'll show you all the pictures I haven't sent you yet."

She patted my cheek and smiled. At least that was one person I could fix things with.

As I drove slowly down the trailer park aisle, I saw a familiar figure. She smiled as she reached her Jeep, and I lowered my window.

"Hey, Allie," I said.

"Hey," she said, coming over and tucking a stray strand of dark hair behind her ear. Her hair was down in waves around her shoulders. I hadn't seen her with her hair down and without her serious work-face on in ages. "I just heard you were back. And my dad was just talking about you, too."

I cocked an eyebrow. "I just got here. Like an hour ago maybe."

She laughed and held up her palms. "News travels, my friend. You know Miss Mavis pulled that thing over and burned up her cell phone the second you drove down Main."

"True," I said. "And your dad was probably telling you my car's always parked wrong," I added, scrunching my face. "There's not much room at the office, but I swear he's taking his walk every time I fudge it."

"No, he was having one of his moments," she said, her face falling. "He's not taking his medicine like he should, and then he gets ornery about it. Anyway, he woke up babbling about money in the trees and Carmen at the big house."

I laughed. "Uh oh," I said. "Your dad used to be kind of spot-on with his dreams. Think I'm going to prison?"

"I hope not!" she said, laughing with me. "Have you been bad?"

Don't go there.

"I plead the Fifth," I said.

"Good choice, counselor," she said. "But I think he was talking about Old Man Bailey's house."

My mouth went dry.

"He used to call that 'The Big House' when I was little. Which I never understood, because I saw it many times and it's not big."

It certainly felt big on the inside.

"Huh," I said, blinking away the memory. "That's weird. Have you ever met Bailey?"

"I used to wave to him from the car, but I never formally met him," she said.

"Probably a good thing," I said under my breath.

"What?"

I shook my head. "Nothing." I wasn't going to explain what happened to someone who hadn't experienced it. I didn't need anyone else thinking I was off my rocker. "So is he doing any better?" I asked.

"Not really," she said, tugging on a lock of hair. "I pull my hair down when I come to see him because he tends to stay in the present more when I do. I'll probably have to move him soon, but that will crush him and break Angel's heart, so I'm holding off as long as I can."

"She's driving now, right?" I asked.

Allie crossed her arms. "She's *aiming*," she said. "At the road. I wouldn't call it driving."

I was dying to ask her what she knew, and she knew it. Allie heard everything. Owning a diner was second only to hairstylists and bartenders on the gossip trail. The difference was that Allie only listened. She didn't talk. Being the gossiped-about outcast at seventeen clipped not only her wings, but any urge to spread or repeat *anything*.

"So, how's your mom?" she asked, nodding toward the office trailer.

"Nosy and into everyone's business," I said.

Allie paused and slipped her hands into her jeans pockets.

"So she's taking over the park from Larry?" she said.

"Yeah," I said. "Interesting, huh? And she's excited about it. Well, except for the renting-from-Sully part."

Damn it, just saying his name out loud came full circle to punch me in the stomach. Kia was right. I was being a weepy-limp-whatever-she-called-it.

"He has it bad for you, you know," she said, her voice dropping to a whisper as if it were a secret someone might overhear.

My heartbeat pounded in my ears.

"Yeah?" I asked, my voice cracking a little. She nodded, and I blew out a slow breath. "I hope he remembers that."

* * *

My room in my mother's small trailer was a hybrid. It was partially still my room—there were traces of color and knick-knacks and a silk flower that used to be in a homecoming corsage still tucked into a corner of a band poster. Along with that now was a craft bench filled with paints and brushes and some weird little pencils. Canvases leaned up against one window, and a desk and computer had been moved in next to the small dresser.

Gerry had a new hobby, apparently. Or a new idea to sell something. Most likely the latter. My mother rarely took the time to do a project if there wasn't a gain in it.

I laid on the bed and stared up at the ceiling, remembering many many nights like this, studying the pattern in the ceiling tiles and wondering if I'd ever get out of this place. *Look at me now.* That young me would never believe I'd come back here looking to settle. No, not settle. Settle *down*. With Sullivan Hart, no less, now business owner renting a house in Charmed.

I glanced over at my dresser and wondered if it was all still there. I sat up and pulled it forward, chuckling when I saw the back panel. Filled with poems, decorative doodles, phone numbers my mom didn't want me to have, and Sully's name written in decorative lettering. It was my private place, my sounding board, my expression. I ran my fingers along the large bubble letters.

Oh, what that naïve girl had yet to know, to learn, to figure out. I used to lay here and either dream about the next time I'd see him, the next time I'd kiss him... then later wonder what went so terribly wrong that he could leave me behind.

Fifteen years later, and the scenario wasn't very different. The "terribly wrong" part was different—I hoped. God, I hoped. But I had to get my head straight. Coming back was spurred by making a decision about Sully, yes, but it needed to be about more than that. I needed to be back for myself, or I had no business being there. I needed to get my ass organized and set up. Work on my house. Start living like someone who planned to stick around a while. Take my job more seriously. Maybe even get involved in the community.

Good Lord, did I just really think that?

But it was true. Regardless of whether Sully ever came back, I had to start living my life, and not waiting for it.

* * *

I had a flat tire, fought with a judge, and came damn near to cussing out two teenage boys in a courthouse hallway for being idiots. All in one day. That wasn't counting the fun week I'd had with the electric company debacle getting my house back on the grid, losing my favorite shoes, and twisting my ankle walking down my front steps. How was that for living my life grandly?

I topped it off by tripping over the rug in my office trying to get to my buzzing phone, nearly face planting with a lamp. I hit the button while my butt was still in the air.

"Lanie, you just about killed me, so I hope this call has purpose."

"*All* my calls have purpose," Lanie said.

"You're right, Your Highness," I said, kicking off the deadly shoes and sinking onto the couch. "I don't know what I was thinking. Please proceed."

"Just seeing what you're doing tonight," she asked.

"Well, it's Friday," I said. "Which means I either can go hit my mom up for a Scrabble game, hang out at Rojo's by myself and gorge on chips, or stay home and watch Netflix."

"Ugh, don't even mention Scrabble," she said. "Nick and I used to play it all the time when we were trying not to have sex. I got so burned out."

"Yeah, rub it in that you're having sex with a god," I said.

"Well, not tonight," she said. "He's playing poker with Bash tonight. They needed a sub and he needs some guy friends, so I told him to play nice with the other boys."

"Alan's not in on it, is he?"

"No," she said. "I wouldn't send him into a den like that. So that means I'm free. If there were only a girls night or something in my future."

"No shit," I said. "Where can we find one of those?"

Lanie giggled. "A grocery run after work for bad food and adult beverages?"

"Absolutely," I said. Just what the doctor ordered to pull me out of my funk. "Meet me at my house, and I have the perfect idea on what to make."

"Make?" she asked. "No, no. No make."

"Believe me, you want this."

"I'm talking about eating things out of tubs and packages," she said. "No work."

"It's called Sex in a Pan."

"I'm in."

Chapter Nineteen

"I have Oreos," Lanie said, dropping them into the basket. She stopped short. "I should make the baked apples."

I thought about it for half a second. "Nah, that's comfort food. We don't need comfort. We're kick-ass women just looking for a good time tonight."

Of course, right as I said that, we passed two teenagers, a mom and her preschooler, and an older man who may have been a pastor.

And Dean. My mouth dropped open.

"Hey Dean," Lanie said, glancing up from studying a package of shortbread cookies. She did the same double-take. "Damn."

Dean had a lumberjack thing going on, and not in a good way. A full beard, baseball cap over scraggly hair, a polo shirt oddly out of place with the mountain-man head, and dirty sneakers. He stood in the produce section squeezing peaches.

"Dean?" I said.

He looked up, then back down, as if those peaches were the answers to all of life's questions.

"Holy hell, Dean, what happened to you?"

"You happened to me," he mumbled.

"Oh, hell no," I said. "I have enough issues without adding you to the roster. You can't blame me for going off your rocker."

"Sure I can," he said, selecting a peach and putting it in his bag. "I can do anything I want. I'm unemployed and have lots of free time."

"Let's walk away from Grizzly Adams," Lanie whispered, looping her arm through mine.

"I heard that," he said as we walked away.

"God, that's sad," I said. It was more than sad, it was depressing. He was still pining over me, and I had pined over Sully for years. No one had ever pined over him. And if he didn't shave off all that shit, take a shower, and stop fondling peaches and committing larceny, no one ever would.

"So, ice cream?" Lanie asked.

I chuckled. "No sympathy for the insane?"

"We can eat it in his honor," she said. "Unless ice cream counts as comfort food."

"It's universal."

"True. Do we have whipped cream for the sex dessert?" she asked as we rounded an aisle. A stock boy stacking cans of tuna turned and stared at us. He looked like he was still in high school.

Lanie threw an arm around my neck and sniffed me. "That's right. We get extra."

The poor boy froze, his hand midway to the shelf as we strolled away giggling like twelve-year-olds.

"You're horrible."

"I'm awesome," she countered.

"What else," I said, looking at my list. "We have both puddings, cream cheese, vanilla, butter—oh, pecans!"

We rounded the end cap, and I tossed bags of pecans in the basket. It didn't matter how many because, one, pecans go great with chocolate ice cream, and, two, more is better.

"Do you have a chopper?" Lanie asked.

"Of course I have—"

"Ladies."

My feet stopped. My mouth stopped. My heart damn near stopped. The two bags in my hand hit the floor. On the upside, at least I didn't walk into him this time. On the downside, I would have loved to walk into him.

Lanie kept going, barely missing a beat. "Two for two. Hey Sully," she said as she passed him. "I'll be in the bakery," she called back to me.

He stood there with a basket full of meat, wearing his trademark T-shirt, jeans and work boots. His hair hadn't grown out, so he must have decided he liked the mid-length look. I liked the mid-length look. But mostly I couldn't look away from his eyes. They had me rooted to the floor in a wary but *holy fuck it's good to see you* way. At least I hoped that's what they said. And all that meat meant filling a freezer and staying a while, right? Wow, how my direction had flipped.

He didn't look completely surprised to see me, so someone must have given him the heads-up. Probably Kia. How long had he been back?

Neither of us spoke for a minute. Finally he stepped forward and kneeled down for the pecan bags. When he rose, his face was only inches away from mine.

Breathe.

Something had changed in that two-second span. His eyes had glazed over; walls had gone up. His feelings were disguised behind a protective layer.

My own walls should have gone up, but they were slow to move.

"Get done what you needed to?" I finally managed to squeak out, holding out my chin so I looked stronger than I felt.

He nodded. "I think so. Did you?"

Cute.

"I think so."

He nodded again. "Good. See you later."

He started to walk around me, and my head exploded.

"Wait, what?"

He turned slowly, exhaling like I was the last person he wanted to talk to. "What?"

Hello? I shook my head, giving him my best "what the fuck?" look. What was he—why was he—what was I missing? Was this reunion a little anti-climactic, or what?

"See you later?" I asked. "After all this time—*see you later?*"

"What do you want, Carmen?" he said.

I wanted my blood pressure to go back down to a safe level, that's what I wanted. He was playing me, right? Getting back at me?

"Um—something?" I said.

"Something," he echoed. "Something like what? My deep relief that you're back?" He held up his hands. "Fine, you have it."

I blinked. "You're mad at me."

He laughed and rubbed at his eyes. "No. I'm just done with the push-pull. You have no idea what you want, Carmen. One second it's me, the next it's the road—no, it's *always* the road."

"Excuse me?" I said. "Who was all about the 'one last night of fun' and 'let's not talk about tomorrow?' I didn't see any heartburn over pushing or pulling when you were getting some—"

"My mistake," he said.

My breath left me in a rush, and I struggled to inhale.

"*Mistake,*" I repeated in a whisper. "Nice."

"I knew you were leaving and went there anyway," he said. "I shouldn't have."

"Well, I told you I loved you—" I said, my throat closing on the words as they hit the air. "I guess I *shouldn't have.*"

"And then drove away," he said. "*Away*." A sour smile crossed his face. "I get it, Carmen," he said. "I do. Payback's a bitch and I was due, but telling me that as you left—"

"And getting tattoos that stood for *forever* the day before *you* left was any different?" I threw back. "Don't be a hypocrite, Sully."

A lady walked by, smiling and then looking at us funny. I grabbed a pack of chopped walnuts off the shelf just to have something in my hand to mangle.

"You made a choice," he finally said softly.

"And then stood outside that door begging you to stop me," I said under my breath.

Something pierced the walls he had up. Just for a second. I saw it. Then Dean rounded the aisle. His eyes went from me to Sully and then closed as he scoffed.

"Of course," he muttered, pushing his basket around us.

I drew in a shaky breath. My chest heaved like I'd run five miles.

"If you didn't want to go, you didn't have to go," he said when we were alone again. "All you had to do was reopen the door."

"I'm opening it now," I said.

His jaw muscles flexed. "And the next time you feel the need to fly?" He shook his head. "I told you that night. I can't keep doing this. I can't give you the road, and live my life in the temporary. I did enough of that. I need the real deal or nothing at all."

"I'm… not… temporary," I said, a little too loudly. "When I said what I said to you, it wasn't just for that moment, Sully. I've loved you my whole damn life." I pointed behind me. "Want to know why Dean looks like that? Because I was the asshole who could never love him like I loved you. I came back looking for you before I even unloaded my car because when you figure out what you *want*, you can't get to it fast enough. I'm not going anywhere. But you know what? I'm not going to do cartwheels trying to prove that to you. You can trust me or not trust me; that's on you."

I snatched the pecans from his hand and walked around him, gulping air, my fingers and lips numb. I was probably having a stroke, destined to die in Brewsters.

"Welcome home," he said to my retreating back.

Don't stop.

"Ditto."

* * *

We bought the damn apples.

"Are you sure you still want to do this?" Lanie asked while we worked on our respective dishes in the kitchen. In pajamas. Because sleepovers are normal in your mid-thirties.

"For the third time, yes," I said. "I'm fine."

"But you could go talk to him—"

"He made it really clear that he's not interested in talking," I said, putting the final layer of pudding on my creation. "Now for the whipped cream layer."

"It's okay if you want to talk about Sully," Lanie said. "I get it. Believe me. Do you remember how messed up I was over Nick when he left?"

"Screw Sully," I said, scooping a big trench out of the Cool Whip tub with my finger and holding it out for Lanie to do the same.

"But you're making his dessert," she said around a mouthful of whipped cream.

"I'm never getting hot sex again," I said. "That was a *mistake*. So why not have the next best thing?"

"Here." She handed me a bowl of the hot steaming apples with cinnamon that her aunt used to make for us. "Eat while you work."

"Mmmm," I moaned as the mixture of hot, sweet, and tart melted in my mouth, soothing my raw nerves. "Aunt Ruby would be so proud."

Lanie beamed. "Now get that finished so I can have a foodgasm too."

We did. And she did. She agreed it was a good sex substitute as well, except that Nick was evidently a porn star in bed and nothing short of him actually feeding this to her while having sex would make this better.

I couldn't argue with that logic.

We were loading up our bowls with a second round, planning out the ice cream for after the sugar crash hit, when my doorbell rang. Lanie and I looked at each other instead of the door, and I tried really hard to mask the anxiety and play it off.

"Did you order pizza?" she asked.

"Nope," I said. "It's probably my neighbor. He locks himself out a lot."

She nodded, a fake pensive frown on her face. "Sure, or it could be people selling Bibles or—hey! Maybe it's Publisher's Clearinghouse!"

"Don't laugh. I actually entered this year," I said, carrying my bowl to the door and gripping it tightly as my heart played table tennis against my ribs.

Somehow, even though I was ninety-eight percent sure who it was on the other side, seeing him standing there as I opened the door didn't soften the squeeze to my chest. I refused to let it show, however, mentally ordering my hand to pick up my spoon and put food into my mouth. It managed to do that without dropping any or putting it in my eye, so I was impressed. At least I was wearing a T-shirt and soft floppy pajama shorts this time, and not flashing my boobs.

"I know you have company, and I wasn't going to do this, but—" he began.

"Excuse me." Lanie scooted past me, robe tied around her waist, purse on shoulder, bowl in hand.

"Where are you going?" I asked, panicking as if we were in the fifth grade and she was leaving me alone to talk to a boy.

"Things to do," she said, winking at me.

"Dressed like that?" Sully asked.

"Don't knock it," she said, holding up a double-loaded bowl. "But I'm bringing this with me." *Call me,* she mouthed.

"You don't have to go," Sully said.

"Oh, I know I don't," she said. "Consider it a gift, and if you fuck it up, I know where you live." She shrugged. "Actually I don't, but this one does, and she'll tell me."

Sully chuckled as Lanie walked down the steps, but when he turned to look at me, his face was serious. I nervously shoveled pudding in my face like someone might snatch it from my hands.

"Can I come in?" he asked.

No. No. Say no. *Say hell no.*

"I'll come out." I pushed past him, trying not to breathe him in as I did. *Get a grip, Carmen.*

I sat in one of my new fancy wooden rockers I bought with some of my unused travel money, thinking he'd sit in the other one. No. He leaned on the railing, facing me, arms crossed. God help me.

"You were right," he said, finally.

"I know," I said around another mouthful. "Want to narrow it down?"

He pulled a piece of paper from his pocket and unfolded it.

"You made a list?" I asked.

"Didn't want to leave anything out," he said. "Number one... about me being a hypocrite."

"Mmm," I said, nodding. "That."

"I felt a little of what you probably did when I left," he said.

"You felt *nothing* like what I did," I countered, scraping the bottom of my bowl and willing my hands to quit shaking. "I looked you in the eye and told you what I was doing. You watched me leave." I shook my head and scooped up the last of the pudding. "I stood in an empty parking lot and waited for someone who never came."

"I can assure you, one's not better than the other," he said.

"Whatever," I said and stood up. "Next?"

"Next," he echoed, stepping forward. I felt that step in my bones. "I wanted to tell you that it wouldn't have mattered."

"What wouldn't have mattered?"

"If you'd opened the door," Sully said, shaking his head. "If you would have asked me to stop you, I still wouldn't have done it."

My bad-assery wavered. My knees went wiggly. *No. Stay strong.* But he was so close, and that damn magnet thing of his was tugging at me. Like I needed to hold on to that beam over there before he pulled me all the way in.

"I couldn't be the reason," he continued. "You had to make that decision on your own."

I nodded. "Okay, fair enough." I held up my chin and forced my expression to stay neutral. "You know, you could have waited to tell me all this. You didn't have to come over here tonight and—"

"Well, you know, when you figure out what you want," he said. "You can't get to it fast enough."

The spoon rattled in the bowl as my trembling hands wouldn't be denied. He was good. Fuck me, he was good.

I cleared my throat. "So," I managed, glancing at the support beam again. It looked further and further away. "Is there a number three?"

Sully looked at the paper for an extraordinarily long moment, before resting his focus back on me.

"Yeah," he said. "I love you."

Chapter Twenty

My spoon clattered to the deck, jarring me from a stunned state of paralysis. I didn't bend to pick it up. It could stay there. I was surprised the bowl hadn't joined it.

I love you.

"Th-that—that's—actually on the paper?" I managed, giving up my last vestiges of playing it cool.

Sully held it up, and even in the low light from my window I could read it.

Hypocrite
Wouldn't have stopped you
I love you
Kiss her

I looked up at him, my eyes burning.

"You forgot one," I whispered.

"No, I didn't," he said, the paper fluttering to the ground as he stepped forward. He cradled my face in his hands as his mouth landed on mine.

Everything stopped. The pain, the hurt, the drama, the world, any possible reason not to kiss him for days. We both inhaled deeply, as if the very touch of our lips seared and sealed the deal. Holy shit, I'd missed him. I knew that every day, but I never knew just how much until I was tasting him, touching him, breathing him in.

My right hand, still clutching the bowl, reached out blindly for the beam in a desperate effort to find the railing and get rid of it. I needed both hands. I needed all of him. Then his fingers twisted in my hair, and he growled into my mouth.

I tossed the bowl over the railing.

I wrapped both arms around his head as we dove into each other, every single nerve ending firing. Needing more. Craving and reacting to every touch.

He loved me. He was here. I was here. No one was leaving. His hands reached under my shirt and roamed my back, groping my ass, picking me up as I wrapped myself around him. This was different from the carnal driving need of before. It was hot, it was delicious... and it was slow.

We had *time*.

"God, I missed you," he breathed.

"I love you," I whispered back.

He exhaled sharply. "Please say that again."

"I will," I said, smiling. "In a little while."

Sully turned and pushed me against the beam, rotating his hips into me.

"Mmm," I moaned softly against his lips. "Do *that* again."

"I will," he said, looking down to watch his hands caress my bare thighs all the way up under my easy-access shorts. When he met my eyes again, they were heavy-lidded with desire. "All night if you like. But I want to see you looking at me from your bed."

"A bed," I said, my hands trailing down his chest as he kissed below my ear. "Have we ever met such a thing?"

"A rock," he said, his lips moving down the side of my neck.

"Love that rock," I breathed.

"A post," he said, pulling my hair gently to give him better access.

"Lots of—posts," I gasped as his fingers came teasingly close to ground zero. "Back seat of your—dad's Cadillac."

"Mmm, good memories in that car." His hands slid around back to pull me harder against him.

"Fuck," I moaned, the sensation driving every pulsing need to that one place. My hands slid up under his shirt, needing skin.

"No," he breathed back against my ear, his voice sounding strained as my fingers unbuttoned his jeans. "No fucking tonight. I'm making love to you." He picked me up from the beam, and I wrapped my arms around his neck. "In your bed."

He carried me through the door with relative ease, considering I was dragging my teeth down the side of his neck. Stopping in the hallway, he pinned me against a wall, shoving hard between my legs and making me groan.

"Keeping doing things like that, and the first round will be right here in this hallway," he said through clenched teeth.

"And that's supposed to punish me?" I kissed him long and deep, squeezing my thighs tighter around him.

He pulled me off the wall. "Not getting off that easy," he said, grinning. "No pun intended."

I giggled as he bumped us into my room, but stopped him as he moved to lay us on the bed. Suddenly I felt his need to make it different. To make it real. To make it solid and permanent.

"Put me down first," I whispered. He obeyed, looking at me quizzically as my feet hit the ground. I wrapped my hands in his hair and pulled his head down. I kissed him softly, tasting his lips and trailing my fingers over his face, his neck, and down his chest. "I want to undress you."

I lifted his shirt over his head slowly, never breaking eye contact, and a smile crept into his eyes. I let my lips follow my hands down his torso, dropping kisses as I went, licking his skin, feeling the rush of adrenaline and female power as my kisses went lower and his abs contracted in anticipation. I lowered that zipper slowly, tantalizing him, knowing full well there was no underwear in the way and what I was unveiling.

His breathing quickened as his dick was freed. I slid down his jeans and untied his shoes in no rush, sliding them off his feet and tossing everything aside until he stood before me, glorious and naked and mine.

Mine.

Heat pricked the backs of my eyes. From my knees, I looked up into his. They weren't just burning with lust, knowing he was about to have his mind blown. He loved me. And sweet God, I was head-over-heels myself. Again.

I stood and backed out of his reach. I slid off my shorts and slowly raised my shirt over and off my body, standing before him in just a thong and nerves running at such a high frequency I could almost hear them hum. I wanted this to be special and amazing, and yet I was teasing myself. His eyes on me were almost as palpable as if his hands were caressing every inch.

"You are so beautiful." His voice was so low I could barely hear it, but its timbre sent ripples of heat over my skin. "Please come here."

I moved forward, but when he tried to touch me, I clicked my tongue in protest.

"Me first," I whispered, letting my nipples graze his chest. The pleasure was so dizzying, I nearly lost my resolve. "No touching till I say so."

Lowering myself slowly, I slid my body down his in a tease so maddening, he cursed my name. On my knees, I looked up at him, then ran my tongue up the length of his dick. Pure carnal pleasure glazed his eyes as he convulsed and grabbed my hair.

"No, no," I said. My tongue circled the tip as his balls filled my hands. "No touching."

He growled, his fingers clenched in my hair. The guttural sound almost undid me. It was heady; it was breathtaking; it was erotic as hell. And when I took him in my mouth and sucked as my hands worked him, his primal moans made my toes curl.

"Please get up," he finally said, his voice gruff and his eyes wild.

I let go of him, raising up as teasingly as I'd gone down. He turned me around, palming my breasts in his hands as he pulled me back against him and planted rough kisses on my neck.

"Mmm, Sully…" I stretched against him, my back arching in response.

"Fuck, what you do to me," he muttered against my spine, his hands pressing down my body, his fingers sliding under my thong and finding me. I jolted as he touched and then circled away. Touched again, and then away.

"Do to *you*?" I gasped. "Oh God."

"Please lay on that bed," he said against my neck. "I need to see that before I lose my shit completely."

It was all I could do to leave his touch. My little game had backfired in a most delicious way. Every sensation was electric. I didn't want to leave his hands behind, but when I crawled onto the bed and turned to lie on my back, the reward was so worth it.

His expression of pure male appreciation was overwhelming. The massive boulder he had ready for me was pretty overwhelming, too. Harder and bigger than I'd ever seen it, it almost looked painful. He didn't look like he was in pain, however. He looked ready to bury himself inside his woman.

His woman.

Those words rang in my head as he moved my thong to one side and ran his fingers across me and inside me, making me gasp and beg before his mouth claimed it.

I arched off the bed as he sucked me, grabbing the sheets into my fists and damn near pulling them off the bed as his tongue and lips drove me mad. I remembered the first time he'd done that. In the pond. His face buried in me as I floated on my back and held onto the dock, screaming his name and lost in the otherworldly sensations crashing over me.

I was almost there when he yanked off my thong, then headed up, leaving me whimpering like a child until his mouth closed around my nipple, sucking and—oh God, he rolled us over, my breasts heavy against his face. He growled in satisfaction as he pressed them harder against his mouth and continued to suck.

Another part of me was too close to euphoria to be denied. I pulled away from his mouth and slid down where the important parts could get reacquainted. Caressing myself along the length of his dick, I moved back and forth where he'd left off.

"Jesus, Carmen," he groaned, watching with crazed eyes as his fingers dug into my hips. "Fuck, I need you now."

I looked up at him, still moving. "What happened to making love?"

He dragged his gaze up to mine. "I love you," he said. "But if you don't fuck me right this second, I'm gonna have a damn heart attack."

I smiled. "Your wish, love."

I lowered myself over him, inch by inch, as every muscle in his body tensed. He watched our union as I moved on him. Sliding up and down on the tip, then letting him fill me up completely, nearly losing it every time I did that. I was close. He had driven me to the point of delirium once already, and now the feel of him deep inside me as he held onto my breasts—it was all too much. Too good.

And then he was up and I was on my back before I knew what hit me.

"I need deeper, baby." Sully's mouth met mine in a kiss that stopped time. "Hold on." He lifted my legs over his shoulders and plunged into me, moaning. "Oh God, yes."

With every stroke, he stretched me out. It felt like a baseball bat as he swelled bigger. Every muscle inside me burned and throbbed, tightening around him, needing the release.

"Sully," I cried.

"Baby," he pushed out, "You're so tight. Shit—so good—I can't hold back."

I couldn't breathe, it was so intense, so hard, so—

Then he touched me. He reached between us and found me with his thumb, and the volcano erupted.

Everything that was trapped built up fast, tensing my whole body as it burst forth in a sea of screaming mind-blowing sensations. Over and over, the waves hit me, Sully joining me as he let go, eyes shut and face contorted with the most exquisite of pain.

We rode the ride down in a tangle of limbs and whispered words, clinging to each other through the lessening waves. Finally, we pulled free of each other to lie side-by-side and gasp for air.

He took my hand, intertwining his fingers in mine, and squeezed.

"When I can move, I'm gonna come tell you that I love you," he said between breaths.

I squeezed back twice.

"No rush," I said, my lungs still searching for more. "I got the gist."

Sully laughed.

"Shit, that was—I have no words."

"Words are overrated," I wheezed. "How can you laugh? It takes oxygen to laugh."

He laughed harder and gripped his chest. "I need to start working out or something," he said. "Do some cardio. Good God, woman, you kill me."

I turned to look at him. "Complaining already?"

"Oh, hell no." He rolled onto his side and blew out a breath. "In fact, you can kill me again in a little while." He winked. "Give me thirty minutes."

I cocked an eyebrow. "Thirty minutes?"

"Maybe an hour," he amended.

It was my turn to laugh, and I rolled onto my side with a groan. "Oh God, you need cardio and I need aerobics," I said. "Maybe yoga. I feel like an old woman."

"I promise you," he said, pulling my free hand to his lips. "You're no old woman." He let go and brushed a lock of hair from my face, his gaze going thoughtful. "So this is you all sexed and naked and satisfied and tousled in a bed."

I chuckled. "Given that some thought, have you?"

"Oh, I used to fantasize about it big time," he said. "Close out the sounds of thirty other trailers full of people around me, and picture you, just like this. Us, all by ourselves, in crumpled sheets."

I traced his jaw. I didn't know how to even put into words how amazing it was for me, too. Seeing him in my bed, feeling his warmth. Feeling the longevity of it—that was the kicker. It wasn't temporary.

"Live up to the fantasy?" I asked.

He shook his head slowly. "So much better."

"Why's that?"

He leaned forward and kissed me softly. "Because I couldn't do this," he whispered against my lips. "And if I started kissing my hand, someone would have thrown something at me."

I laughed out loud and kissed him back, relishing the feel of his hands on me. Of him under mine. Lazy and unrushed.

"This is…" I began, unable to find the words. "Amazing isn't enough."

"Forever," he said, touching the tattoo on my breast. "How about that one?"

Unbidden tears came to my eyes, and I ran my hand over the matching one on his arm. Forever had burned me before. It was a hard thing for me to buy into.

"Forever is a pretty word," I said, smiling as I tried to blink back the tears. "But it's not a guarantee."

"Waking up tomorrow isn't a guarantee, either," he said. "Driving across town isn't a guarantee. Life is life, love." He stroked my cheek with the back of his fingers. "Forever is what we make it. And it's an awesome thing to aim for."

I studied his face. The face I spent a lifetime trying to forget and never could. The face I still couldn't completely believe was back here in front of me. That I could possibly wake up to every morning.

"And if the Lucky Charm is a dud?" I asked.

He frowned. "That's sacrilege, you know."

"Just saying."

"I'll pretend you didn't *just say* it," he said, passing a hand between our faces and making me laugh.

"What the hell was that?"

"Carnies are superstitious people, babe," he said. "You can't curse me like that."

I laughed harder. "Curse you? I thought you didn't believe in all that mumbo jumbo."

"I may not buy into all the heavy crap," he said. "But fate is something else. You don't tempt it by planning for things to go wrong."

I propped my head up on my elbow. "Fate is what we make it," I said, echoing his words.

A reluctant grin spread across his face, and his hand slid around my back, pulling me closer. "So it is," he said.

"Besides," I said. "Lucky Hart is about more than this project," I said. "The carnival has to be pretty profitable—well, except for your brother."

He took a deep breath and let it out. "Actually, it's two separate entities now. Lucky Hart Carnivals and LH Industries are now unrelated."

I frowned. "What?"

"That's what I was doing," he said. "Severing ties." Sadness mingled with relief passed through his eyes. "The carnival is now one hundred percent Aiden's. I'm out of it. LH Industries is mine."

My jaw dropped. "Oh my God, Sully. What—why?"

"It was time," he said. "I can't be responsible for him anymore. I can't be his savior anymore, and keep bailing out the same boat he's sinking. It's on him, now."

"Are you—okay with that?" I asked.

He nodded slowly. "Ironically, yes. Carnie'll always be in my blood, but I've never felt so free as the moment I signed that paper."

"So the Lucky Charm—"

"Has to succeed," he said, chuckling. "Or I'll be bussing tables at the Blue Banana."

I kissed him, feeling the weight of everything he'd turned upside-down to stay in Charmed. After I'd left, even. He did that not even knowing if I would come back. That was kind of major. But also didn't leave him much reason to stay if things went south.

"I love you," I said, watching that land on him. "And I need to know that no one is bailing, just as much as you do." I threaded my fingers into his hair.

Sully looked into my eyes. Suddenly, it was like that long ago night, back at the carnival when he slid off the fence, locking eyes with me. That night, with just that one look, he left no doubt that I was it. That I was the only one in his world. This was that same look, telling me we were locked in. We were permanent.

"Carmen Frost, no matter what happens from this day forward, what my company does, what we do, where we are, or when one of us has a name change—"

My belly tingled at the hint, and nervous laughter fell out of my mouth.

"You're changing your name?" I asked. He pinched my ass. "Ow!"

"It's always been you and me," he said. "Even when it wasn't. I'm here. My home is wherever you are."

I smiled and kissed him. "Carmen and Sully's Great Adventure, huh?"

"Right here in Charmed," he said, pulling me on top of him.

I giggled. "I don't think it's been an hour yet, sir."

His hand came behind my head as he kissed me, grinning.

"Carnie time."

Keep reading for a special preview of the
next Charmed in Texas romance,

Once a Charmer

Coming in October 2017 from Lyrical Press!

Chapter One

"Damn it, Bash, get out of my head."

It wasn't the first time I'd muttered that sentence over my travel mug lately on the way to the diner, but it was the first time it had made me late.

Actually, my teenaged daughter was the culprit on that, attempting a sick day and dragging the morning out, but the not hearing my alarm part was on me. Or on Bash. My best friend. My really hot best friend who I couldn't quit having very vivid dreams about.

Yes.

Those kinds of dreams.

About Sebastian Anderson doing things to me I had no business thinking about him doing. Thoughts you aren't supposed to have about someone who's been your rock, your buddy, your confidant, and who has literally had your back for everything for fifteen years. Until a few months ago, when I stupidly showed my hand in a moment of weakness. A really old, never-supposed-to-be-seen-again hand, that came out waving during a crisis and now spent the twilight hours slapping me silly with fantasies. Before leaving me tossing and turning in frustration until the alarm went off. Too many nights of that, and the alarm ceases to matter.

I rolled my head on my shoulders as I walked through the front doors of the Blue Banana Grille, shaking off all the rest. I couldn't think any more about sex dreams or Bash Anderson. *This* mattered right now, whatever was going on here. My diner. My legacy, passed to me by my father, and hopefully one day to my daughter, Angel. After she finished college, of course, and medical school, and joined the Peace Corps and saved the world. Maybe then she'd want to come back and relax and run a small-town diner in Charmed, Texas.

Assuming she got off her phone long enough to finish high school and quit trying to play hooky.

I smiled at Lanie McKane, Nick's wife, who looked up from a crossword puzzle and cup of coffee to wave and mouth a *Hey, Allie!* at me. Nick McKane was my star head chef, and had patrons coming day after day to devour his creations. He was also easy on the eyes, so while his wife was most likely just waiting for him to take a break, I had a feeling she also liked making an appearance now and then. I didn't blame her. Running a diner, I'd seen almost everything at one time or another, and if there was one thing I knew for sure, it was that women can't be trusted.

No, I wasn't selling out my people. I just called things as I saw them. And most of the women in this town had sold me out a long time ago.

I nodded at a few of my regulars that came several times a week for Nick's breakfast specials, and I picked up the napkin that had fallen from old Mr. Wilson's lap for probably the twelfth time. Our ex-mayor, Dean Crestwell, sat by the window on the far end eating his eggs and looking like he wanted to hide under his jacket and beard. My every-morning-at-the-counter-for-coffee old salts were already perched on their stools, flannel shirts tucked in and white socks peering out from underneath trousers that were a little too short.

I glanced to my right, and *bam.*

Kick to the belly with all the tingling feels, as a certain pair of major blue eyes looked my way and did a little head nod. Bash sat there talking to another man. *Shit!* I was instantly transported back a few hours to a particularly lusty dream in which those same eyes were heated and dark and looking up at me from—

"Oh my God," I said under my breath, turning away immediately, my hand going directly to my messy bun—for what? To see if I looked okay? "Jesus, I'm pathetic," I added, yanking my hand back down.

I looked at them sideways after getting behind the bar and tying on my black apron. I didn't recognize the other guy. Not that that was weird. Bash met with many people at the diner, as plenty of others did. It was a good central location for all kinds of meet-ups, plus the food couldn't be beat. Bash Anderson was a major presence as the owner of the largest bee apiary in the area, and he could easily be talking to a new investor or client. Anderson's Apiary kept the town and probably a quarter of Texas supplied with honey, beeswax products, and bee hives for hire. But while my not knowing his breakfast partner over there wasn't a stand-out moment, the guy himself practically glowed with *I'm not from here.*

We were a pretty relaxed lot in Charmed. Casual was the basic dress plan, and stepping up—at least in my opinion—just meant nicer jeans and maybe some killer shoes. Guys didn't even need the shoes. In stark contrast, this guy with Bash wore black slacks and a sweater, what appeared to be leather penny loafers on his feet, and he had too much hair gel making his locks shiny. He looked like he belonged in a J. Crew catalog from the nineties. More than that, he had a leather bag slung over the back of his chair like a purse.

Definitely not from here.

Kerri, a waitress I'd hired two months ago, who still hadn't learned to memorize orders, came rushing over.

"Miss Greene, Nick said to tell you he needs to talk to you ASAP," she said.

"Okay," I said, glancing through the open window section to the kitchen where Nick was cooking with a scowl on his face.

"Also, that section over there by the ficus and the bookshelf?" she added, pointing.

"Otherwise known as tables ten through fourteen?" I asked.

Kerri nodded. "Yes. It's leaking over them again. Has been ever since we turned on the heat."

Great. I made a mental note to call someone out to get up on the roof, or maybe Nick would do it later. I nodded toward J. Crew and lowered my voice.

"Who's that with Bash Anderson? Someone about the Lucky Charm?"

Charmed was getting an overhaul in the form of an entertainment complex along our pond. The Lucky Charm was the baby of Sullivan Hart, an ex-carnie from the Lucky Hart carnival that had frequented our town for decades who had come to town a few months back. Restaurants and shopping and rides and a boardwalk—it was already partially underway with a few rides and shops, and the town was in a constant state of chaos. Contractors, investors, businesspeople wanting to expand or kick off startups, they were all as stirred up as an ant pile. For the diner, this was a good thing, as most all of them met up under my roof for a good meal.

Kerri followed my look. "No idea, but he was asking for you earlier."

I looked at her with a question. "For me?"

"Right before Mr. Anderson showed up," she said, nodding. "Nick talked to him for a minute, though, so maybe he knows."

I frowned back in the men's direction, where Bash looked to be hanging on every word J. Crew was saying. Bash did a quick double-take my way, which sent the butterflies skittering again until he said something and pointed and the other guy turned toward me with a polite smile.

A smile that didn't quite reach his dark eyes. They remained distracted, and a weird familiar metallic taste filled my mouth as I looked into them. A déjà vu that wasn't pleasant. Which was ludicrous. I'd never seen this man before.

"Good deal," I said, also taking in the manicured hands, the fork in his left hand that was just poking at the food instead of eating it, and the expensive watch on his right wrist. "Get them some more water. Stand toward the new guy's right to fill it."

She frowned, glancing his way. "Why?"

"He's a leftie." She looked at me blankly and I sighed. "He's new here. He's barely touching his food. So he'll be more approachable, less defensive, and more likely to leave a good tip if you serve him on his weaker side."

Kerri's eyebrows lifted. "Wow."

"Yeah, it's rocket science," I said under my breath as I pushed open the doors to the kitchen. "What's up, Nick? You know Lanie's out there, right?"

He didn't look up, focusing instead on folding some cream into a bowl of sliced strawberries that would go into his famous strawberry cake. That's what I loved about this guy. It was strawberries and cream, and he treated it like it came straight from a cow with a golden udder.

"Yep," he said. "I was just waiting for David to get here so I can run to the bank with her to do some paperwork."

I tilted my head. "She's taking her break from the bank to come here to get you on your break, to go *back* to the bank?"

"That's what I said, but Lanie said if she waited for me, I'd get caught up in what I was doing and forget." Nick shrugged. "And she's probably right."

"You do get a little tunnel visioned," I said.

"So did he introduce himself?" he asked, picking up a spatula to turn the strawberries gently.

"Who?"

Dark eyes darted my way. "The guy out there who looks like his mom dressed him to get beat up at school," he said.

I choked back a laugh as I plucked a strawberry slice from the bowl and popped it into my mouth. "No, he's meeting with Bash about something." I moaned around the berry. "Oh man, I need about forty more of these."

"I have the feeling you might want to double that," he said, frowning as he grabbed another bowl. "This guy—something's up."

I rose from the stool I'd just rested on. "Why?"

"I don't know, he's odd. He only wanted to talk to you, but now he's eating with Bash?" Nick said, shaking his head as he worked.

"What did he say?" I asked.

Nick glanced up. "It has something to do with your dad."

Something that felt like cold little fingers traced a path down my spine. Something old and familiar and not welcome.

"W-why?" I asked, resisting the urge to reach out for the wall, the door, the sink nearby. Anything tangible and touchable that could ground me and yet make me vulnerable at the same time. *Don't show weakness.*

"He said he was here to talk to you on behalf of Oliver Greene."

On behalf of...

I stared at Nick and nodded slowly as I turned for the door. The man's face came into view as I emerged on the other side as he shook hands with a smiling Bash and the two men parted ways. J. Crew came up to the counter in front of me and sat on a stool, lacing his fingers. Instantly, I knew what the taste had been about, the unpleasant sensation, the déjà vu. I'd never laid eyes on this man before, but I'd seen the others before him and they all had that same useless look about them.

I held out my hand.

"Allie Greene," I said. "What did he lose?"

* * *

My father was a good man. He had a heart of gold with hands of steel and had worked hard his whole life before illness stripped him of that. He also had a weakness. If there was a deal or a scam, a poker table or a get rich quick scheme within ten miles, he couldn't resist. If he had five dollars in his pocket, it would burn a hole until he was forced to spend it, and frequently that was aimed at something with chips or a bigger pocket. Especially during stressful times.

I loved my dad with everything I had, but I had watched him gamble all our savings away after my mom died. The only new truck he'd ever owned was trailered and gone, and our house—I would never forget the man who came for that. I was seven, and that man's face would forever be etched in my memory as the person who took away my room with the purple flowers and sent us to the trailer park.

This man had the same empty eyes.

"I'm Landon Lange," he said, gripping my hand. "I'm an acquaintance of your father's."

A tall woman with big blond hair came through the door and strode straight up to the counter. "Hi!" she said, her voice perky, teeth flashing. "Can I get a cup of coffee?"

"Sure thing," I said, letting go of the man's hand and reaching for the nearby coffee pot robotically, pouring a cup. "Sugar and creamer is right there," I said, pointing without looking.

"Thanks, hon," she said. "Great place."

I met her eyes. Another stranger. I guessed bringing in a tourist attraction was going to bring that in, too.

"Thanks," I said.

I felt my eyebrows lift, looking back at Lange. "So, an acquaintance," I said, smiling. "That's a new one. Although I'm curious how you know him recently since he's been home-bound all this last year."

"It's actually been a little while," he said. "I was hoping maybe he'd come through."

"How much?" I asked, closing my eyes and shaking my head.

Landon Lange appeared to study his manicured nails on the countertop and then pulled a piece of paper from his man-purse.

"I own fifty-one percent of this diner," he said.

My eyes popped open. My *everything* popped open.

"What?"

"There's this—" he began, smoothing the paper on the counter. My counter. The counter I'd cleaned 4,394,839,409 times and now held a paper that said—

"No," I said. "That's not—"

"Miss Greene."

"That's not possible," I said, bringing the word down to a whisper. A hiss. An utterance of no-fucking-way. "This is my diner. It's ours. It belongs to my family. It doesn't go on the table—ever."

That was the deal. That was always the deal. *Please God, don't take away the deal.*

"Miss Greene."

"Stop saying my name," I said, hearing my voice rise but unable to control it. It was like someone else held the remote and I was watching the show. The blond lady moved as far over to the right as she could, and Lanie moved slowly up to take her place as if she might need to vault it and kick somebody's ass.

"Everything okay?" she asked quietly.

"Why don't we go in your office," Nick said, miraculously appearing behind me.

"I have this signed—" Landon began again.

"I don't care what you have," I said. "It's not happening."

"Allie, please," Nick said in a low voice. "Let's take this in the back."

Nick was right. He was being the cool-headed logical one. Acting like management, taking charge of the situation. He was being me. And I was having a mental breakdown next to the coffee pot.

I own fifty-one percent...

Oh my God.

What did you do, Dad?

The walk to my office felt like the walk of doom, as the cold chill of things shifting washed over me. It wasn't my office if this guy owned—

The hell it wasn't. It had been my mom's and dad's before me and fuck if some man-pursed asshole was going to take it from me.

I spun around.

"Mr. Lange, my father has put a lot of things on the line over the years," I said, focusing on the tone of every word as it left my mouth. He couldn't have really done such a thing. I had to believe that. I had to hold on to that hope. "I've seen too many things lost, including my home, and he made a promise to me after that. The Blue Banana would never be jeopardized."

"Well, I'm sorry," he said, walking in and setting the paper on my desk without hesitation. "It is what it is. Signed and legal. He can verify it."

It is what it is.

Hope left the room. It peeled itself from every surface and floated away. My father did it. He lost it. He lost our everything.

I couldn't breathe.

"He—" I cleared my throat. "My dad can't verify anything. He's got dementia. Some days he isn't sure of his own name."

"Sorry to hear that," Landon said. "He was a nice guy."

"He's still a nice guy," I snapped.

Landon held his palms forward and then picked up the paper and held it in front of me. "Can you just look at the signature and see for yourself?"

My feet felt rooted to the floor. I shut my eyes, feeling the tightly wound control I valued so much begin to slip away. I didn't have to look. I didn't want to. I'd know my father's writing in a heartbeat, and I knew with just as much conviction that it would be on that paper. Still, I needed to see the proof. The stinging slap to the face. I felt Lanie's arm link through mine and Nick's hand on the back of my neck, and my eyes fluttered open to a watery image of a yellow form. A deed transfer. Of majority percentage of the Blue Banana Grille to Landon Lange. Signed and dated in a hard right-slanted hand by Oliver Greene, Owner.

I didn't have even a tenth of a percent to my name. I ran it as my own because it was our baby. My mother gave birth to it, my father raised it, and I took it on. Now this stranger who had never set foot in here before today had controlling ownership. Had been in control for a while, and I never knew it.

"This was signed last year," I said, my voice not much more than an exhausted whisper. "Over a year ago, actually. Why are you here now?"

He never changed expression, just set the paper down on my desk when I didn't take it from him.

"Honestly, I like your father, Miss Greene," he said. "He's straightforward and truthful, and I don't see much of that in my line of work."

"I'll bet," I said.

"What exactly is your *line of work*?" Nick asked from behind me.

"He's a bookie," I said.

"I'm a private loan officer," Landon amended.

"He's a bookie," I repeated.

"So," Landon continued. "I didn't want to capitalize on his bad luck. Thought I'd give him a while to straighten out his affairs, but he never contacted me again."

"His *affairs* are sitting at home watching war movies and sports and taking walks from one end of the trailer park to the other," I said, cutting off the tears that wanted into my words. "Most likely, he doesn't remember any of it."

"That's unfortunate," Landon said, then shrugging. "Or fortunate, perhaps. Spares him the drama."

"What do you want?" I asked, swiping a rogue tear as it fell and letting that one little piece of weakness be my staff. I took a step forward. "You don't strike me as the diner type, Mr. Lange. I don't see you having any interest in a small town like Charmed or any of its establishments."

His lips tugged into an almost-smile. "On the contrary, Miss Greene," he said. "I see a lot of opportunity here. I've recently made a couple of lucrative investments here in Charmed—I figured why not since I own the majority of the most popular eating establishment." He smiled, and my skin prickled. "Give back, is what I always say."

The image of this man sitting across from Bash, shaking his hand, crossed my thoughts.

"What do you want?" I repeated, crossing my arms over my chest.

His smile grew curious. "Are you suggesting that I'm open to a payoff?"

"I'm *suggesting* that anyone able to so glibly take a man's livelihood with a piece of paper is probably just soulless enough to throw something else out there," I said, refusing to blink.

Landon clapped his palms together and rubbed them in a fast motion. "Oooh, an insult and a challenge all in one sentence," he said. "You do make it interesting, Miss Greene."

"How much?" I asked.

"Oliver was in to me for fifty grand," Landon said finally, setting my skin on fire with his oily words. "Not all at one time, mind you. I let him skate by a time or two. But things add up after a while and Oliver—well, he couldn't seem to get on the right side of it."

Fifty grand.

Sweet Jesus.

"But that was before I checked on it," he said. "The Blue Banana appraises for just over seventy-five thousand."

I stared at him, not really seeing him anymore. Seventy-five thousand dollars. We were done. I was done. I couldn't get that kind of money if I wanted to. I basically worked for him now.

"You—want Allie to cough up that kind of money to buy her own diner back?" Lanie asked.

Landon shrugged. "Makes no difference to me one way or the other." He turned to go. "But I have to ask—The Blue Banana?" He screwed up his face in dislike. "What's with that?"

My chest squeezed around my heart and I briefly wondered if cardiac arrest might be in my near future.

"It's personal," I pushed out.

He shook his head as if pondering it. "I'll give it some thought. We can do better than that."

And he was gone.

Nick and Lanie were talking to me. I felt hands and hugs and something resembling comfort. But all I could see were the eyes of another man taking something from me. The sound of his words telling me that my life's plan had just flipped on a dime. The feeling of what had always been solid ground under my feet being wiggled away one tug at a time.

"What are you going to do?" I heard Lanie ask.

"Counters need wiping," I said breathily, forcing myself to walk. "If Dave's back, go do what you have to do, Nick. We'll take care of it."

"Allie."

"Go," I said, looking back but not really focusing since the world as I knew it was dissolving into confetti. "Business as normal."

Normal.

Whatever that was.

Sex in a Pan (Sully's dessert)

Ingredients:

Crust:

1 cup pecans, chopped
3 Tbsp. white sugar
1/2 cup butter
1 cup flour

Cream cheese layer:

1 8 oz. package cream cheese
1 cup powdered sugar
1 cup whipped cream or Cool Whip

Vanilla pudding layer:

1 package of instant vanilla pudding (5.1 oz. or 144 g)
3 cups milk

Chocolate Pudding layer:

1 package of instant chocolate pudding (5.1 oz. or 144 g)
3 cups milk

Top layer:

3 cups whipped cream or Cool Whip
Shaved chocolate (enough to cover; took me 3 Hershey bars)

Directions:

Preheat oven to 350 degrees.

Spray a 9×13-inch baking dish with cooking spray.

Mix the crust ingredients together and press the mixture into the prepared baking dish. Bake for about 20 minutes.

Prepare the chocolate and vanilla pudding as per the instructions on the package.

In a mixer, combine the cream cheese, powdered sugar, and 1 cup of whipped cream. Mix until light and fluffy.

Let the crust cool. Spread the cream cheese mixture evenly over the crust.

Spread the chocolate pudding over the cream cheese filling, then the vanilla pudding over the chocolate. (I sprinkled a light layer of additional chopped pecans between the pudding layers just because we are nutty freaks over here, but that's a personal preference)

Top with the whipped cream and sprinkle with the chocolate.

Refrigerate for a couple hours until set.

Oh my my my…

Photo Credit: Leo Weeks Photographers

Sharla Lovelace is the bestselling, award-winning author of sexy small-town love stories. Being a Texas girl through and through, she's proud to say she lives in Southeast Texas with her retired husband, a tricked-out golf cart, and two crazy dogs. She is the author of five stand-alone novels including the bestselling *Don't Let Go*, the exciting Heart Of The Storm series, and the fun and sexy new Charmed in Texas series. For more about Sharla's books, visit www.sharlalovelace.com, and keep up with all her new book releases easily by subscribing to her newsletter.

She loves keeping up with her readers, and you can connect with her on Facebook, Instagram, and Twitter @sharlalovelace.

Did you miss the first Charmed in Texas Novel?

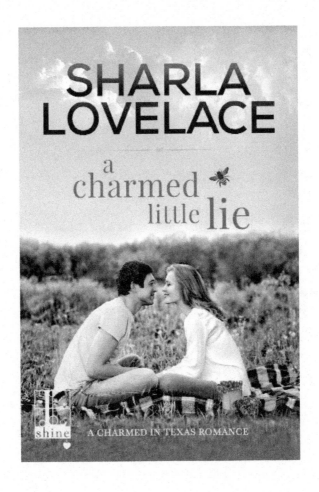

CPSIA information can be obtained
at www.ICGtesting.com
Printed in the USA
BVOW04s0402020617
485574BV00003B/12/P